Foreig

Roslyn McFarland

Foreign Attachments

For my sister Jan

Foreign Attachments
ISBN paperback: 9781740272636
ISBN ebook: 9781740273787
Copyright © text Roslyn McFarland 2024
Cover image: Frissell, Toni, photographer: *A couple walking along the Seine River in Paris* Toni Frissell Collection, Library of Congress, Prints & Photographs Division, Washington DC. USA
Author photo: Tricia Koffel

First published 2024 by
GINNINDERRA PRESS
PO Box 2 Bentleigh 3204
ginninderrapress.com.au

The present is the only reality.
—*Stella Bowen*

The human dilemma…is that most of our decisions are well and truly made by our ancient, limbic, emotional system before our frontal reasoning cortex even becomes aware of it happening.
—*David Williamson*

Prologue

December 2019

He'd always given danger a wide berth. Well, up until today, that is. He checks his watch. Almost 4 p.m. Not the time to start analysing why he's behaved so recklessly. He needs to act quickly, which means getting her out of here as soon as possible. Somehow. But what on earth is taking her so long?

And then he hears the toilet flush. Enfin!

He grabs his underpants from the divan and puts them on. He turns around to find her standing there – still naked and all smiles. He takes a step back and is about to say: I don't want to hurt your feelings, but I love my life, the way it is. Or was, before this afternoon. And I don't want anything to change that.

But she speaks first: I really enjoyed the last hour or so we've spent together but I'm sure you'll agree it was a mistake.

This isn't what he'd expected but he's relieved she hasn't caused a scene. His breathing steadies. You're right, he says. I feel the same.

Merveilleux! Let's draw a line beneath this afternoon then and agree never to mention it again. She takes a step closer to him. It will be our little secret.

He's not sure she can be trusted but says: I think I'd prefer if it was just a pleasant memory that fades into oblivion.

Of course, she murmurs, giving him an enigmatic smile. I suppose I'd better find my clothes and get going.

That's when he hears a key in the lock and the door opening. The studio floods with light from the landing, bringing with it a fierce clarity of vision. Precisely what he's dreaded. Reality turned into nightmare. The stupidity of the afternoon.

Part One

February 2015

As the A380 started making its gentle descent into Charles de Gaulle Airport, I couldn't help thinking how Stella Bowen's arrival to Paris was so different to my own. She'd lived through World War I and the Spanish Flu epidemic and then, at the wintery end of 1922, had sailed from England in a cross-channel steamer with the love of her life, the writer Ford Madox Ford and their two-year-old daughter, Julie.

Whereas I'd just left the searing heat of an Australian summer and was about to land in a city still traumatised by the Charlie Hebdo terrorist attacks. I was also expecting to be greeted at the airport as promised by the man I loved. But only his voice was there. As I joined the queue at the passport control gate, he called my mobile phone. Of course, he was full of apologies, but I was too tired and numb from the flight to tell him how disappointed I was.

I'd been awake since leaving Sydney. In the gloom of that aeronautical no man's land, my rebellious, over-active brain could not be quelled. Most passengers had dutifully fallen asleep when the crew plunged the cabin into a fake dark night. But not me. Every time I closed my eyes, all I could think about was the fury my mother, Rachel had unleashed when I'd told her I was quitting my job at the gallery and moving to France to live with Antoine, a man my mother had never met.

All things considered, her reaction hadn't been surprising. What I hadn't anticipated was the intensity of Rachel's histrionics. At first, her objections had been harmless enough. Even mildly amusing. It was clear she knew very little about Antoine and kept referring to him as a minor French celebrity musician, who'd only use and abuse me, then toss me aside like some day-old baguette.

When I told her there was nothing minor about Antoine Tribolet, she'd chortled scornfully. Ah-ha, she said, so what you're telling me is that he's great in bed!

That's not what I meant, I said, and you know it.

Well, can you please tell me why you're the one who has to turn your life upside down? Why must you accommodate him? Why can't he come and live here in Australia? She emphasised he and here. They sounded like sneers. That's when things got a bit nasty.

I tried to explain that I wasn't turning my life upside down, that I was in the process of making my life. My way. I'm making a commitment to someone I love, I said, which is something you know very little about.

My mother was suddenly wordless, her expression unreadable.

I blundered on: Antoine and I have discussed this at length. Unlike you, we both know what it means to give and take. And because my career will be less affected by a relocation to another hemisphere, the decision for me to move to Paris has been pretty simple to make.

Oh God, please stop. This is worse than I thought. You're completely delusional. You haven't fallen in love, girl, you've fallen for that worn out, romantic myth that's tied women to the kitchen sink for centuries.

I took a deep breath. I didn't want to lose my temper. I hardly ever disagreed with my mother about anything, but what she'd been saying had cut deeply. And I'd had quite enough of her stubborn belief that she knew best. No, you stop, I said calmly. Whether you like it or not, I'm going to Paris to live my life according to my own script. Nobody else's. And while I know you tend to view all men as potential tyrants, there's nothing you can say or do that will change the way I feel about Antoine.

Rachel looked thoughtful, then pacing the room like a caged, wild thing, started railing against Antoine, calling him the epitome of the older, successful man, a Rochester or a Mr Darcy for our times. Obviously, you see yourself as the muse to the musical genius, she had said, but the only thing you'll be doing is turning yourself into a doormat. And while you're propping up his ego and playing hostess at all his after-concert soirées, do you honestly think you'll find time to write that novel of yours, aye? Or are you just going to abandon the whole idea now? Is that it?

And on she went. Full of questions: Did I intend to be a kept woman, or would I support myself financially? And how was I going to get by on my schoolgirl French? Until, with a deep sigh, Rachel plonked herself down on the old leather couch.

It was time now for me to respond. I drew up a tub chair opposite my mother and began by reminding her that I'd soon be turning thirty and was perfectly capable of choosing my own destiny. More than this, my credentials and experience would surely score me a job in any one of the many galleries in Paris, especially now that I'd been granted EU citizenship by descent, thanks to Gran having been born in Dublin. And when it came to my novel, what better place was there to research and write my fictionalised version of Stella Bowen's life than in the city Stella loved most? But because I already knew how my mother would respond, I chose not to say that Antoine had offered to support me financially while I worked on my novel. Instead, I told her he'd set up a study for me in his apartment.

My mother sniffed: I bet you'll need more than a room of your own, my dear. Her fury may have been spent, but her contempt remained. I've done my best to raise you as an independent woman, but clearly my best efforts failed. Then she muttered something about millennials dashing her hopes for a different world order in the future.

But I had stopped listening. Although I wanted to tell her that I'd been taking French conversation classes, I decided to save my breath. I knew it didn't matter what I said, I wouldn't be getting any support from her. Not right now, at any rate.

Rachel stood and made for the door, then turned and said: One day you're going to regret being so impetuous. And I hope for your sake, it'll be sooner than later.

To her retreating back I shouted, spitting out the last word: I know what I'm doing. I'm not an idiot, Mother!

When Antoine called me at the airport I understood he'd been delayed through no fault of his own, so there was no point in beginning our life together by complaining about something I couldn't do anything about. Especially on the phone and in a public place. Besides, I was starting to look forward to a long, soaking bath and an even longer sleep. I could hear the desperation in his voice as he told me he'd been called back to the recording studio in the south of France, where his latest album was being produced. There'd been some kind of problem with the sound mix that only he could resolve. He really had no choice but to go. He apologised again and promised he'd explain everything when he got back to Paris. Which, he assured me, would only be in a day or two at most. He also told me I wasn't to worry. He'd organised everything. A driver named Gilles would be waiting for me near the exit in the Arrivals Hall. He said Gilles would be holding a sign with my name on it and that he'd take me to the apartment.

It's your new home now, *chérie*, Antoine said. Make yourself comfortable and get some rest. Then his voice became a breathless whisper, and he told me he loved me and that he'd show me just how much he did when he got back to Paris. Again and again, he said. You wait. I'll make it up to you. *Ne t'inquiète pas.*

I had no reason to be worried, so I told him I wasn't going to. The bond between us was strong and rare and true. That, I was sure of.

As we entered the outskirts of Paris, Gilles pointed out Père Lachaise Cemetery. Up until then, he hadn't said a word since we'd left the airport, which didn't bother me because his French was extremely rapid, and I couldn't help thinking my level of comprehension was about as sophisticated as a French toddler's. It wasn't long before he spoke again though, and all I could make out was something about taking *un petit détour*.

That's when he turned right into a set of narrow, fairly nondescript one-way streets before suddenly stopping the car at a small T intersection.

Look Miss Palmer, look down the street, he said in very passable English.

Please call me Neve, I said. Then doing as I was told, I saw that part of the road was cordoned off and most of the footpath was heavy with flowers, drawings, candles and cards.

Ah! So this is where the offices of Charlie Hebdo are, I said.

Yes, as you can see, we Parisians are still mourning. Everyone keeps coming here. It's like a pilgrimage, to pay our respects and to try to understand this horror. Why were Kalashnikovs used against people who only ever used a pen as a weapon? It makes no sense.

He shook his head then fell silent. I turned around to look through the limousine's rear window and could see a number of vehicles had lined up behind them. No horn beeped impatiently.

Gilles gunned the engine and drove off. I hope you don't mind me taking you here, he said. It was on our way, and I thought it might help you understand the mood of the city right now.

Very thoughtful of you, I said and thanked him. I wasn't sure what else I could say.

My first sight of the Île St Louis, my new neighbourhood, was from a distance. But even then, I was knocked out by what I saw of this peanut-shaped island in the middle of the Seine River. A light dusting of snow covered its slate rooftops so that all its stately stone mansions, what the French call *hôtels particuliers,* seemed to gleam in the morning light. But despite the cloudless, clear blue sky overhead, I was well aware that the weather was quite frosty outside and made a mental note to expand my winter wardrobe as soon as possible.

When I stepped out of the car, the breeze was indeed biting, but I scarcely felt it because Gilles hurried me through the entrance of the corner building and led me up the beautiful spiral staircase with its black metal handrails to Antoine's apartment. An apartment that took up the entire second floor.

Once inside, I immediately noticed that all the external shutters on the windows had been opened. Obviously to enhance the impact of the interior, a study in minimalist elegance and light. Gilles excused himself to fetch my luggage from the car, but he wasn't long because, by the time he returned, I hadn't even moved from the open plan living and dining area. He pointed towards the kitchen and informed me it was well stocked. Next, he gave me the security code for the ground floor entrance and the keys to the apartment. Then he smiled and wished me well.

I must go now, he said. I work for Sacha Durand, Antoine's friend and manager. So no doubt we will meet again.

As soon as he was gone, I swept back the sheer curtains from the nearest window and stood for some time staring out over the Seine. There to my right – the flying buttress end of Notre-Dame – and directly across the river – Stella's beloved Left Bank with the distant dome of the Panthéon beckoning me.

But the apartment's phone started ringing so answering it had to take precedence. It was Antoine – checking to see I'd arrived, wanting to know if everything was OK and if I found the apartment agreeable. A stupid question really. Who in their right mind wouldn't like it?

We didn't talk for long. He only seemed to want to tell me he loved me and that he'd be home soon. Later, all I could remember saying was I hope so, I really do.

First I thought it best to familiarise myself with my new living arrangements. I loved the parquet flooring and the way the L-shaped configuration of the apartment took full advantage of the marvellous French floor-to-ceiling windows. Every living space, apart from the narrow hallway, was flooded with light. Antoine had set up a desk for me in what looked like a cosy lounge-library. And there were two bedrooms, each with its own adjoining bathroom but the larger one of the two was obviously meant to be ours. It had its own dressing room, and this was where Gilles had deposited my bags.

I sat down on the edge of the bed, not sure if I was tired or simply overwhelmed. I remember thinking I should've been jumping for joy like some feather-headed nobody in one of those schmaltzy rom-coms, who'd finally snared her prince – a super-rich and talented French one at that! It all seemed too good to be true. I reminded myself that I needed sleep, but I also knew if I were to adapt as quickly as possible to my new time zone, I had to stay awake. At least until the early evening. I hoped a brisk walk around the perimeter of the tiny island would do the trick.

And of course it did. Once I left the building, I'd headed east down to the quai de Béthune and watched several barges drift along the watery blur of the Seine. Taking the rue Saint-Louis-en-l'Île, I cut through the middle of the island and passed by chic boutiques, quaint speciality shops and several small art galleries and restaurants. I even stopped by a *petit bistrot* and ordered *steak frites*.

As I walked back to the quai d'Orléans and rounded the corner to the entrance of Antoine's apartment building, I realised that apart from the waiter, I'd spoken to no one else. And I couldn't have cared less. I felt refreshed, clear headed. Yes, I had no friends in Paris and hadn't even set eyes on Antoine yet. But my life had changed. And I felt exhilarated by that. Despite my mother's dire warnings, I knew I was up for the challenge. I was also determined to prove her wrong. I wasn't only going to make my relationship with Antoine work, I'd also get stuck into my novel as soon as I could. That was my promise to myself.

Before meeting Antoine, my life had been pretty uneventful – I had a wide circle of friends, a job I loved and, thanks to a legacy left to me by my maternal grandparents, a small mortgage on a little semi-detached house in a tree-lined street in Newtown, where I'd lived for several years with my old boyfriend, Sam. That is, until we broke up. Our split had been completely amicable. There were no scenes, no tears. It was easier that way. We told our friends we'd drifted apart but in reality, neither of us was willing to admit we'd never really been suited in the first place.

Only Rachel had seen the separation as a cause for celebration. Brandishing a bottle of champagne, she'd dropped by the afternoon Sam moved out. Let's toast your return to independence, she'd said, as she sat back in the old rattan chair in my tiny rear courtyard. It's time for you to play the field, to spread your wings and live a little. You don't need to live with a man to feel fulfilled, you know.

Of course, I did know this. Only too well. My mother had raised me single-handedly and instilled in me a strong sense of self. She'd made sure my childhood was happy and carefree, for which I was grateful. I'd been showered with love and lacked for nothing. Except perhaps, a father. But then I'd never felt I'd missed out on anything by not having one.

As the late afternoon sun sank slowly behind the jasmine covered back fence, we'd drained that bottle of champagne with me assuring Rachel that I was in no rush to meet anyone. For that was my intention. It was only later that I realised it's not possible to predict when or where you'll fall in love, or with whom. But when that thunderbolt of feeling hits, it's the random and unpredictable nature of it that makes it so irresistible. At least that was my experience when I met Antoine a few months later in August.

He'd been giving a series of one night only concerts in major cities across the Asia-Pacific region. The final show of his tour was to be in the Concert Hall of the Sydney Opera House. While I'd heard of Antoine Tribolet, mostly because of the Oscar he'd won for a film score he'd written, I didn't know much about his music and had no idea he was one of the most admired and respected composers of contemporary music in the world. That's why I hadn't considered going to see him perform until my good friend, Tamsin invited me to come along. Her lighting designer boyfriend Finn, who worked at the Opera House, had given her two free tickets. With no plans for the evening, I agreed to go.

Of course I'd been to lots of concerts, but none had been as extraordinary as this one. I can only describe it as other worldly –

a sonic showpiece – dissonant one moment, hauntingly melodic the next. More evocative than poetry, more passionate than jazz – it moved me in ways no other music had ever done before.

At the end of the ninety-minute performance, there wasn't a single person in that packed concert hall who remained in their seats. The standing ovation seemed endless, but Tamsin and I waited for the audience to disperse before heading to the northern foyer, where we were to meet up with Finn for what he'd said would be post-show drinks. It turned out to be a little grander than that.

A couple of hundred people stood about laughing, talking, sipping their drinks. It wasn't long before Finn appeared and asked us to follow him. There's someone I want you to meet, he said. Nearby was a group of about ten people – one of whom was Antoine. Introductions were made and after some polite but perfunctory chit chat, someone said: Look at that view! All eyes turned towards the floor-to-ceiling glass panels that laid bare the ballet of sparkling lights on the harbour beyond the Opera House windows.

I think Van Gogh would have liked this scene, came a voice close behind my left shoulder. The voice had a distinct French accent. I turned and faced Antoine. Up close, I reckoned he had to be in his forties, which made him at least ten years older than me. But whatever his age was, he was an extremely attractive man. I smiled and agreed with him, saying I thought Van Gogh's interpretation of Sydney Harbour by night would've been beautiful.

He pushed back his dark, collar-length hair from his forehead and said he was sure of that, then told me he had half a mind to compose something about it himself. That's when I noticed he'd changed his shirt since the concert. This one was crumpled and deep blue in colour – like his eyes. Oh, I think you should, I said, hoping the conversation wouldn't lead him to ask what sort of music I usually listened to. I couldn't quite see him dancing wildly round the lounge room to roaring rock'n'roll.

Instead he fixed his eyes on mine and admitted he hadn't caught my full name. The thought crossed my mind that the two of us could well be the subject of other people's attention, but I wasn't about to shift my gaze to check if others were watching us. I also had a feeling that he was impatient to know me better. So I sped up the social niceties and stripped down my life to the bare essentials: telling him my name and that I currently worked at the Art Gallery of New South Wales.

He smiled as I spoke, while his eyes moved discreetly over my face. He was still smiling when I stopped talking. So, Neve Palmer, he said, what kind of work do you do at this gallery?

I explained how I was part of the research and curatorial team there, that I specialised in portraiture, thanks to a six-month internship in London's National Portrait Gallery.

He looked impressed and laughing, said he was glad he'd mentioned Van Gogh then.

Antoine's English was excellent. Yes, his French accent was unmistakeable with the *th* sound pronounced *ze*, but I couldn't help thinking no matter the language, any conversation with him would be easy going. He then asked me if I'd come to the concert alone. I told him about Tamsin and Finn and looked around to see they were immersed in conversation with another couple nearby. That's when I said it was his turn to tell me about himself.

He spoke of his childhood in Paris and about his father, who played a number of musical instruments and who'd encouraged him and his twin sister, Thérèse, to do the same. But unlike me, he said, she preferred to sing. He paused for a moment and lowered his head.

I wondered if he was struggling to find the right words, but then he looked at me and spoke of his love of the piano and especially the work of Chopin and Liszt and that from an early age he began studying harmony, counterpoint and composition, which in time led to him being accepted at the Conservatoire de Paris. Then he broke off. I don't want to bore you, he said.

I wanted to say that that'd be impossible, that I could listen to him all night. But right then, I caught sight of Tamsin waving to me. I raised my hand to wave back but she gave me a conspiratorial wink, then performed a discreet little mime, letting me know she and Finn were about to leave and that she'd phone me tomorrow.

Antoine noticed me looking away and said: Ah, but I see I am boring you.

No, no. Not at all. It was Tamsin signalling me that she and Finn were about to leave.

Pas de problème. I should be going too. He seemed to force a smile. I returned it as warmly as I could. As you can imagine, he said, I'm exhausted. I need to get some sleep.

Of course, I replied, sure that I'd blown it and wouldn't be seeing him again. I then added that I'd enjoyed meeting him. And that's when he asked me if we could get together some time on the weekend.

I gave him my phone number, hoping I didn't appear too eager. He said he'd ring the next day, which was a Friday and then took my right hand in his. For one second, I thought he was about to shake it, but he used it to pull me a little closer, then kissed me lightly on both cheeks.

Until tomorrow, he whispered then disappeared into the crowd.

I then made my way out of the Opera House. I needed fresh air. I needed to go home and I needed to think. The connection between us had been immediate. And I was certain he'd realised that too.

But the thought occurred to me: what if I'd been misreading the signs? Sure, Antoine was charismatic, but what if the art of seduction was part of his musical genius? What if I was just another girl in yet another city? A naïve one at that, who believed his eyes were the eyes of a man who understood me, who saw who I was, and who I wrongly thought was the real deal.

By the time I turned the key in my front door, I'd convinced myself he wasn't going to ring and that I was a fool to have thought he would. But around three o'clock the next afternoon, I received a call from the gallery's reception desk that someone was waiting for me in the foyer area. I raced upstairs to find Antoine standing in front of Brett Whiteley's *Self-portrait in the studio.*

What a surprise! I wasn't expecting to see you here, I said.

I thought it was better than a phone call…to see where you work, I mean. And I like it very much. Especially this painting here, he said, pointing at the Whiteley.

I told him it was one of my favourites too and mentioned Whiteley's use of cobalt blue, before launching into a brief rundown of his life and death and how his last studio was now an art museum managed by the gallery.

Antoine's eyes lit up and he asked me if we could go there this weekend. Then he added: Perhaps, I should've mentioned it last night, but I fly to Cairns on Monday for a little diving vacation before I return for work in Paris.

To say I felt disheartened by this news would be an understatement. But I hoped I didn't show it when I said that anything was possible.

Formidable! What time do you finish work today? Because the sun is shining, and we can walk back to my hotel and have dinner together in the restaurant there – if that's what you would like?

And in that very Gallic way of putting forward a suggestion, he raised his shoulders and eyebrows in expectation of a positive response.

Give me five minutes, I said.

We strolled through the Botanic Gardens down to the water's edge, then followed the path round past the Opera House that was glowing with late afternoon light. We stopped to watch a monstrous cruise ship cast off from Circular Quay's overseas passenger terminal.

Quel spectacle! Antoine turned to me; his face flushed. He was excited like a little boy. He wanted to know if Sydney winters were always as mild as this one.

Compared to winters in most of Europe, I guess they are, I answered. I couldn't help feeling a weird sense of pride that my city was working its charms on him. He took my hand when I told him the sad story of Bennelong, who was kidnapped back in 1789 by Governor Arthur Phillip, on orders from King George III to set up a relationship with the local Aboriginal people. As we continued to walk towards the Rocks, Antoine kept asking me questions, not just about the early colonial years of Sydney but also about the present state of relations between the First Peoples of Australia and the rest of the population.

But later, when we stopped for a drink in a tiny bar off a cobblestoned laneway, his questions became more personal. He asked about my father – had I known him? I told him the truth, that in my teens, I'd asked my mother about him – like who he was and what he was like. And how she'd told me straight up that she wasn't sure of his identity because around the time she fell pregnant, she'd only had casual partners – some of whom she knew nothing much about except for their first names.

And you accepted this? he'd asked, sounding surprised.

Of course, why not? Then suddenly I found myself trying to explain how my mother was a free spirit, who preferred having serial boyfriends, and that ever since I could remember there'd always been a man in her life, but none ever stayed around too long, which in Rachel's case said more about the way she chose to live her life than about her choice of lovers.

Antoine raised an eyebrow. You call your mother by her first name?

I wasn't surprised he asked this question. I knew it was somewhat unorthodox but simply said yes, then changed the subject and asked him about his sister, whether or not she'd pursued a career as a singer.

He laughed. The only singing Thérèse now does is in her local church choir. Like her husband, Étienne, she's extremely devout. She decided years ago to be a full-time wife and mother, so she had nine children by the time she was thirty-six years old. Something my parents found difficult to comprehend.

And what did you think?

I think she's crazy. But it's her life. Besides, Étienne treats her well, and they both seem very happy living in Canada. So in the end, we've all had to accept her choice. And when my father died, my mother went to visit them and has visited several times since.

This time it was Antoine's turn to change the subject. And when he did, he shifted the mood of our conversation as well. He spoke with passion about the power of music, how it can trigger emotions and activate the brain and even enliven the human heart and soul. That's why, he said, every single culture on this planet of ours has managed to develop some kind of music.

Yes, but music isn't the only art form that's emerged in civilisations.

He'd sat there smiling as I spoke. You're right, but I am, as you anglophones say, one-eyed when it comes to music. Why don't you tell me what attracted you to the world of art?

My love of reading, I said. And then told him how I'd spent my childhood with my head in books – all kinds of books – everything I could lay my hands on. I also spoke about my mother's influence. How as a journalist, Rachel knew reading expanded the mind and developed the imagination, and that she also strongly believed in the transformative power of the arts – how music, painting, drama and dance made life more bearable.

You were very lucky, he said.

I think so too. From an early age, my mother took me to concerts and the theatre and dragged me off to major art exhibitions. She wanted me to make connections, recognise and appreciate beauty, proportion and grace. Which I learnt to do, but it was in galleries where I both lost and found myself at the same time. That was where I was happiest.

It sounds to me like your mother is truly *remarquable*.

I had to agree and left it at that. I wasn't ready to talk at greater length about Rachel. Besides, we'd finished our drinks, and Antoine was on his feet, ready to go.

As soon as we arrived at his hotel, he suggested we go straight to his suite. So we can both freshen up before dinner, he'd said. I felt quite taken aback by this. Did he actually think I'd believe that the sole reason for going straight to his suite was to use the bathroom? Was this the way he intended to lure me into bed? If it was, it was all a bit too obvious and lacking in finesse. So much for the seductive charm of Frenchmen, that I'd seen represented in films.

A worse thought then crossed my mind: maybe he was hoping that when it came to love, I might be like my mother. Standing in the middle of the giant-sized living area of his top floor suite, I got to thinking that perhaps this was all part of an elaborate routine he played out in every city and town he passed through. That to him, I was just another concert groupie, up for a bit of sexual dalliance with the musical genius. Yet at all other times, he seemed so sincere. Had I misread his intentions? If I had, it was more than disappointing, it was offensive. And if that were the case, what kind of fool did he take me for? Charged with this emotional cocktail, I tried to figure out what I'd say when he made his first move. I'd never had a problem steering clear of manipulative, toxic men before this, so why not now?

But just then I became aware of music playing softly behind me. Hope you like Chet Baker, said Antoine, who was opening the sliding doors to the balcony. And there before us was the twilight vista of green and yellow ferries plying the waters past the Opera House. He'd turned to face me and moving closer, pulled me to him. We didn't speak but swayed together, dancing in time with the music until the light in the room grew ever more dim. After a while, we kissed. Once. Twice. He whispered that he'd wanted to hold me in his arms from the moment he saw me, then murmured something incomprehensible in French. That's when all my qualms floated out onto the balcony and into the bustle of the harbour.

Next morning, I woke slowly to the light. I felt clear headed despite the chaos of clothing and the debris of room-service littering the bedroom. Antoine was still asleep beside me. I made no movement – just listened to him breathe. For the first time in my life, I understood the meaning of the word contentment and realised I wanted to open myself up and let life come in. When I kissed him lightly on the cheek, he stirred and opened his eyes.

Grâce à Dieu. Tu es encore là !

Of course, I'm still here, I said. Where did you think I'd go?

And so, we never did get to Brett Whiteley's studio. Except for the time it took to take a cab to and from my place to pick up some fresh clothes, Antoine and I spent the weekend in his hotel bed. My first thought though when I woke on Sunday morning, was that today would be the last day we'd be spending together. I felt pretty miserable but gave myself a strict talking to in the bathroom mirror and decided to stay upbeat and not wreck the day. I needed fresh air and suggested we take a ferry ride and maybe have lunch somewhere by the harbour. Which was precisely what we did.

Later that afternoon, while walking back to the hotel, I told Antoine that I'd recently started writing a novel based on the life of Stella Bowen. Of course, he'd never heard of her.

You're not alone, I said. She's not widely known even in this country. She was an artist who left Australia just before the outbreak of World War I. And she had one hell of a life.

So how did you get to know her?

My mother took me to an exhibition of Bowen's paintings at the Australian War Memorial when I was in high school. There was something very moving about her work that I didn't quite understand at the time – a visceral response, I guess. But it wasn't until I was at university that I became fascinated by her. Her name kept popping up in unexpected places.

How? What do you mean?

Like when I learnt about the curious life of Jean Rhys who, at the age of seventy-four, while living in a shack made of tar paper and corrugated iron, managed to write Wide Sargasso Sea, the novel that wrenched her from obscurity.

Ah, he said. I've heard of this book. I think in French it's called La Prisonnière des Sargasses. But what has Jean Rhys got to do with your Stella?

Well, quite a lot. Back in 1925, forty years before Jean wrote that novel, their lives collided in Paris in a very bizarre way. That's when I became really intrigued by Stella. So I started reading everything about her life that I could find. And after reading her memoir, I felt absurdly connected to her.

Why absurdly? he asked.

Well, apart from the fact we're both Australians and share the same birthday – 16 May – we really have very little in common. Even so, a tiny nugget of an idea took hold in my brain. If I found her life so fascinating, maybe others would too.

So what did you find out about her?

I gave him a brief run-down, highlighting the years she spent in France with her lover, Ford Madox Ford. And Antoine then agreed with me that Stella's life was calling out to be fictionalised.

Besides, he said, everybody is interested in *les Années Folles*, those crazy years of the 1920's when artists of all kinds flocked to Paris. It was such an exciting period in the cultural life of my country – a time of experimentation in all things. And he rattled off names of composers who'd been there at the time. I'd only heard of a few, like Ravel, Stravinsky and Gershwin. At some point I told him that the working title of my novel was The Only Reality.

And why have you chosen that, he asked.

Because they're Stella's words. She wrote: 'The present is the only reality' near the beginning of her memoir, and the first time I read that sentence, I was struck by it for it seemed to me then, as it still does, that it sums up her entire approach to life. She'd always endeavoured to live in the moment, relishing everything around her and not dwelling on the past or worrying about the future.

It's not a bad philosophy, said Antoine, with a tilt of his head. Perhaps we should follow it. What do you say?

I'm not sure I know what you mean, I said.

We were almost at the hotel entrance and as we turned to face each other, he said: What would you say if I cancel my flight to Cairns tomorrow and stay with you for two weeks?

You mean at my place in Newtown?

He took my face in his hands, nodded and smiling, said: Do you want me to beg?

Sensing something momentous was taking place I put my mouth to his and gave him my answer.

Giddy with love, we let desire overwhelm us and lived every moment of those two weeks in tender sexual mutuality – something I'd never experienced before. While I managed to get myself to the gallery each working day, it wasn't where my heart wanted me to be. But on my return home each weeknight evening, Antoine greeted me with a glass of wine. He usually had dinner already prepared and he enjoyed telling me about the sights and sounds he'd experienced during the day when he'd been exploring the streets and laneways of Newtown and its nearby suburbs.

I had never known a composer before, particularly one with a long Wikipedia page. So it came as a complete surprise when, on the night before his departure, he told me he'd been busy working on a new piece, a piano sonata. Then on his keyboard, he played what he thought might end up being the first of three movements. It was to be called Reflections of Neve.

So what do you think? Do you like it?

What a stupid question!

With Antoine's return to France, I returned to my regular life. Work at the gallery kept my mind occupied but when not there, I found it difficult to concentrate on anything. I was missing him badly. Even when working on my novel, I'd sit for hours in front of my computer screen writing, deleting then rewriting the same sentence over and over again. All I could think about was Antoine. And no amount of flowers, daily phone-calls, text messages and steamy Skype sessions could alleviate my suffering. Or his. These only served to highlight the intensity of our feelings for one another. Put plainly – we just wanted to be together.

In December, we managed to meet up for a week in Hanoi. Antoine booked us a suite in the luxurious Hotel Metropole. To my shame, I'd never heard of it so knew nothing of its grand history. And it was there that Antoine had suggested we should live together.

From the moment our eyes met that night in the Opera House, standing in front of that glorious view of Sydney Harbour, I knew that something incredible was happening to us, he said, and I knew you felt it too. But we can't go on like this. Each of us is responsible for our own destiny and because the two of us are miserable when we're apart, don't you think we should do something about it?

It sounded like common sense to me. You're right, I said. Let's do it.

The decision to make Paris our home hadn't been difficult. It was obvious that it would be so much easier for me to re-locate than it would for Antoine. He had commissions to fulfil, long standing contractual engagements, and musicians who relied on him for employment.

In Paris, he said, you can write your Stella novel every day, *si tu veux*. You won't need to work. Unless of course you want to. But I'd be happy to support you. *Pas de problème*.

I smiled and knew that he knew that I rather liked the idea. That's when he murmured that he hoped one day we might have a child.

So we started making plans. When we said our goodbyes at the airport, he presented me with a pair of pearl earrings as a parting gift. Naturally, I was thrilled but apologised for not having anything to give him in return.

Perhaps you could let me read your novel, he'd said.

But I'm not even half finished yet.

Smiling, he tenderly cupped my cheeks in his hands and said: It's OK, *chérie*. I understand if you'd rather not show it to me.

I wasn't sure how to respond. I knew I couldn't say I was fearful of his criticism when there wasn't a whit of judgement in his touch. So I told him the truth: that I hadn't shown anyone my work because I really didn't see myself as a writer. I don't have any credentials, I said. I'm just an art curator, who had an idea that the jam-packed life of a relatively unknown, long-dead, Australian woman artist might make fascinating reading if it were turned into a novel.

Antoine removed his hands from my face and ever so lightly placed a kiss on the tip of my nose. Don't worry, he said. I should never have asked.

In the face of such sensitivity, I promised that as soon as I got back to Sydney, I'd email him everything I'd written so far.

Hopefully, I'll have it read by the time you get to Paris in February.

And that's how I came to leave my ordered, unremarkable life in Australia to follow the dictates of my heart.

Part Two
1906 – 1922

The Only Reality
by
Neve Palmer

an obedient child

A sprawling two-storey house sits upon a hill looking down on extensive parklands and beyond to the black chimney stacks and shipyards of Port Adelaide. There, in the drawing room, a dark-haired, twelve-year-old girl is suffering. Although baptised Esther Gwendolyn Bowen, everyone calls her Estelle. It's Sunday afternoon – the usual family time for the singing of hymns.

The child's mother is dressed in her usual Sunday widow's weeds. Her eyes are closed as she pounds the keys of the piano. Standing to attention on either side of her are Estelle and her younger brother, Tom. The boy bellows out the words: Rock of Ages, cleft for me, let me hide myself in Thee, while his sister does her best to stay in tune. She knows she's failing. They both are.

Let the water and the blood, from thy riven side which flowed…

She wonders why her mother can't see that this weekly regime is not only pointless, it's also torture – for all three of them. Estelle despises these Sunday sing-alongs even more than having to practise daily on the piano for two whole hours. If she's learnt nothing else, she knows she has no gift for music.

Even this hymn doesn't rhyme!

Be of sin the double cure, cleanse me from its guilt and power.

Mid-second verse, her mother stops playing. Her eyes spring open, and she rounds on her daughter. 'Oh Estelle, can't you hear yourself? You're singing quite off key. Surely you can't be that tone deaf.'

'Well, I must be,' is what Estelle wants to say.

But Mrs Bowen is not about to wait for her daughter, a mere child, to respond. Instead, she turns suddenly to Tom and dismisses him. 'You may go to your room and amuse yourself until I call you for tea.'

Estelle waits in silence as her brother scurries off. She knows she's in for it.

'My dear,' her mother says, rising, then moving to the old rosewood settee and inviting her daughter to sit down beside her. Once they're both seated, she asks: 'What is to become of you, Estelle? You are the worry of my life.'

Estelle, hoping for some kind of paternal guidance, looks up at the large portrait of her late father that looms above the mantlepiece in all its black, oval framed mourning. His face stern, a mask really. She'd never really known him, having died when she was three. But she vaguely remembers his huge moustache that tickled her cheeks when he bent to plant a goodnight kiss on her cheek each evening. She wonders if things would be different if he were still alive.

'I'm sorry, Mother. I really am,' she says.

'Well, I'm sorry too because,' and here she takes a breath, 'I don't believe you're sorry at all. For if you were truly repentant Estelle – you'd make some sort of effort and try to do something about it!'

'But I don't know what to do about it. I've tried my very best to improve my singing, but I'm not very musical, Mother. I don't like it.' She wishes she could tell her that singing only hymns is a boring pursuit which gives her no joy. No joy, at all.

'What utter nonsense, my girl,' comes the reply. 'I've watched you at dancing class, and you clearly enjoy the music there. Everyone remarks how you have an excellent sense of rhythm. Which of course means to me that you are indeed musical.'

At this point Estelle knows it would be foolish to argue. Any discussion between them is now over. Her mother has clearly outwitted her. For Estelle does love her dancing classes with Miss Young. In truth, she adores everything about them, conducted as they are in a ballroom with floor to ceiling mirrors and panels of crimson brocade and immense crystal chandeliers. There she is taught the polka and the waltz and best of all, she's able to dream of larger, grander, more glorious ballrooms that would surely be in plentiful supply in England, which she hopes one day to see for herself. One day when she's grown up. With this thought, Estelle now smiles.

'So, can I take from your expression that you'll stop this wilfulness and try a little harder with your singing in future?'

'Yes, Mother.'

Mrs Bowen is about to stand up but changes her mind. 'Ah, yes… and while we're here, there's one other matter I wish to speak to you about.' She pauses and as she does, Estelle rummages through her brain, wondering what that 'matter' might be. 'I'm also extremely concerned about the inordinate amount of time you seem to spend with your head in a book.'

'But Mother, you know I love reading and you've always said I may read any of the books we have here at home.'

'But not to excess, Estelle.'

'Yes, yes. I do understand.' And now she speaks quickly for she knows that without pleading her case, her mother might well put a stop to her reading altogether and that would be unbearable. 'But I've only just started reading Mr Dickens, as you suggested Mother, and I still have George Eliot and Charlotte Bronte to go. And I solemnly swear to you I won't ever go near Adam Bede or Jane Eyre, because you've forbidden me to. And I never, never, ever read on Sundays…'

'Please stop, Estelle,' Mrs Bowen says, shaking her head. 'I've heard enough and I'm quite sure all you say is true. But my concern is that you spend every available waking moment of the other six days a week absorbed in gratifying this unwholesome desire to read and get lost in some kind of senseless dream world.' She pauses to look at her daughter, but as she doesn't return her eye contact, she sighs and presses on. 'What's more, you obviously think you're fooling me when you read in bed at night against my orders, but I'm here to tell you Estelle, that I am fully aware that you extinguish your candle when you hear my footsteps in the hallway. And I wouldn't be at all surprised if you relight it after I've walked away!'

Estelle straightens her back, blinks and bites down hard on her lower lip.

Her mother continues: 'I see that you cannot deny it, which is a hopeful sign, for I fear for you, Estelle. Reading morning, noon and night…being late for school because of it…it's nothing but self-indulgence. And you must endeavour to curb it, my girl. Otherwise, who knows what may become of you?'

Lowering her head once more, Estelle stares at her hands which she's clasped together in her lap. 'I'll try to, Mother,' she says. 'I promise.'

But Estelle believes her mother is a saint and she already knows that she'll never be as virtuous as she is.

only this

Estelle rolls onto her back and studies the black lacquered, wood-panelled ceiling. Because she'd had her own bedroom back home, she'd taken her privacy for granted. But not anymore. Not since she'd been allocated this single-berth cabin and realised that solitude was a privilege. Most unaccompanied passengers on board hadn't been so lucky and were forced to share a cabin with total strangers – a situation Estelle knows she'd hate.

At twenty years of age, she appreciates having time to herself – to rest and reflect, to recharge and rejuvenate without banal interruption or feeling compelled to converse with one's cabin-mates. And knowing it will take a while to absorb all that she's seen and experienced since her departure from Australia, she intends to take full advantage of her good fortune while at sea.

She smiles just thinking how awkward she'd felt when she boarded the ship. It had been rather an ordeal meeting other passengers for the first time. Especially when they tried to engage her in polite conversation by asking her about her life in Adelaide. What on earth was she supposed to say about her birthplace that would be of any interest to anyone? Did they really expect or even want an honest response from her?

And because she had been raised from an early age to be polite and courteous in behaviour and manner, she'd mumbled responses about bathing in the bluest of seas. She spoke of the bountiful fruit trees in the backyard and all the loveliness of the flowering plants – of wattle, bougainvillea, hibiscus and roses. But not a word did she say about drought, flies and mosquitoes and how she truly believed that Adelaide was a stultifying, provincial little town that had the audacity to call itself a city. One only had to look at its geography, how it desperately clung to the coast, while its citizens filled its many churches every Sunday to pray for the deliverance of rain.

As far as Estelle is concerned, the life she's led before boarding the ship was as uneventful as a series of two-dimensional images in a cheap novelty flip book. But after everything she's experienced in the last thirty-six hours, she's certain her life is on the brink of becoming much more thrilling.

On the previous morning, she had chosen to disembark early – as soon as the ship had docked at their first port of call. And what a revelation that was! The first thing she noticed was the weather. It was certainly hot but so much more pleasant than it was in Adelaide. And she was surprised to see that despite the heat, no one in Colombo appeared to exert themselves. She'd taken a rickshaw ride through the city and discovered it was full of men in white linen suits, who were by no means in a hurry. In fact, they seemed to glide through the streets, leaving a careless perfumed trail of curry leaves and cinnamon in their wake.

It was all so strange and unfamiliar and excitingly foreign. She was taken past temples and colourful markets, as well as an enormous red and white mosque. She was beguiled by a smooth-talking Hindu tailor, who offered to run up a replica of one of her favourite garments in less than twenty-four hours…for a song, he'd said, for a mere song. Estelle declined and was rushed away to enjoy morning tea in a grand restaurant that had striped canvas punkahs swaying above the dining tables.

But then later, her Sinhalese rickshaw driver carried her through the never-imagined poverty of a nearby quarter with its squalid alleyways crawling with tiny, brown-skinned beggars. Estelle was shaken by what she'd witnessed and all she could think to do was ask to be returned to the ship.

It had certainly been a day of surprises, but she knew she needed to take stock, perhaps even take a nap, before she threw herself into preparing for the evening ahead. Which was precisely what she did, for she'd been invited by several other young passengers on board to attend a ball with them. It was to be held in Colombo's elegant Galle Face Hotel, that overlooked the Indian Ocean. She could hardly refuse.

Before leaving Adelaide, she'd had two very simple evening dresses made for her in taffeta and lace. One in the palest of pinks, and the one she'd chosen for this ball in pale blue. Her dressmaker had fashioned two rather fetching, matching headbands to complete the look.

Fastening the clasp of her mother's pearl necklace around her neck, Estelle had taken a final look at herself in the mirror. Pleased with the result, she smiled at her reflection and couldn't help wondering if her mother would have approved. But that didn't bear thinking about. She intended on having an enjoyable evening. After all, she was about to attend her very first ball. Little did she know that it would also be her first taste of cosmopolitan life with all its romantic possibilities.

Once at the hotel, beneath the coloured twinkling lights that were half-hidden in the foliage of towering palm trees, she began to relax and enjoy herself. Backlit by the moon, a small orchestra played dance tunes while a troop of immaculately attired waiters served tropical cocktails and canapés. Conversation had soon turned lively. And she found herself talking to Bertie, a rather handsome man twice her age, who worked in 'Trade' in some kind of official capacity for the British Government. Tea, rubber and spices were briefly mentioned.

Estelle had been charmed by his accent, his sophistication, his confidence. There was not a hint of arrogance about him, and when he guided her onto the dance floor, she knew she was in expert hands. As they waltzed together, he pressed her to his chest and she felt like she was flying, flying.

Afterwards on the terrace, looking out at the midnight sea, she told him of her desire to further her skills in art once she was in London. He smiled and holding her in a gentle embrace, suggested she change her name to something befitting her new independent start in life. She had laughed at this and said that Estelle wasn't even her real name; that it was Esther, after her mother, but so as not to confuse the two, the family had called her Estelle, instead.

'Naming one's children after oneself – such an absurd Victorian custom,' said Bertie, 'if you don't mind me saying.'

'Not in the least. I couldn't agree more.'

He leant in towards her and when his moustache lightly brushed her lips, a surging tide of warmth washed over Estelle. They kissed once, twice. But then he pulled back.

'I'm truly sorry,' he said. 'I can't…rather I shouldn't, be doing this. You're just too lovely. Too lovely. And I was carried away. I forgot myself. I do hope you'll forgive me.'

It was then he told her – he had a wife and two small children in Kandy. That she, Estelle, being so young, had plenty of time so needn't be hasty to be too grown up. 'For I'm certain,' he continued, 'truly certain, that you have a grand future in front of you, without getting mixed up with the likes of me.'

Three sudden short blasts of the ship's horns interrupt Estelle's thoughts. The ship is about to leave Colombo and set sail again. They'll soon be halfway to Europe. Oh, how she loves the endless days at sea! To think, to dream.

She rolls back onto her side and looks across the room. Framed within the porthole's window is a giant yellow moon. And there on the little desk in the far corner of her cabin is the basket of fruit that had been delivered earlier that day. The card, still attached says:

Thank you for a delightful evening. I shall not forget it in a hurry.
Nor you, dear Stella – for that's the name I'll remember you by.
Stella – the finest star in a constellation of dancing partners.
Stella – a strong and modern woman for our changing times.
With every good wish for the journey ahead,
Bertie

She'd read the message several times, always re-attaching the card carefully to its basket. Such demonstrations of gallantry were rare in Adelaide. And having never been given a gift like this before, she wants to preserve it, just as she'd found it when she'd returned to her cabin after breakfast.

Up until yesterday, her life had been quite sheltered. Protected. Almost circumscribed. And if truth be told, had her mother not died last year, she probably would have ended up being married off to some serious young man and forced to settle down to a life of boredom and unenviable predictability. Thankfully though, she'd managed to convince Uncle Charlie, her mother's brother, to let her go to England.

And in this way she fulfilled her art teacher's prediction, that she would one day flee the petit bourgeois atmosphere of Adelaide. For Miss MacPherson, who was later to be known as Margaret Preston, often railed against the place to her pupils, claiming it was nothing but a cultural and intellectual backwater, hemmed in by a vast forbidding desert on one side and by wind-racked waters of the Southern Antarctic Ocean on the other. And there'd never been a single student who dared to challenge Miss MacPherson's point of view. How could they, when she'd studied in France, Italy and Germany and had paintings hung in the Paris Salons? Surely, she of all people, would know how Adelaide compared to the rest of the world.

Estelle well remembers how liberating and inspiring her classes were, and how brave and uncompromising Miss MacPherson was, especially when she pleaded with her mother to allow Estelle to quit piano lessons so she could pursue her talent in art. And what a joy it was when her mother finally relented.

'But only in moderation,' she'd insisted. For it was common knowledge that Miss MacPherson was the only artist in South Australia to employ a nude model. A practice Mrs Bowen thought was highly inappropriate. 'One thing's for certain, you won't be going full time to her classes. I simply will not permit it, Estelle,' said her mother sniffing. 'You may attend Miss MacPherson's studio two days a week. That is all. I believe I'm being more than reasonable. The subject is now closed.'

And those two days never disappointed. In fact, they'd filled her with excitement. There may have been many people who considered Miss Macpherson 'a red-headed firebrand', but none of her students cared. Especially young Estelle, who made a silent vow to be forever grateful to her teacher for being the embodiment of all that was possible.

But then quite suddenly Miss MacPherson upped and left. She'd returned to Paris, leaving her students bereft. That was when Estelle begged her mother to allow her to continue her studies in Melbourne at the National Gallery School just as Miss MacPherson had done. Predictably, Mrs Bowen dismissed such a preposterous idea.

'Oh Estelle,' she had said. 'I pray that one day you will appreciate why I dislike that woman's undue influence upon you.'

But a lot had happened since then. Estelle yawns. Her mother's terminal illness and the horrific realities of her disease were hard to forget. They'd put a sudden stop to all talk of pursuing her art education. She'd been silenced by the force of filial duty to tend to her mother's needs. Of course, the last thing she'd wanted was for her mother to die. But die she did – with courage and composure, fervently believing she'd be joining her husband straight after her final breath released her from pain. Such was the power of her faith.

Estelle shuts her eyes against the grimness of these recollections. While she admired and respected her mother, she'd never really shared her mother's religious fervour. Long before her mother even became ill, Estelle had applied the blowtorch of logic onto the teachings of the Church and had decided that free will was a precious commodity, not to be pruned and reshaped into some pious design. Intellectual freedom is what she believes in.

And now she's well on the way to attaining it. The trustees of her mother's estate, having agreed to allow her to go to England for one year, until her brother Tom finished school, gave her a return ticket, an allowance of £20 a month and arranged for her to stay as a paying guest with the Addington family in Pimlico. Finally, the world was opening itself up to her.

For here she is – free and beholden to no one – on the cusp of an autonomous future, where she could follow what her mother called her unhealthy obsession with art. Surely this feeling, this moment is the only thing that matters. For she's come to believe that the present is the only reality – a credo she intends to live by once the ship docks in England.

'Thank you, Bertie,' she whispers to nobody. 'And I shall leave my old name in this cabin and take a new one for my new life.'

shock of the new

When Miss Stella Bowen boards the boat-train in Southampton bound for London on a wet and foggy day, the possibility of the world being plunged into the horror of war is the last thing on her mind. Her main worry is the weather. It isn't what she'd been expecting in the month of April. Her borrowed Baedeker Guide to London and Its Environs, which she'd frequently consulted before leaving Adelaide, had stated quite clearly that London's celebrated rose gardens always crawled with colour by late May because of the abundance of spring sunshine. And so for that reason, she'd crammed a good selection of white muslin dresses and matching white shoes into her suitcase. And nothing much else. Except of course her hopes and dreams.

So when the miserable weather continues unabated for several days without any appearance from the sun, she feels drained of her usual optimism.

'You're not to be worried, my dear,' insists Mrs Addington, during supper one evening. 'Rain, hail or shine, you'll still be seeing the sights tomorrow morning, as planned.' She turns her head toward the pasty-faced, young man seated beside her. 'Isn't that so, Percy?'

'Yes, Mother.'

Stella can't help feeling sorry for poor Percy. He's on his term break from Oxford, and his parents have charged him with escorting her around London on foot. He's clearly embarrassed and probably ill-equipped to perform the task as well. But Stella manages a smile and, sweeping her eyes around the table, addresses the family in general: 'I really do appreciate your kindness.'

She hopes she sounds sincere. Mrs Addington nods her approval.

'A pleasure. A pleasure,' mutters her husband, while taking another slice of cake.

To no one's surprise, the skies are grey and forbidding when the pair set off next morning. Percy strides ahead but at the first intersection he stops and waits for Stella to catch up. Then without a word, off he goes again. This becomes the pattern for the entire excursion.

Stella does her best to maintain his pace, but it's virtually impossible in the rain, which only helps to underscore just how inappropriate her choice of clothing is. She fears she looks ridiculous because her umbrella hasn't saved her from becoming wet and bedraggled. Still, she stubbornly presses on through the streets and laneways without a murmur of complaint. A whining colonial is the last thing she wants to be. Besides, the inclement weather turns out to be the least of her grievances.

What pains her more is the city itself. Everywhere she looks – Bond Street, Park Lane, Oxford Circus – is dirty, dank and grim. Even the air she breathes is foul. But what intensifies her disappointment are her living arrangements, which become increasingly unbearable as days pass by.

The terrace house, where the Addington family live, is in Pimlico's St George's Square, not far from the murky Thames River. It is, by anyone's standards, a dark and uncomfortably pokey dwelling. Not at all what Stella is used to. And although the family members are well-mannered and kind, she finds nothing exceptional about any of them. The two daughters are both dull, stay-at-home types, who never seem to be invited to parties, let alone balls, as Stella had hoped. Instead, these girls, along with their mother, work tirelessly for the Church and expect Stella to follow suit. Which of course she does, believing that as long as she remains a lodger with the Addingtons, she has little choice in the matter. But at night she lies awake, hoping an alternative might come her way.

After three dismal weeks in Pimlico, she decides she has to do something. She just can't keep sinking in the quicksands of inertia. She must take charge of her life and she's sure a change of scenery will do the trick. She knows that a break away from the city would do her good. So thinks it might be time to pay her respects to her brother's godfather, Bishop Harmer, who along with his wife, Mary, was a close family friend, when he was the Bishop of Adelaide years ago. Now as the Bishop of Rochester Cathedral, he lives with his family in Kent. At Bishopscourt, no less.

So she writes to him, and a visit is arranged. She is to take the train, and the good bishop will collect her from the station. And that's precisely what he does.

The day is warm, and Stella encounters the crisp, clean air and verdant beauty of an English spring from the passenger seat of the bishop's silver Rolls Royce roadster. Of course she's delighted, even more so by the Harmers' residence, which is an imposing Georgian house surrounded by the sweeping lawns and banks of rhododendrons of Bishopscourt itself.

Although her first weekend there, enclosed by such delightful gardens, is a pleasant relief from the gloominess of St George's Square, she soon learns that the atmosphere within the house is just as constrained as the Addingtons' terrace house in Pimlico. During her second stay over supper one evening, she foolishly expresses her desire to study art, which is met by pale, disapproving faces and a stern suggestion from the bishop that she ought not to think in that way.

'I'm afraid you're going to have to understand that the pursuit of art should only ever be considered to be an interesting hobby. Especially for a young lady.' Smiling, he pats his lips with his napkin then placing it back on the table, addresses his wife. 'So my dear, what are we having for pudding tonight?'

When Stella leaves Bishopscourt and returns to Pimlico, she feels as miserable as the grey-flannel sky that seems to her to encase London. One thing though is clear. Both residences are stuffed with fixed ideas. Unless in the service of God, independent thought is outlawed and displays of spontaneous joy are frowned upon. She may as well have never left Adelaide.

It happens without warning. The Pimlico family needs her room. A much-loved son is about to return from India. Stella must find new lodgings, which, oddly enough, she does through Bishop Harmer's wife. It just so happens that her niece has a friend – an artist by the name of Peggy Sutton, who lives in a studio flat in King's Road, Chelsea with her civil servant husband and their baby. Naturally enough, Stella is relieved that she's finally escaping the dreary oppressiveness of St George's Square.

On the day Stella moves in, Peggy, who is full of life and energy, announces they will go out that very evening to celebrate her arrival. Stella is thrilled. Her life has taken a turn for the better.

'Well, here we are!' exclaims Peggy. 'You do know, don't you, that many people believe the Café Royal is still *the* place to be?'

A bored looking waiter shows them to a tiny white marble topped table in the far corner of the room. Peggy orders two absinthes and then removes her wire-framed glasses, placing them on the table. She leans closer to Stella and asks in an audible whisper, 'So what do you think?'

Stella's heard a great deal about the Café Royal, made famous for attracting famous dramatists such as Oscar Wilde and George Bernard Shaw, but now it looks like it attracts an altogether different type of crowd. Her first instinct is to confess she's feeling somewhat dismayed, but she senses that such a reaction simply won't do. It's obvious that Peggy expects her to be delighted.

She forces a smile and lets her eyes sweep the extravagant room, with its mirrors and gilded caryatids and red plush seats. 'It's awfully stylish,' she says, hoping her new friend will be fooled by this little charade. For Stella thinks the décor is in fact quite charming but in an old-fashioned way. It's the bizarre clientele that Stella is shocked by. She'd certainly never seen such exotic creatures in Adelaide and doesn't know what to think. Even the waiter who delivers their drinks seems odd.

'Bottoms up!' says Peggy, raising her glass.

Stella follows suit, downing the cloudy pale green liquid in a single gulp.

'It's always the quiet ones.' Peggy shakes her head but sounds and looks pleased.

The absinthe isn't at all pleasant to taste, but at this point Stella really doesn't care. She's happy her new friend has failed to detect how appalled she really is by their surroundings.

Peggy signals the waiter to bring another round. 'But I'd take it easy, if I were you,' she says, her face so close to Stella's, she can feel the warmth of her breath on her cheek. 'It's going to be a long night.'

And she isn't lying.

Their next stop is the Crabtree Club in Greek Street, only a short stroll from the Café Royal, but a million miles from respectability. On the way there, Peggy tells Stella all about the club: that it's the brainchild of Augustus John, the most bohemian of painters; that it hasn't been open long and is meant for the exclusive use of artists, poets and musicians.

'Whenever I've been here,' enthuses Peggy as they climb up four flights of rickety wooden stairs, 'there's always been something wonderful going on. I'm sure you'll find it frightfully amusing.'

But as far as Stella's concerned the scene before her is nothing of the kind. She surveys the poorly lit, smoked filled room with its flimsy card tables and bench seating as the only furniture. There are no waiters and there's not a single person wearing evening dress. Many women are in trousers. Some even have page-boy haircuts. But at the far end of the room there's a piano sitting on a platform which is being played by an anaemic-looking young man with kohl-ringed eyes. Several couples are up dancing, but Stella can't help thinking the way they're moving together in time with the music is quite indecent.

She looks away, glancing at the empty table beside them and notices there's a skinny lad passed out beneath it. Nobody seems to be the slightest bit worried. But then there's a sudden burst of clapping and whistling as a scantily dressed, gypsy-like creature with wild, black hair and painted red lips takes to the platform. With the pianist accompanying her, she begins to sing 'My Little Popsy-Wopsy'. When she's finished, the patrons cheer and yell for more. So does Peggy.

'Don't you just adore this place?' she asks, clapping furiously. Stella nods, but she's never seen such immoderate behaviour in her life. Surely, most reasonable people would consider this club to be a den of iniquity. But how can she possibly say that to Peggy? She doesn't want her new friend to think she's some kind of censorious Victorian prude. It's just that this place and these people seem so…so…extreme.

Peggy's voice interrupts her thoughts. 'Don't look now,' she says, 'but over there, by the door…do you know who that is?'

'Of course I don't, silly,' says Stella, doing her best to sound light-hearted, but sincere. 'I hardly know a soul in London, let alone someone who comes here.'

'Well, the fellow closest to the door is Jacob Epstein. He's a really interesting sculptor. And the older chap beside him just so happens to be the painter and teacher, Walter Sickert.'

Stella senses that she ought to be impressed, but their names mean nothing to her. Just as she's weighing up what she should say in response, Peggy says: 'You've never even heard of them before, have you?'

'You're right. I haven't a clue who they are.' The truth is out. And to Stella's surprise, she feels relieved.

'Never mind. I have a feeling you're a fast learner. You're bound to know everybody in no time. I can tell.' And then Peggy informs her new friend that Sickert is a terribly important artist, whose work has been included in a new exhibition of contemporary British Art at the Whitechapel Gallery. 'You really ought to go along and see it, Stella. I'm sure it would be worth your while.'

'I have no doubt about that.' And Stella makes a mental note of the name of the gallery.

'As for Jacob Epstein, he seems to court controversy wherever he goes. Even in Paris!' Peggy takes a sip of her drink, while Stella waits, knowing there's more to come. 'He was commissioned to create some kind of stone monument for Oscar Wilde's tomb in Père Lachaise cemetery, but when it was completed, it caused a huge hullabaloo. The French authorities thought the sculpture was completely inappropriate, what with the exposed genitals on the statue's mythical winged man. So they had the offensive appendage plastered over. Can you believe it?'

'Well, to be frank, I can well believe it – coming from Adelaide, as I do.'

'Oh, but of course.' Peggy laughs and waves her hand towards the rest of the room. 'And I suppose all this must seem awfully shocking to you.'

Stella grins, comforted in the knowledge that Peggy understands her feelings.

'But you'd think Parisians would be much more broad-minded than you colonials.' She adds, draining her glass then placing it back on the table. 'Anyway, I think we'd better be heading home,' she says, patting Stella's hand. 'Heaven only knows what that rascal of a husband of mine might be up to!'

wartime

Stella isn't affected too much when the heir to the Austro-Hungarian Empire, Archduke Franz Ferdinand is shot dead by a lone assassin in Sarajevo. She's not too sure where Sarajevo is but she does know it's far from the head-on collision of values she's experiencing in London. Nothing seems to align with the way she'd imagined. True, she's glad to have loosened her domestic ties with god-fearing, narrow-minded, puritanism. But she often feels uncomfortable, or worse still, out of her depth in this bohemian milieu. Surely it can't be the only alternative.

Everyone she encounters seems to be on a mission to defy convention in some way or other. She's met girls from highly respectable families, who don't think twice about visiting a man's room unchaperoned. And even more astonishing is the way their carefree behaviour has no effect whatsoever on their reputations. She can't imagine what on earth her mother would have thought about that.

But when Britain declares war on Germany, everyday life changes for everyone overnight. And Stella is no exception. She's dragooned into volunteer work with the Children's Care Committee in the East End of London. And although the grinding poverty and horrifying conditions of the slums depress her, surprisingly it's through this work that her spirits take a turn for the better.

It all starts one afternoon at the Care Committee's office. She'd returned there to write up her report of the disastrous morning she'd just spent in the Outpatients Department of Hackney Hospital, where she'd taken a young child with ringworm. Trying not to cry, she'd sat down at her desk and stared numbly at the blank page in front of her.

'Well, hello there,' came a light-hearted voice. 'I must say, you're looking rather glum!'

Stella flinched and straightening her back, looked up to see a pale-skinned, smiling face with vibrant deep-set eyes and a shock of scarlet hair. This face continued to speak in the cheerful way that it had started. 'Now don't tell me. I bet you've had a harrowing morning – one you never wish to repeat. Am I right?'

Stella blinked, nodded and listened.

'My name's Mary – Mary Butts.[1] I'm a student at the London School of Economics. That's why I'm here – to gain some practical experience. For what precisely, I'm not quite sure,' she said with a laugh and perched herself on the corner of the desk. 'You see, I intend to be a writer. And a famous one at that. I write every day, you know, and I consider myself a Socialist as well, much to my mother's disgust.' Then leaning closer to Stella: 'She and I don't get on. All she ever cares about is the opening of the next village fête and all she ever wants to talk about is how wonderful that inbred and incompetent bunch of parasites the Royal Family is! I tell you, she's an utter disgrace!' Suddenly looking startled, Mary hesitated a moment, then continued. 'Oh dear, I've forgotten my manners, haven't I? Do forgive me. I do tend to blather on, but you did look so forlorn, sitting here. I thought you might need some jollying along. Anyway, you must tell me about your morning. And I promise I shan't interrupt.'

Mary's like a Roman candle, thought Stella, shooting off streams of exploding balls of light. She may be opinionated and shockingly irreverent, but the passion of her convictions is quite invigorating. So Stella told her about the draughty, over-crowded hospital's waiting room where she and the little boy had been kept for hours until they were finally sent away without any treatment by an uncaring doctor, who told them to return in four weeks' time. 'The whole experience was a nightmare!'

---

1. **Mary Butts:** (1890 – 1937) English Modernist writer, pacifist, nature conservationist and life-long non-conformist.

'I don't doubt that in the slightest,' said Mary. 'But I hope you realise that what you encountered this morning is the daily experience of the poor. No matter where they are. No matter where they go. And when you learn from this case and others like it, you'll be able to use it for the greater good.'

Stella couldn't help wondering what it was about redheads that made them such outspoken, fiery creatures. She was reminded of Miss MacPherson back in Adelaide. Both women didn't seem to mind sharing their opinions with anybody who'd listen.

And so it happens that over the next few months, Stella begins to feel less lonely. She becomes Mary's willing ear, listening to her many theories about the Poor and the Working Man. And although Stella thinks many of her ideas are extreme, Mary becomes a lively and entertaining presence in Stella's life.

At the end of that year, Stella receives a cable from her brother, Tom informing her that he is about to enlist in the 10th Battalion of the AIF, and that her return to Australia is therefore considered optional. This is just the spur she needs. Cheered on by Mary, she immediately sells her return ticket and follows her dream to enrol as a full-time student in art school. And thanks to a glowing reference from Bishop Harmer, she's accepted as a boarder in an exclusive student hostel in Kensington.

Despite the war, everything seems to brighten.

It's in the hostel's drawing room one rainy Saturday afternoon that Stella meets her next friend. Phyllis Reid is from Birmingham and is an extremely attractive young woman with a mane of light brown hair and enormous green eyes that light up whenever she speaks.

'You're new here, aren't you?' Her diction is clear, her voice hearty, her smile warm and self-assured. The two girls exchange names. Then Phyllis rushes on, 'I'm studying voice production and dramatic art at Miss Fogarty's school at the Royal Albert Hall. What about you?'

'I'm at art school.'

'Oh, what a blessed relief! I just hate being on a competitive footing with friends.' She shivers and re-adjusts her woollen shawl around her shoulders. 'I don't suppose you fancy some cocoa and a bit of a natter upstairs?'

Stella is immediately won over. 'That would be lovely,' she says, wishing she had some of the warmth and natural enthusiasm Phyllis displays.

'Follow me then. I might even have a biscuit or two.' She winks and starts to cross the room towards the door, but suddenly turns around to face Stella again. 'You know, I've never met an Australian before. But I've got a very good feeling about you and I think we're going to end up the best of friends.'

The afternoon speeds by in a stream of cocoa, conversation and a great deal of laughter. They swap tales of their childhoods and discover how similar their upbringings are. They share the same values, and even though Phyllis is much more of an extrovert than Stella could ever be, there is an instant rapport between them.

'We're definitely kindred spirits,' Phyllis announces, not knowing then there'd be many more evenings spent this way, sharing their life stories.

Stella is the happiest she's been for some time. She feels she now has a real confidante, each of them willing to exchange her views of the world – Phyllis on the Suffrage movement, which she knows quite a bit about, and Stella on Chelsea's bohemian set and of course the indomitable Mary Butts.

Winter that year is long and cold but talk costs nothing and warms both their hearts.

As the war rages on across the Channel, the two friends receive an offer to share a Kensington studio that's owned by an artist, who has gone as a soldier to the front. It's too good to refuse. And around the same time they move in, Stella realises she isn't achieving much at her current art school.

'If I have to draw another nude in charcoal, I think I'll scream,' she complains to Phyllis. 'That's all that's ever promoted there.'

'Sounds very boring to me. If I were you, I'd jolly well do something about it.'

Stella doesn't need convincing and first tries the Slade but she finds the professor who interviews her intimidating. And so she chooses the Westminster School of Art, believing they will assist her in discovering what and how she, and she alone, wants to paint.

What's more, the great Walter Sickert teaches there. She remembers seeing him at the Crabtree Club and knows he's fallen out of favour with several contemporary critics who, in line with the current style of Matisse and Picasso, are championing the notion that art is separate from life. But this doesn't bother Stella in the slightest. What counts is that she's seen some of Sickert's work and she admires what she sees.

And so her formal education in art finally begins. Sickert inspires her. From the very beginning he teaches her to open her eyes and trust what they tell her. He believes that creating life in a single touch is the greatest gift any painter can have.

He tells her to be still and observe things more closely. 'You mustn't be afraid of the canvas,' he says. 'Trust in the beauty of spontaneity.'

Stella soaks it up.

It's Peggy Sutton who suggests the girls host a party. 'Don't you think it's about time?' she argues. 'I mean, it's such a wonderful studio you have here. So much more spacious than ours. So light, so airy. It's utterly perfect for parties.' Stella and Phyllis sit mesmerised, while Peggy paces the room, barely pausing for breath. 'And besides, it's for a jolly good cause. A fellow artist off to war. He should be given a send-off to remember. Wouldn't you agree?' And then with eyes downcast, 'Who knows? He may never return.'

The girls are not just convinced, they relish the idea of having their studio filled with happy people. Of course, Peggy promises she'll assist them in any way she can. But later, over tea and toast and after their friend has gone back to her place in Chelsea, Phyllis delights Stella with a scornful but hilarious impersonation.

'Oh and I want you both to know, that I'll do absolutely anything to help out,' she cries, her voice throaty, just like Peggy's. Then continues with her arms extended in a theatrical pose, 'I'll start by drawing up the guest list for you and I can assure you that everybody who's anybody will be included.'

When Stella stops laughing, she praises Phyllis's talent for mimicry but feels it necessary to express her concern that people might well be frightened to venture out at night, what with Zeppelins appearing over London now with alarming regularity. 'And perhaps no-one will turn up, and the party will be a complete flop,' she says.

Phyllis chides her. 'Fiddlesticks! You wait and see. I reckon everyone's just like us. The war's not going to end any time soon, so we might as well enjoy ourselves instead of moping about and feeling miserable about it.'

And they certainly do enjoy themselves. The party is a huge success.

From the very start, the atmosphere had been relaxed, thanks to the strategic placement of candle-lights and the inspired addition of a gramophone that Phyllis insisted on purchasing. Most of the guests dressed for the occasion. Everyone mingled. Many grew dizzy from dancing and when that happened, someone read a poem.

But the life and soul of the party was an American chap by the name of Ezra Pound, a published poet no less. He was tall and gangly and wore a large earring in his left ear. And he continued to dance well into the night, while others preferred to look on, amazed by his frenetic abandon and his unique dance style, which consisted of sudden movements and a complete disregard of the rules of ragtime and fox-trot. He literally kicked up his heels and swayed wildly from side to side about the room, often not in time with the music at all. He was a sight to behold.

Much later, when only the stragglers were left, Ezra had held court. Phyllis, who had a genuine passion for poetry, sat at his feet with several others, while Stella looked on from a nearby sofa, where she'd seated herself next to Ezra's wife, Dorothy.

'All art should enhance the appreciation of life. Otherwise it's of little value for anyone.' He held his head aloft as he spoke. With his slender, golden tuft of hair on his chin and his long, crinkly hair swept back and up from his high forehead, he was indeed the very model of the Romantic poet. He was mesmerising.

'Bad writing,' he had continued, scattering bombshells of emphasis on unlikely words and phrases, 'like all forms of bad art, can destroy civilisations. And it's for this reason that we must study the past so that we may discover the principles of good writing, of good art and then make it new again.'

Abruptly he stood up to make the night's final pronouncement. 'But remember, technique is the test of sincerity.' He suddenly smiled, nodded to Dorothy and walked with a swaggering vigour to the door, where he wrapped his sunflower yellow scarf around his throat, put on his velvet coat and waited for his wife to say her good-byes.

They were on the point of leaving when Ezra turned from the entrance and faced the studio interior. 'By the way Phyllis, I forgot to say – that gramophone is an excellent investment in your future. Dorothy and I will most definitely come again.' And then he disappeared.

From that time forward, the girls' social world swells. Together, they slowly begin to accumulate an assortment of friends – artists, writers, performers, intellectuals and conscientious-objectors. And when Ezra invites them to his weekly dinner club at Bellotti's in Soho, Stella, while thrilled to be in the company of extraordinary individuals like the poet, T.S. Eliot and popular novelist and suffragette, May Sinclair, she's a little surprised that Dorothy rarely attends these events.

'I rather like my solitude,' she later tells Stella. 'Besides, it's impossible to keep up with Ezra's relentless pace. So I'm fairly picky about where I go along with him to.'

Stella admires her cool detachment and takes it as a personal compliment when Dorothy accompanies Ezra to several dance parties she and Phyllis hold in their studio.

But between these social occasions, Pound takes it upon himself to further the girls' education. He starts by urging them to read more innovative works like Joyce's A Portrait of the Artist as a Young Man and Eliot's 'Prufrock'. He also encourages their continuous curiosity in all the arts, although he's scathing about artists like Walter Sickert, who aren't experimenting with form.

Nevertheless, the war dominates every aspect of a Londoner's life. While soldiers are being slaughtered or wounded in their thousands, DORA, the Defence of the Realm Act, gives the government unprecedented powers. Curfews are imposed. Many people, who are deemed to be 'causing alarm', are arrested. Women are manning the factories. Beer is watered down. Pubs have their opening hours slashed. Prices soar. Essential items like butter, meat and sugar are rationed. London is under attack from the night sky. Fear stalks the streets.

And the ever-increasing numbers of casualties weigh heavily on Stella's mind.

broken

What the officer remembers when he returns from the Somme is that after he was blown into the air, he couldn't remember a thing – nothing about his past, not even his name.

He'd been at the back of Bécourt Wood with his battalion's first line of transport. Right in the middle of the strafe. Because they were bombarded at least two or three times a day, he'd almost become accustomed to the noise. Nothing seemed to happen of any consequence. But this time it was different. The shells were screaming right above him.

Nearby, one of his men, a mere lad, was blasted backwards into a truck, his stomach ripped open, his mouth a silent O. He was about to go to him when wham! He was lifted skyward. Up, up. This wasn't how it was meant to be. To die like this.

When he fell back to earth, he'd landed flat on his face. And was out cold.

Later he was told that he'd been unconscious for over three weeks. He had no idea. He didn't have a clue who he was. His identity had been erased by a high-explosive shell. And his teeth and mouth were a mess.

It takes a while before his memory starts to return. Whole patches of his life seem to have been erased. Firstly, he remembers his name and that before enlisting he'd been a writer, but he's told he is now Second Lieutenant Ford Madox Hueffer of the Welch Regiment.

When his battalion goes to rest camp, he's moved to the Casualty Clearing Station in the small town of Corbie, where what he later calls 'the nerve-tangle of war' begins. All day long he's beset by nightmares and grotesque hallucinations. With enemy planes dropping bombs all over the field hospital, he can't distinguish dream from reality.

Immense shapes in grey-white shrouds, whispering murderous plans, loom over him. Dead Red Cross nurses are carried in stretchers past his bed. There are times he's sure the Germans have taken him prisoner and that he's lying on the ground, his hands and feet manacled. Sometimes his long-dead father appears to admonish him again and again as he once used to do when he was but a boy.

'Look at you!' he booms. 'You've made a thorough mishmash of your life. I always knew you were an extremely stupid donkey.' Then he vanishes. But his laughter echoes like a bully's puerile taunt: 'Mad ox…mad ox…mad ox…'

These are memories Ford doesn't want to recall. But somehow he knows that if he's to regain his sanity and his intellect, he has to retrieve his past, so he can move into the future. That, he understands. Then a revelation comes to him one night.

A severely wounded soldier lies screaming and crying three beds down from him. His bandages are soaked in blood. And before anyone knows what's happening, he rolls out of bed and has his hands around Ford's neck trying to strangle him. The orderlies manage to pull him away, but the man starts to shout a single word over and over again: 'Faith! Faith! Faith!'

At first Ford thinks the soldier's calling out the name of a woman. His dying words a call to the love of his life or perhaps, for love in general. Next, he wonders if it's some kind of religious exhortation. And if so, faith in what? God? But which one? Or is the repetition of the word meant only as a simple plea to believe in oneself?

He lies there terrified that he may never be the same again, while asking himself if perhaps he hasn't been a little mad all his life. He doubts he will be able to move forward with his altruistic sense of patriotic duty, of the British stiff-upper-lip, of being courageous in the midst of uncontrollable panic induced by the horror of war. But he's a writer and now he knows he wants to write again. But this thought makes him even more frightened and anxious. Would he ever be able to transform his experiences of war into a convincing narrative?

Still in this disturbed state of mind, Ford is deemed fit for action and is sent back to the front to join the 9th Battalion. This time near Kemmel Hill in the Ypres salient. His Commanding Officer doesn't like him, believing him too old for the job. Ford perseveres. Knowing he is the only writer his age to be at the front, he decides to take a literary view of the war. He will bear witness.

Until he becomes ill again, that is. His shattered teeth are causing him problems, and he's having trouble breathing, exacerbated by his exposure to mustard gas. In a letter to his mother he informs her that he's wheezing like a machine gun, then adds that he'd prefer to be dead. It isn't only the physical damage to his lungs that plague him, it's the nervous breakdown brought on from being blown up by a 4.2inch artillery shell.

On the edge of unreason, Ford is sent to convalesce in a hospital by the Mediterranean in Menton and then is invalided home shortly after. For the rest of the war he will mostly serve as an administrator and lecturer in a training command at Redcar, on the Yorkshire coast.

What he doesn't yet know is that the fear of fear will plague him for a long time after the war has ended.

an invitation

The summer of 1917 begins with Germany launching a strategic campaign of terrifying bombing raids over London. Gone are the Zeppelins that attacked by night. The new Gotha bombers boldly strike in broad daylight. Often in waves, they fly in formation thundering down upon the capital. Civilian casualties are high, and the material damage spirals into hundreds of thousands of pounds. Understandably, the British people are not amused. Anti-German feeling is so high, King George V decrees the Royal Family's surname will no longer be Saxe-Coburg-Gotha and changes it to Windsor, a thoroughly British sounding name.

Still, one Sunday morning in August, Stella and Phyllis wake early and over breakfast they chatter about the previous night's fancy dress party, which had been a riotous outpouring of fun and giddiness, with lots of dancing and singing of bawdy songs.

'I'm sure everyone's trying to forget how utterly terrible this wretched war is,' Stella says, some toast still in her mouth.

'Oh, let's not get all gloomy and talk about the war.' Phyllis puts down her cup and eyeing her friend's crestfallen face, quickly back-peddles. 'I mean there has to be some joy in the midst of all the horror.' She swallows a mouthful of tea and says: 'But are you alright?'

'Of course, I am.'

'No, I mean really. Are you happy? Really, truly happy?'

Stella manages a smile. 'That's an easy question to answer when there's room to express some doubt.'

'So don't keep me in suspense then.'

'Well, I'm quite content, if that's what you mean. I'm still able to enjoy myself. Like I did last night. But if I were to be completely honest with you, I'd have to say I'm not so sure I'm someone who'll ever find true happiness.'

'Why on earth would you think that?'

'Oh, you know… I think it's pretty obvious that I'm destined to be the eternal wallflower.'

'Ah! So that's what this is about.' Phyllis raises her eyes in imitation of someone about to swoon with joy and then breathlessly spells out the letters: 'L.O.V.E.'

Well-used to her friend's jokes and theatrics, Stella slow-claps her hands. 'Very amusing. But I do sometimes think that the man of my dreams may not actually exist.'

Phyllis shakes her head in disbelief. 'What a load of old tosh! Where on earth do you get some of your ideas from?'

'Don't worry, you're not the first to say that, and I bet you won't be the last either.' Stella rises and collects their plates and cups and saucers. She wants to put an end to this conversation and makes her way to the kitchen. It really makes no difference what she says, Phyllis will always have her own view of things. As it should be. And besides, there's no use talking to her, especially when it comes to affairs of the heart. Phyllis has always been the expert. She's also remarkably beautiful. Everybody says so. And she has more suitors than she knows what to do with. She's forever falling in and out of love. Passion could well have been her middle name, for she hardly ever shows any emotional restraint.

Aware that some people think she's rather dull compared to Phyllis, Stella doesn't mind in the least. What really bothers her is the fact that she's been in London for four years now and hasn't met a man she's found even vaguely attractive, let alone someone she could call her sweetheart. Whereas all her close female friends have fallen in love at least once and most of them are now being courted. Some of them, like dearest Mop,[22] are even having affairs. Not that Stella considers herself

---

2. **Mop**, nickname for **Dame Margaret Postgate Cole:** (1893 - 1980) Poet, novelist and significant figure in the British Socialist movement, notably during WWI when she joined the peace movement along with her future husband, **G D H Cole**. She abandoned her pacifism with the rise of fascism in the 1930s. A champion of comprehensive education, she was awarded a DBE in 1970 for services to local government & education.

judgemental anymore about that sort of thing. But there's been the odd occasion, like this morning, when she's wondered if her Adelaide inhibitions are still lurking within her, keeping at bay any inkling of romance.

A few weeks later, Stella receives an invitation to another party. This time she goes by herself because Phyllis wants to spend a few hours alone in the studio with her latest boyfriend. As soon as Stella arrives, a good-looking young man approaches her and asks her to dance.

Delighted, she readily accepts, not knowing that he's another woman's escort for the evening. And what's more, the woman in question is none other than Violet Hunt, the wealthy socialite and novelist, now in her mid-fifties but still impossibly glamorous. She no longer enjoys dancing herself, so sits at a sulky distance with a clear view of the dancing couple, who look like they're enjoying themselves a little too much. And although Violet isn't in love with her escort, it doesn't stop her from being seized by jealousy. Alone in her corner, she feels slighted and neglected and continues to fume until Ezra, typically late, arrives just as people are beginning to leave. Violet watches him as he surveys the room.

'Ah, there you are!' he cries out, sounding even more boisterous than usual, thanks to a sudden lull in the music. Having spotted Stella, he rushes towards her. 'Come along, come along,' he says, grabbing her hand and almost dragging her across the room towards Violet. 'There's someone, I want you to meet.'

Ezra has absolutely no idea that Stella has been unwittingly dancing with Violet's escort and so he blunders through his introductions, while Violet, her face impassive, sits upon the sofa like a gilded monarch receiving her subjects. The two women exchange awkward pleasantries. Violet's regal manner and striking good looks unnerve Stella, who feels decidedly drab in comparison. But having already suggested to several other left-over partygoers that they should come back to her studio for more dancing, she thinks it only good manners to extend an invitation to Violet as well.

'Why, thank you,' comes her icy response. 'But I really must decline, as I'm frightfully tired and have an early engagement in the morning.' She then takes her leave and goes home alone, taking her petulance to bed with her.

Later, once her temper abates and she's reflected on the evening's events, Violet realises she'd behaved badly at the party. And wishes she hadn't gone at all. She'd accepted the invitation because she'd thought being in the presence of so many young people, all full of energy and stamina, her spirits would lift, and her morale given a much-needed boost. But no such luck.

They were all too busy enjoying themselves to pay her the slightest bit of attention. She thinks perhaps they weren't aware of who she was and that was why they'd ignored her. Or worse still, maybe they did know and simply didn't want to be in her ageing company.

Surely, she'd suffered enough already. For too long now, people she'd thought were friends had cruelly snubbed her, thanks to all the newspaper placards plastered with her photograph screaming her name. She'd become a persona non grata overnight, which had hurt. Deeply. And now Ford's claiming he no longer loved her with the passion he once did. Well, it's all too much to bear. What she needs to do is to make some new friends. Friends who are dependable, loyal, sensible. And most importantly, good company.

So Violet decides to seek out young Stella Bowen, for at least she seemed pleasant and courteous. She'll wait a few weeks then invite the young woman for afternoon tea at South Lodge, her London residence.

Intrigued and somewhat flattered, Stella accepts the invitation. After all, Violet is seriously famous. She'd grown up surrounded by Pre-Raphaelite writers and artists. The painter, Alfred William Hunt was her father, and her mother was the novelist, Margaret Raine Hunt. Violet was also known to have a large circle of friends in the literary world, Henry James among them. And as for lovers, it was rumoured she'd had quite a few, including Somerset Maugham and H.G. Wells. But her most notable was of course Ford Madox Hueffer, who was ten years her junior. Together, over several years, they'd set outraged tongues wagging by causing a series of public scandals.

Months ago, Ezra had urged Stella to read Hueffer's novel, The Good Soldier. She'd liked it a great deal and learnt that Hueffer, having worked for years with Joseph Conrad co-writing and editing, was considered an influential critic as well. He'd established the prestigious English Review that introduced Pound to England and published the early work of the young and ambitious writer, D.H. Lawrence. But up until she'd met Violet, who now seemed bent on taking Stella into her confidence, the scandal had been of little interest to her.

'Oh, you can't imagine, my dear, what I've been through,' Violet says, returning her cup and saucer to the marble-topped table beside her. 'I've been so desperately unhappy for such a long time; I scarcely know where to begin…' Her voice trails off melodramatically and then returns, 'but I don't wish to bore you.'

'Please don't think that.' Stella hopes she sounds reassuring. 'I'm not in the least bit bored.'

'I can't tell you how relieved I am to hear it.' At this point she leans closer to Stella and searches her eyes. 'I can tell instinctively that you are someone I can trust.' There's a slight upward inflexion in her voice, a cue for Stella to respond.

'You have nothing to fear from me. Nothing at all.'

And so Violet tells her new friend how she met the great Ford Madox Hueffer. 'He was in dire financial straits you see, estranged from his two young daughters and their dreadfully vexatious mother, Elsie. He'd been living alone in a squalid maisonette above a slaughterhouse. Can you imagine it, Stella? A slaughterhouse!' She pauses, blinking back tears then continues. 'He was so terribly, terribly depressed. And without a word of a lie, if it hadn't been for my hasty intervention, he would've no doubt committed suicide. I'm positive of that.'

Violet rings a small bell, and on cue a maid appears. 'Some muffins please, Clara,' who scurries away only to re-appear seconds later with muffins, which she offers to Stella. Placing one on the bread-and-butter plate that's resting on her lap, Stella picks at it from time to time as Violet continues her story.

'Ford's a genius, you know. And while all geniuses can be difficult, he is extremely so. But back then, I didn't know what I know now. I also didn't think the difference in our ages could or would ever be an impediment to our future together. After all, we had so much in common.' Another little pause to check Stella's interest. Then off she goes again. 'Did you know his maternal grandfather, who helped raise him, was the painter, Ford Madox Brown? So you see, from the very start we were absolutely suited. I can't tell you, how hopelessly in love with one another we were!'

She begins to fiddle with the amethyst brooch pinned to the collar of her dress. 'And I don't mind admitting to anyone either that he's the greatest love of my life. You see, he promised to marry me as soon as he was divorced. But when Elsie petitioned the courts for the restitution of her conjugal rights and won the case, Ford became the butt of jokes all around London, and by implication so did I. The whole thing was grotesque. My reputation was in tatters, and I felt utterly humiliated.'

She breaks off then and from beneath her bodice frees a white lace handkerchief, which she uses to dab at her nose. 'The shame and indignity of it was enormous. But did Ford do anything about it? Of course not! He was like some blasted ostrich with its stupid head in the sand! He just locked himself away to edit the novel I'd just finished writing. Perhaps you've read it – The Wife of Altamont? At any rate, he ignored every court order that was made against him. Until that is, he was charged with contempt of court and so spent a week in Brixton Gaol.'

Violet pours them both more tea and tells Stella how they'd decided, after Ford's release from prison, that a trip to Germany was in order.

'We were both of the opinion that a legal end to his marriage with Elsie was the only solution, and if she refused to divorce him in England, well it was up to Ford to try to secure one in Germany, the land of his ancestors. He stayed there for some time, waiting for the divorce to be finalised, and so it wasn't until the spring of 1911 that we were able to marry.'

Violet rises from the chaise longue and begins to pace up and down in front of Stella. 'I know you'll find this hard to believe, my dear, but the absolute worst thing happened.'

Stella can't imagine things getting any worse.

'You see,' continues Violet, 'apparently a German divorce wasn't granted after all and what's more, neither Ford nor I could find our marriage papers. We had no proof we were man and wife even though we knew we were in our hearts.' She stops pacing and looks directly at Stella. 'I suppose you are shocked. And think me immoral. A woman of easy virtue?'

'Absolutely not. I think you're very brave.' In fact, Stella thinks Violet is quite the progressive new woman. She also can't wait to read one of her novels.

Violet sits back down next to Stella and grasping her hand, lifts it to her lips and kisses it. 'Thank you, thank you. I truly appreciate your understanding. For I'm afraid there's still worse to come…'

And off she goes again, detailing how Elsie had won a libel suit against her for using the title Mrs Hueffer and how the press had hounded her, with Ford again thoroughly traumatised by it all. 'He simply couldn't cope,' says Violet, 'detesting all the unwanted attention on what he believed was a very private matter. And it all took a terrible toll on our relationship. I was constantly bailing him out of his financial problems. But before long he turned against me, claiming he was tired of it all and no longer loved me as he'd done before.'

Her eyes narrow. Her voice sours. 'But I can assure you Stella, he always knew where to run to when he needed something, and I suppose I always knew he was tied to me no matter what he thought. And then the war started. I was ill at the time, but Ford being Ford and in some sense old school, felt it was his duty to enlist. That was when I knew he was retreating from me, but I wanted to hear him say it.'

Stella notices an inconsistency in what Violet had just said. She also wonders why Violet feels the need to use a military expression when it comes to questions of the heart, so asks: 'You wanted to hear him say he was retreating from you?'

'Not in those exact words, silly. No, I wanted him to tell me straight, that it was over between us. Finished. Kaput. I realised he was no longer attracted to me in the same way he once was and thought he'd enlisted to get away from me. I know he thinks he'd like to be free of me. But he can't do it. He hasn't got the intestinal fortitude. He wants me to be the one to break off. And I'm not about to give him up.' She clicks her fingers. 'To be honest, I want him to do the right thing. To be a man. For once in his miserable life.'

Malice has entered the room, and Stella feels uneasy. The thought crosses her mind that there may be more to this story than the one she's hearing.

'I suppose you think I'm being spiteful. But I can assure you, my friends would think me rather tiresome if I weren't.' She changes the subject. She knows she's said enough for one day. And she certainly has no desire to reveal to young Stella what many people don't know and hopefully never will and that is – she has advanced syphilis. Luckily for Ford, he'd never contracted it, for when their affair began, Violet was already in the tertiary non-transmissible stage of the disease. He'd only been informed that she suffered from it back in 1914, when her doctor insisted on examining him. Just in case.

And it was from that moment that Violet sensed he was repulsed by her as well as the disease. Not that she would ever say that out loud. And although Ford had been sympathetic enough and tried to be kind to her, she doesn't want his pity. Or his compassion. She wants something much more physical than that.

So afternoon tea comes to a very abrupt end. And Stella is free to go.

a gift

Towards the end of October 1917, Stella receives another invitation from Violet to attend a weekend gathering that she's hosting down at Knapp Cottage, her country retreat by the sea in Selsey.

'Ford will be there,' she declares. 'So you'll be able to meet him at last. He's got leave. Mind you, it's only for forty-eight hours, but I know he'd relish some youthful company. So please, do say you'll come along.'

Curious, Stella agrees to go, mainly because she's heard so many different opinions about this Ford Madox Hueffer. At least by going down to Selsey, she'll be able to judge for herself what he's like. Especially since Violet's constant carping about him is making her question everything she's heard. So much so, Stella had even raised the topic of the bizarre nature of the couple's relationship with Dorothy, when she'd recently visited the Pounds.

'I find it astonishing that Violet professes her love of Ford to anyone who'll listen but then in the same breath says the most monstrous things about him.'

Dorothy rolls her eyes. 'You're not the first person to have noticed. I suppose that's why Ford's tried to break off the affair so many times. But every time he does, Violet launches a fresh campaign of accusations.' Stifling a sigh, she adds: 'Have you read her novel, The House of Many Mirrors?'

'No, but I will, if you recommend it.'

'Well, you're in for a treat.' More rolling of eyes. 'I have to say though, it's a nasty, vindictive piece of work. She portrays herself as a beautiful, wealthy widow, who's years older than the man she's married – a profoundly selfish but brilliant architect called Alfy, who's clearly based on Ford. I can only imagine how he must feel about it.' She pauses and smiles at Stella. 'At any rate, I'm sure once you've read it, you'll understand why he wants little to do with her.'

'I'll get myself a copy this afternoon.'

'For goodness sake, don't buy one. I've got a copy somewhere and before you go, I'll see if I can dig it out for you.' Dorothy breathes deeply. Stella can see her friend is choosing her words carefully. Both women know that Ezra would disapprove of the conversation they're having. 'I've no doubt the fact that they're both writers must be awfully problematic for Ford.'

'How do you mean?'

'Well, Violet's prolific. And her novels are sexually frank, so they sell extremely well. But by any measure they're not what you'd call high art. Whereas Ford's work is ground-breaking. I mean, look how inventive The Good Soldier is with its time shifts, its form… But did it sell well?' She shakes her head. 'By God, it must be extremely galling for Ford when her trash just walks off the shelves, whereas his work gathers dust.'

Stella's immediate thought is that merit doesn't always guarantee popularity or financial rewards but not wanting to state what she believes is obvious, she simply agrees with her friend that it would indeed be demoralising for any writer of Ford's talents and skill.

But it's time to go. At the door, Dorothy hands Stella her copy of The House of Many Mirrors. 'Don't bother returning it. Consider it a gift.'

by the beautiful sea

A nondescript, stucco, three-bedroom house surrounded by towering trees – Knapp Cottage isn't what Stella expected. But then neither is Ford. Being a pacifist by nature, she's fairly sure he'll be a militarist. So even before she meets him, she decides to avoid conversations about the war as best she can and to try to keep an open mind while making the most of the fresh sea air.

She arrives late in the afternoon with Violet greeting her in her usual effusive manner.

'Follow me, my dear, and I'll show you to your room.'

As soon as she opens the door, Violet sweeps across to the large bay window opposite and throws open the tango red, heavy linen curtains exposing the view of a magnificent Wayfaring tree, heavy with clusters of black berries.

'Oh, how beautiful!' exclaims Stella. But she isn't merely referring to the external garden scene but also to the room itself. Everything about it is theatrical. The walls are papered in jade green and purple, complementing the crimson and yellow velvet patchwork quilt on the large four poster bed. An old wooden washstand is painted in gold. Cushions are scattered about and in one corner there's an inviting armchair, draped in some kind of colourful oriental fabric.

'I'm glad it pleases you,' says Violet. 'But I need to tell you that it'll just be the three of us this weekend – you, me and Ford.' She flutters her eyelashes as she speaks, which Stella thinks extremely odd. 'You see, yesterday I was feeling very, very poorly and I feared I wasn't up to having too many guests, so I had Mrs Child wire everyone to tell them not to come. Except for you of course. And now here you are…' She raises her arms to indicate resignation. 'I do hope you don't mind, dear. To tell the truth, I was fairly certain you'd prefer it this way.' More fluttering eyelashes.

Taken aback by this disclosure, Stella hardly knows what to say. She's been given no choice in the matter. How dare Violet assume she knows what she prefers! Then she wonders if Violet is manipulating her in some way. Perhaps there's some agenda she's not privy to? But to what end?

She starts to feel uncomfortable and out of place, which really isn't a promising start to the weekend.

'So once you've freshened up, come and join us in the parlour. Mrs Child will shortly be serving tea. We're only having whiskey and sandwiches, I'm afraid.' And with a smile, Violet is gone.

Bearlike in stature, Ford is an imposing figure of a man. Stella had imagined he'd be in uniform but instead, he looks more like the gardener who'd just dropped by to discuss the benefits of composting fallen autumn leaves. He isn't handsome either.

Though there's definitely something solid and dependable about his demeanour that Stella thinks is appealing. His voice is soft and warm as well.

At first, he reminds her a bit of Ezra. Not physically, but in the way he speaks with such authority on so many subjects. She's always loved stimulating conversation, but this is something else. She finds she could listen to his stories all night long. But is it any wonder? He's known so many fascinating people and seen and experienced so much in his forty something years.

Nevertheless, she thinks it best to retire early. Violet hasn't said very much all evening and when her eyes meet Stella's, her gaze has been icy. Once in bed, Stella is kept awake by raised voices, most of which are Violet's, that are only silenced with the sound of two doors slamming. One after the other.

Next morning at breakfast, it's convivial enough. But just as the three of them are about to discuss the day's possible activities, Violet's nose begins to bleed. With napkins pressed to her face, she rushes from the table, upturning a chair. Ford stands up and says, 'I best go after her.'

He'd not gone long before he returns to inform Stella that Violet has taken to her bed and will stay there for the remainder of the day.

'And so Miss Bowen, I'm at your disposal.' He gives a quick bow of his head then waits to check Stella's response. 'I thought a stroll by the sea would be nice. And you must see my vegetable patch and the orchard out back. What do you say?'

She smiles broadly and replies, 'I think that sounds lovely.'

While Stella and Ford are enjoying each other's company, Violet broods between bouts of impotent rage. Her doctor had advised her to accept the fact that her now frequent nose bleeds are caused by the slow disintegration of her septum, yet another ailment caused by syphilis. And this knowledge only fuels her despair.

But it isn't the only thing.

Alone in her room, she realises she's seriously miscalculated. She only introduced Stella to Ford in the crazy hope of reviving his affections for her – Violet. But instead, she'd placed herself in the hideous position of witnessing Ford's eyes burning with desire whenever he spoke to the younger woman. How could she have been so deluded? It had been a long time since he'd last looked at her that way.

Yes, there's no denying it now. He's grown tired of her.

But she really doesn't know how she's going to cope without him. Firstly, she'll be the laughingstock of London. The older woman scorned and tossed aside. That's how the world will see her. And if her illness becomes common knowledge, God forbid, there'll be no end to the social hostility she will have to endure.

Oh, why can't Ford maintain appearances? Surely, he could show some loyalty. To her. After everything she's done for him.

By afternoon's end, she's resolved to confront him. She'll wait till Stella has gone to bed and then she'll remind him of his obligations to her and to her alone. Which is precisely what she does.

But this time, Stella can hear almost every word of their overheated exchange. Violet starts pleading with Ford to show her some tenderness. 'At the very least, you owe me that.' Then minutes later, her voice begins to grate like a high-pitched violin. 'You're only ever affectionate when you want money. You have used me badly. Badly, do you hear?' Then the sound of breaking crockery.

'Good God, woman. Will you behave yourself? Have you forgotten we have a guest?'

'How could I forget?' Sobbing follows, then some muffled noise before Violet starts up again. 'But I'll tell you one thing for certain, if you turn your back on me, I won't be giving you a penny more. Not one! I don't care how hard up you are. How will you like that?'

There's a short silence before Ford responds. 'I will tell you what I don't like and that is your disgusting exhibitions with your creaking door voice, hoping to belittle me at every turn. Don't you realise that all you manage to do is humiliate yourself in the process?'

More tears, then a sudden about-turn, with Violet begging to be forgiven. 'All I want from you is a little loyalty, Ford. Is that too much to ask?'

'Loyalty? You want loyalty from me when you give none? You must be joking.'

'But I've always been loyal to you. And you know it.'

'You don't know the meaning of the word.' His clear voice has become a deliberate hiss. 'What do you call your all too obvious portrayal of me in The House of Many Mirrors, then? Do you call that loyalty? Because I don't. I call it betrayal - venting your feelings about me in your novels. Airing all your grievances in print. Your appalling indiscretion has destroyed my reputation and ruined me socially.'

'It's rather late to start complaining, isn't it? Why on earth did you agree to edit it then?'

'How was I to know what the book's contents were? You're so full of your own importance, Violet. You really are. You care nothing for others. Nothing. I have tried to love you and have offered you companionship, but you make it impossible.'

'But don't you see, I don't want companionship or your love. It's your passion I want.'

'Of course, you do. With your bedroom mind that's the only thing that makes sense to you. But if you really wanted me to be attracted to you in that way, you'd be making yourself attractive and cease all these silly tantrums at once!'

'Oh, why me? Why must it always be me who suffers so dreadfully by brutes like you?'

Ford doesn't immediately respond. Then very calmly says: 'I tell you what. Why don't I stay well away from you for a couple of months, and we can have a quiet time until I get some leave at Christmas? Perhaps by then, I'll be able to make love to you.'

Stella hears a smash of glass, followed by several loud footsteps and a door banging shut. Then no more voices can be heard.

The next morning Ford takes the train to London. So does Stella. It seems natural to them both that they should sit together in the same carriage. Even so, Stella is somewhat on edge in case he should raise the issue of his and Violet's ruckus the previous night. Which would be quite embarrassing, to say the least. But she needn't have worried. He never mentions Violet's name and scarcely refers to the weekend's events.

However, he does tell her that he has an important meeting with army personnel in the city, which explains why he's in uniform. It had been the first thing Stella noticed about him that morning - how fetching he looked in khaki. When she asks about his war experiences, he speaks briefly about his duties at Redcar and even more briefly about his time on active service. He also tells her that all he really cares about right now is for Germany to be defeated. And as soon as possible.

'You know Miss Bowen, I have a recurring dream about finding a rural sanctuary, once this blasted war is over, where I can live off the land and write to my heart's content.'

Stella smiles. 'I think that's a very fine dream to cling to.'

'And cling to it, I shall.'

When he asks her questions about her life, his China-blue eyes smile back at her which make her even less reserved than she'd been the day before. She gives him a potted history of her life, her family and growing up in Adelaide. He listens, genuinely interested in everything she says, including the reasons why she'd left Australia, her passion for painting and the work she's been doing for the war effort.

By the time the train arrives in London, Ford is completely smitten.

Naturally, Stella can't wait to tell Phyllis all about the last few days. What a weekend it has been! Her view of Violet has definitely changed. Having overheard the terrible rows, she's convinced Violet is quite unstable. And as for her cruelty to Ford - well, to reveal the private affairs of the man she professes she loves in such a public way is unconscionable.

Once back at the studio, she doesn't mince her words. 'The pair are absolutely incompatible. I really think there's something wrong with her.'

Phyllis shrugs and pulls at the little gold chain that hangs around her neck. 'Love can do strange things to people, you know. So tell me about Ford? What did you think of him?'

Stella lowers her eyes and blows steam from the top of her teacup, biding her time while she weighs the pros and cons of telling her closest friend what she can barely admit to herself. But then she blurts out: 'I've never met anyone like him before.'

'Ooh, aye! It must have been all that fresh sea air.' Phyllis tries not to appear too surprised. In the theatre world she's come across all sorts of people. And nothing much surprises her anymore. But even though she knows Hueffer is admired by many for his great intellect and especially for The Good Soldier, she's also aware that he's been persecuted by a bombardment of gossip mongering. Some of it extremely unkind. Even at a recent party, she'd overheard someone talking disparagingly about Ford's appearance - that what with his ruddy complexion, sandy hair and a mouth that continually drooped open, he looked more like the village idiot than a man of letters.

'I know what you're thinking,' says Stella. 'I've heard some dreadful things about him too. But wait till you meet him. You'll see.'

'So pray tell,' her eyebrows raised, 'when's that likely to be?'

'For heaven's sake, Phyllis. It's not like that. All I said was that I'd never met anyone like him before. Which is the truth. He's the perfect gentleman. Everything was completely above board. Honestly.' And she makes a tiny sign of the cross on her heart.

Phyllis purses her lips. 'Very well, but tell me this: did he ask for your address?'

'Yes he did, and yes, I gave him my card.'

'Oh my lord, you're blushing!' Her voice is jubilant. 'I knew it! I knew it!' She claps her hands. 'Well, if he likes you and you like him, why worry about what I or anyone else may think? It's no-one else's business, but yours.'

And with that, she lifts her skirt to her knees and starts to dance around Stella, singing:

By the sea, by the sea, by the beautiful sea.
You and me, you and me – oh, how happy we'll be![3]

Stella can't help laughing. She's always loved Phyllis' sense of fun. Even when it was at her expense.

Once Phyllis had stopped spinning and singing, she throws herself down on the sofa and says: 'I tell you what though, I bet you anything that you'll hear from him within the week.'

Stella shakes her head. 'Oh, you do carry on.' But Phyllis is right.

letters

A letter from Ford arrives six days later. Somewhat short and to the point, it opens with the polite salutation: Dear Miss Bowen but becomes playfully flirtatious, by referring to the sunshine of Stella's smile.

And so begins a friendly correspondence – she from London, he from Redcar. Meanwhile, Stella continues to see Violet on occasion, but tells her nothing about her communication with Ford. She doesn't know why but she feels she ought to protect him from any further pain that Violet may choose to inflict upon him. At the same time though, Stella can't help feeling sorry for her, what with her stubborn refusal to see what others can plainly see – that her so-called marriage to Ford is an empty fiction. For Violet has told her she can't let him go; that she loves him with her entire being. But as a woman scorned, she will show him no mercy and she's determined she won't allow him to discard her like some old dish rag.

When in the summer of 1918, Stella leases a little cottage in the market town of Berkhamsted, thirty-odd miles northwest of London, Ford pays her a visit, and their relationship shifts gear. Now in his frequent correspondence, his Dear Miss Bowens disappear and are replaced by:

---

3. ***By the Beautiful Sea:*** A popular song, published in 1914. Music by Harry Carroll. Lyrics by Harold R. Atteridge.

My dear Stella. And before too long, he's making declarations, writing that he belongs to her completely – and to her only, and for good, and all. That is the truth. He pleads with her to believe him but he also uses his novelist's keen eye to tell her about his day-to-day military life in Redcar. He encourages her to paint and feeds her hunger for ideas by expressing with absolute candour his values and attitudes to a myriad of subjects: religion and morality, love and marriage, art and politics.

He dries rose petals and adds them to his letters. He makes it clear that he wants to disentangle himself from the mess of his past and forge a future with her – Stella. That all he really wants more than anything in the world is her and a little cottage, in a valley, not too far from a market town. He confides that: 'I write to you as I never took the trouble to write to any other soul' and begins to refer to her as 'my darling', who is the reason his confidence is returning and miracle of miracles, he's begun to write a new novel.

He'd always believed in the power of the written word and now he has proof. Thanks to his skill in composing letters, the ever-sensible, rational Stella finds him utterly irresistible. And before too long, they're making plans to live together once the war is over.

In her spare time, Stella begins to re-read The Good Soldier. She wants to make sure she completely understands Ford's character. Because he's the man she intends to spend the rest of her life with. About halfway through the novel, she finds a passage that she keeps returning to. It speaks so directly to her that she draws two thick pencil lines against it in the margin of the page. She tells herself she must remember every word:

"For, whatever may be said of the relation of the sexes, there is no man who loves a woman that does not desire to come to her for the renewal of his courage, for the cutting asunder of his difficulties. And that will be the mainspring of his desire for her. We are all so afraid, we are all so alone, we all so need from outside the assurance of our own worthiness to exist." [4]

---

4. *The Good Soldier:* Novel by Ford Madox Ford, Penguin Books, 1988 p.109.

She wonders if these words, written back in 1914, were meant as a message to Violet - advice she'd failed to heed. Whether they were or not, the passage confirms to Stella everything she knows to be true. It isn't humiliation and distress that Ford wants. It's tenderness, stability, reassurance and moral support. And that's precisely what she's determined to give him. After all, he's the brilliant man that she'd crossed the globe to find.

And so when the guns fall silent on the Western Front, Ford writes to his darling from Redcar: 'Just a note to say I love you more than ever. Peace has come.'

And she is happy beyond measure. For they'll soon be living together far from the hurly-burly of the city. They will live off the land and do as they please. He'll be able to devote the rest of his time to writing. And she'll be the painter she's always yearned to be. Her grown-up life is about to begin. In earnest.

But right now, here she is all alone in London on Armistice Day. And like everyone else, she wants to celebrate, so she rushes out of her studio and drags Ezra from his Kensington flat and onto a packed, open-topped bus that's edging its way towards Trafalgar Square. The streets are crammed with cheering, flag-waving people. Suddenly, Ezra starts banging his cane on the side of the now stationary bus and yells down to the masses: 'It's over! It's over! The war is bloody over!' The chanting begins. Everyone is delirious with joy. None more so than Stella.

But up in Redcar, visions of the dead and dying continue to disturb Ford's sleep.

red ford

It is Stella who finds it – a rustic hideaway buried near Pulborough in Sussex, far from Violet's prying eyes and Ford's other worries in London. Owned by a local farmer, this old, moss-covered, red-brick, red-tiled cottage, tucked beneath a red sandstone cliff, faces a meadow that slopes down to a stream. And its name, Red Ford sounds particularly auspicious. The price is right too. For a mere five shillings a week, it's perfect. They take it immediately. But as charming as it appears initially, it is in fact pokey and dilapidated.

As soon as Ford sees it, he realises the cottage needs a great deal of work. At the very least, a new roof, ceilings and support beams. The walls and floors will have to wait. As for the garden – it's over-run by weeds and rabbits, and it'll take some time and effort to set it right as well. So it's decided. Stella will continue to live with Phyllis in Pembroke Studios, while Ford moves into the cottage. Stella will follow – hopefully in April. That way he'll be able to have everything in reasonable shape before Stella joins him, which as it turns out, won't be till June.

But the sorry state of Red Ford isn't the only reason why this arrangement suits them. Their relationship is not yet public knowledge. Only a select few are aware they are lovers. And Violet of course is not one of them. Her obsessive attention and continual demands are relentless. Ford has had enough and is desperate to remove himself from her almost daily assaults on his privacy. He's adamant that she means nothing to him anymore.

'I don't want her having any idea where I am,' he says to Stella. 'I've told her I'm going to live in the country, and as far as I'm concerned that's all she needs to know. End of story!'

And on top of this, Tom, Stella's brother, unexpectedly comes to stay with her. He's the aide-de-camp to an Australian general at the peace talks and has not yet been demobbed. And although she's thrilled to see him, she's reluctant to tell him about her plans to live with Ford, fearing he'll disapprove of such an unconventional liaison. She knows only too well how easy it is to be quick to judgement when it comes to other people's morality. In recent letters to Ford, she herself has been complaining about Phyllis' sexual behaviour and all the emotional distress it's been causing.

'I don't want to upset Tom,' she tells Ford. 'And I hate to think what scandal the news of our situation might cause my family back home.'

'For heaven's sake my dear, in the grand scheme of things none of it matters in the slightest. What we do or don't do should be of no concern to anyone but the two of us. So if it's my advice you're looking for, say nothing to your brother, or to anyone else.'

Ford's unconventional ideas on this issue are not new to Stella. He believes that a man of good breeding and refinement should never apologise and never explain his conduct to anyone. So when others criticise him or spread vile rumours about him, Ford rarely comments or defends his actions. Stella decides to take his advice.

Nevertheless, just prior to Tom's return to Adelaide, she finally informs her brother of her affair with Ford and is relieved when he accepts the news calmly and wishes her well.

On the day Stella moves in, Ford decides to mark the occasion by once again legally changing his name. This time he takes on his maternal grandfather's first name for his surname. And while Ford Madox Ford has a memorable ring to it, the change is not a simple act of re-naming. It's an act of post-war reconstruction. A clear break with his past – not just with the German-sounding surname Hueffer, but also with his unhappy marriage to Elsie, as well as with Violet, who very much liked describing herself as his wife. It's a rebirth of sorts and signals his new life with Stella. Or Mrs Ford, as all the locals will now call her.

He's also managed to make Red Ford reasonably habitable and has almost tamed a great deal of the garden. He's planted an astonishing array of fruit and vegetables – peas, beans, lettuces, beetroot, carrots, onions, spinach and radishes, marrows and melons, herbs of all types and of course, sunflowers and sweet peas as well. Stella's more than pleased with all his improvements and the two of them excitedly set about making the place even more homely. And when a couple of friends visit for the weekend and proclaim the place a primitive hovel and their entire venture an absolute folly, neither Ford nor Stella is the slightest bit perturbed.

They are far too much in love to care what others think. Besides, they're living their own glorious dream, a version of which many men, after experiencing the horror and chaos of the front, had brought back with them to England.

During that first summer, it becomes their habit on warm evenings to leave the front door wide open so they can stand together and look in awe as the spectacle of stars begins its nightly passage across the late twilight skies. Ford often tells her then how wonderfully happy she's made him and how he's never ever remembered or imagined such happiness. And Stella smiles and says that making him happy is the loveliest thing that has ever happened to her. And she believes this to be true.

And when one evening they're greeted by a bright white crescent moon hanging above them, she knows for certain she has no regrets. That she is not ashamed of her shamelessness. Not anymore. For she's reminded of another night when Ford had visited her not so long ago at the little cottage she'd leased in Berkhamsted.

That was the first time they'd been alone together. Only a few months before the Armistice. They'd gone out for an evening stroll around the village and as they walked up the garden path, they'd been startled by the brightness of a bow-shaped moon high above the woodshed. They stood side by side for some moments until, as if programmed, they turned to face each other. Stella's smile was radiant but even so, Ford's first kiss was tentative.

When she didn't draw back from him, he wrapped his arms around her drawing her closer to him. His kisses became less cautious, and it seemed to her that the cavernous, velvet night was embracing them both. She could feel his entire body, the strength and shape of him pressing against her.

Let it not end. Please let it not end. The soft feathering of his moustache on her earlobe, his breath on her neck, his tongue, his fingers, this rush of love…

And then everything stopped. He'd dropped to his knees and looking up at her said: 'I love you so much. So very, very much.' He was breathing heavily. 'I want to kiss you. Do you understand? Kiss every part of you…'

She replied by stroking his hair and whispering his name. Once. Twice. Then Ford raised her skirts above his head, and she leant her head back against the woodshed.

Later that night lying naked, side by side in bed, they talked till dawn. With his right hand idle between her thighs, he spoke of his marital problems and all his worries about money. He told her about being shelled at the Somme and about his continuing lung problems, having been gassed, as well as his consequent convalescence in the south of France. He mentioned his fears of not being able to write again and revealed his hope of living more simply, of having his very own bolt hole somewhere in the country and becoming a subsistence farmer. Finally, he confessed his deep desire to have another child.

'You know, from the moment I first saw you at Selsey, I felt sure we were meant for each other. And despite my being a tortured soul, I know we'll be happy together. And I think you know that too. So what do you say, Stella? Would you consider being a part of my life?'

Knowing this was the only sort of marriage proposal he could possibly make; Stella didn't say a word. She just moved to lie on top of him. And in this way, sang her song of commitment.

It wasn't till they rose mid-morning that she became ashamed of her brazenness. When Ford brought her a cup of tea, he found her teary. 'I suppose you think I'm a wanton hussy,' she sniffled.

'Oh, you funny little thing,' he said, placing a hand on her shoulder, for he knew from the sheets she was nothing of the kind. 'What happened between us last night is what a man and a woman do when they're in love as much as we are. There is no shame in that. You should be smiling, my darling, for you were magnificent.' He sat down on the edge of the bed. 'You must believe me when I say I love you, for I do – very, very much. And together, we shall see the great world and find that cottage that will be our very own temple of love and of art, where I will write again and you, you, who are so clever, shall be the painter you've always wanted to be. I know for certain we can do this. You and I.'

Understandably, she felt flattered and proud. After all, this genius of a man, this colossus of literary and artistic wisdom had chosen her – little Stella Bowen from the cultural backwaters of Australia – to confide in and be his consort. She was quite convinced he could have anybody. But it was she he wanted and her he chose: 'my very own darling from Horsetrylia', as he sometimes teasingly called her.

But summer turns to autumn soon enough, and there's still a steady stream of visitors coming to Red Ford. The Pounds, the critic, Herbert Read[5] and his wife, the Postgates, Mary Butts and her new husband, the young poet, John Rodker, and Phyllis of course, are among them. Most come for the conversation, which they're sure to get from Ford, who can't help being convivial. Even so, he's slowly beginning to realise that the frequency of guests, however welcome, often deprive him of both energy and precious writing time. He even begins to complain about this to Stella, as if it's a problem for her to solve.

Nevertheless, they both take pleasure in everything they do. Their tastes are the same, and they find joy in the tiny world around them: the two brass candlesticks that sit on the rough dining table that Ford made from planks of oak; a jar of flowers from the garden; the comforting scent of evening wood smoke; the pig, muddy in its pen; the dazzling view; the blue, blue sky; and yes, even the unpredictability of the weather.

But after living through an extremely harsh winter, these small joys can't minimise Red Ford's obvious defects. And when in the spring of 1920, Stella learns she's pregnant, Ford is thrilled by the news, but all the property's imperfections are clearly untenable.

In the beginning Stella pleads for certain improvements to their domestic conditions. 'For our son, for our son!' she cries, convinced as is Ford, that their yet-unborn baby will be a boy. The kitchen and

---

5. **Herbert Read:** (1893 - 1968) English art historian, poet, literary critic, philosopher.

pantry are too small. The oil stove belches smoke and soot. The floor of the cook-house floods whenever it rains. Overnight, the couple's focus changes. The entire house suddenly appears make-shift and beyond repair. Moving somewhere else becomes a much more pleasant option. But to manage that, they need a reasonable sum of money. And this they do not have.

pennies from heaven

At first, the pain is tolerable. It isn't as bad as she'd thought it might have been. It'll be a while yet, a nurse tells her, then suggests she should try to get some rest.

Stella closes her eyes and wishes she was back in Sussex in their new home. Even though winter would now have set in, there'd be fewer guests so there'd be more time for her to paint, and of course for Ford, to let his spirit truly fly and write and write and write to his heart's content.

They'd found Coopers Cottage close to the tiny but profoundly beautiful village of Bedham. The cottage itself was three hundred years old and made of oak beams and white plaster. Larger and less dilapidated than Red Ford, it had an orchard full of wild daffodils, a small wood scattered with bluebells and an immense sweeping view. They'd both fallen in love with it at first sight. And thanks to the unexpected windfall received from the sale of the film rights to a novel Ford had written with Joseph Conrad back in 1903, their ability to purchase the property doubled their joy.

But it was only two months since they'd finally moved in. Stella knew she'd never forget that day. There she was, her belly huge with baby, sitting with Ford on top of their cart full of furniture riding through the country lanes. And there it was. At last. A place of their own.

And to help make them more self-supporting, Ford decided to invest in some pigs, including a Black Sussex sow and what he was told was a 'champion' Angora goat, which he duly called Penny. 'Because it reminds me so much of Pound,' he told Stella, laughing at his own wit. She, like most of their friends, found this amusing too.

Meanwhile, Stella was growing fatter and happier every day. That was until Violet was seen hanging over the garden gate, peering in at Ford as he was feeding the pigs. Ford was furious. 'How in hell's name did she manage to track us down?'

Too upset to care about how Violet had located them, Stella started to cry. 'It's all so pointless. Why does she keep doing this?'

'She's to be pitied, my dear. You mustn't worry yourself. The woman can't be reasoned with. She's impervious to anyone else's suffering except her own.'

Stella was calmed by Ford's reasoning, but several days later when they discovered that Violet had hired the local carpenter's wife to spy on them, Ford took immediate action. He consulted his lawyers to inform her that he would have nothing more to do with her and would only discuss matters of business in the presence of his attorney.

But no law existed that could quell what Violet called her 'unholy passion' for Ford and that obsession would last until the day she died.

Stella emerges from a dark, shadowy sleep. Her eyes are half-closed against the brutal, searing hospital light overhead. She wants to vomit, but the feeling soon passes. There are no other parts to her body. She's only one giant belly.

And now here it comes again: she's sure someone has wrapped a blacksmith's belt around what was once her waist and is pulling it tighter, tighter. One notch at a time. She's on the rack. Heaving, groaning. Her mind has relocated and can't be found. There's a woman screaming nearby, but maybe the voice is hers. She wants this agony to stop. The cramps are coming in waves. Unstoppable. Wave upon wave. Naked and sweating, she's certain she's going to die. This pain is too, too much. I surrender, surrender, she says. And counts to ten. To fifteen. Twenty. Please, please let it end. She *is* the pain. She doesn't even know her name anymore. Kill me, she begs. Now.

She can hear the mid-wife issuing instructions. But her voice is faraway. Something about the waters. And she is wet. The sheets are soaked. She must be bleeding. She feels suddenly light in the brain. She may well faint. The pressure inside her belly. Like an earthquake ripping her apart. Never. Ever. Again. Lightening down her spine. Her face a hot, purple gargoyle.

A tiny body is pulled from her body. She hears a baby cry. Sudden relief. It's a girl, says the mid-wife, it's a girl! She has a daughter. Stella begins to weep.

Later she wonders what on earth she's going to tell Mop and Phyllis, who've both recently married, about her dreadful experience of childbirth. Both of them are pregnant with their first babies and are due to give birth any time soon. Stella doesn't want to frighten them, but she also refuses to perpetuate the myth that mothers are quick to forget the horrors of birth. There's no way she'll ever fail to remember that brand of pain and terror.

And what of Ford? She knows he's been terribly concerned about her. Will he be disappointed? He'd so wanted a son. But then they both did. The continuation of Ford's family line and all that. She hopes he'll take the news well when it arrives. He's staying with the Coles in nearby Chelsea, and if his reaction's negative, she hates to think what George and Mop may think of him.

As for her baby daughter, now that she's holding her in her arms, well she's just lovely. On several counts, Stella feels blessed. She's in love and unlike many other women of her post-war generation, she considers herself lucky to have a child of her own.

Meanwhile back in Chelsea, it's been a protracted and difficult birth for Ford too. Over the previous two days, he's complained bitterly of chest trouble and so takes to his bed in the Coles' spare room, where he and Stella had been staying prior to her being admitted to hospital to give birth. He's in a frightful state of agitation and calls for sirloin and a clear soup with plenty of oysters, that being the only diet he believes will relieve his suffering. Margaret thinks it all rather pathetic and says as much to her husband.

'There he is – wallowing about like an obese cockatoo, while everyone else is worried sick about Stella. I tell you George, it's obscene the way he carries on, as if he's the one giving birth, for heaven's sake.'

'I can see why you're indignant about these selfish theatrics of his. And it's no wonder he's disliked by so many people. But I'm almost certain his suffering is genuinely felt and that he does truly care for Stella and the baby.'

'Oh, no doubt you're right. I ought to be more tolerant of others, I suppose.' Margaret loves her husband for his objective and measured approach to everything. When she goes into labour, there'll be no way George would ever act like Ford. He's made of sterner stuff. She tells herself that she must remember that Ford is a true Artist – in every sense of the word. He's passionate about literature as a vital force in the world and he's a lover of freedom too. And sadly, there aren't too many like him around anymore.

But what the Coles fail to realise is that while Stella is well aware of Ford's over-sized ego, she also understands that that same ego is often afflicted by overwhelming anxiety.

Ford and Stella name their baby Esther Julia but call her Julie. Ford dotes on her. The weather that November in 1920 is marked by heavy rain, so they remain in London till after the new year before returning to Bedham with their newborn. And although there's no electricity, running water or any other modern conveniences, they have each other and Lucy, the young maid to assist with domestic duties.

But life becomes especially tough in the brutally bleak and wet days of winter. Mud and slush everywhere. The pipe that brings the water from the nearby spring freezes and bursts. The cottage is draughty and very cold. The nights' blackness begins at 4pm. After a hearty stew, there's gentle lamplit conversation around the open log fire about the Way, the Truth and the Light in Art. All kinds of Art. And Stella paints a portrait of Ford. And another of the barn. But that's about it. What with the demands of running a home and caring for baby Julie, she has little time or energy to do much else.

And once the warmer months arrive, Ford retreats to the top of the orchard where he's built a makeshift hut. Here he writes, sometimes into the night and lets it be known he can't be interrupted. Under any circumstances. For he must re-establish his writing career and that means he can't allow anyone to derail his train of creative thoughts. Without a steady source of income, they will most certainly face financial ruin. And he can't have that. Not now, with Julie to consider.

One evening over supper, when Stella tells him of yet another outstanding bill that needs to be paid, he asks her to please stop talking. 'I can't bear discussing this kind of thing anymore,' he says. 'It's just too upsetting, and if I'm to write for monetary gain, I simply can't become upset. I need to remain calm and focussed at all times. All this talk of bills and bank overdrafts won't achieve a damn thing. We need to stay positive and not be so worried all the time. You must trust me, my dear. So please, no more of this.'

But in truth, Ford is deeply troubled. He dares not speak of being on the brink of bankruptcy, not only because he fears it just might become a reality but also because he'd then have to admit that his grand scheme of becoming a self-sufficient writer-farmer has been utterly delusional. And that, he simply cannot do.

But he does start making demands on publishers for money, which become increasingly frantic and unreasonable. He sends off rushed manuscripts and handwritten, almost illegible stories and is repeatedly rebuffed.

By the summer of 1922, when The Marsden Case is rejected by several publishers, Ford begins to feel disheartened. Still, he knows in his heart that this novel is worthy of being in print, so he sends the manuscript off again. This time to the independent publisher, Gerald Duckworth, while assuring Stella, that should he accept the book, their financial situation will not be so grim.

Whatever the outcome, they decide another miserable winter

in England is unthinkable. They've had enough. They decide to go abroad, where the living is cheaper. Their friend, Harold Munro, who owns the Poetry Bookshop in Bloomsbury, offers them the use of his tiny villa in Cap Ferrat in Ford's beloved Provence. Stella is delighted. There's no hesitation. No turning back. They'll stay for a month in Paris before heading south.

But there's much to be done before they go. Livestock to sell. Threadbare clothes to mend and make presentable. And Ford will write a long poem of farewell to England, or as he calls it 'this dreary land', where critics don't like the kind of Art he admires and whose middle classes dumbly disapprove of genuine love.

Part Three

2015 – 2017

On the morning of my second day in Paris, Antoine called me to say everything seemed to be going to schedule, that he'd be home the next day. Sometime in the late afternoon, he said. And we're going out to dinner. I think we need to celebrate.

I didn't argue.

But the following day, just before noon, I received another call. There'd been an unavoidable delay. Nothing he could do about it, blah, blah, blah. He was full of apologies and declarations of love, but the reality was: he wouldn't be back until Friday – another two fucking days away. Pretty upset, I let him know it.

So much for his promises! I threw myself on the bed. *Our* bed. The bed he should've been sleeping in two nights ago. I sobbed for a good while – wallowing in my own misery, wondering why I wasn't Antoine's first priority. My fevered brain started concocting all sorts of hypothetical scenarios that might've been going on in the recording studio. None of which, of course, had anything to do with technical hiccups. They were more of the sexual kind involving flute playing floozies and sultry sopranos.

But once I'd exhausted my imagination, my rational brain took control. I stood up and told myself I was being ridiculous. Antoine wasn't like that. He was far too sensitive and intense to be disloyal. And sitting around the apartment moping, rehashing all my mother's misgivings about my choice of men, or better still hers, was not the smartest thing to do right now.

So I grabbed my coat and handbag and headed out the door.

When I returned, it was just after 11 p.m. Before I'd even put the key in the door, I could hear the phone ringing. But it stopped just as I was about to pick up the receiver. Minutes later it rang again. It was Antoine. He'd been worried sick as he'd been calling me since early evening. Where have you been all this time?

I went for a walk. I only intended to go as far as Place des Vosges and back. But once I'd crossed the Pont Marie, I got lost in a tangle of streets in the Marais.

Didn't you take your mobile phone with you? I've been ringing that too, he said.

I apologised. I hadn't heard it. It was in my handbag. Still is, I said. I wasn't expecting you to call me.

But why did you stay out so late? It's dangerous to be wandering the streets alone and lost at night.

I laughed and tried to reassure him that I'd felt perfectly safe; that I'd dined in a little bistro. Not far from rue de Rivoli, I said. A very kind *monsieur* sitting next to me on the banquette struck up a conversation. When we finished eating, he offered to accompany me back to the Quai d'Orléans.

There was a moment of silence on the other end of the line. I quickly added that *ce monsieur* was very old.

It was only then that Antoine said that he wanted me to understand that he'd done everything in his power to get back to Paris, that all he wanted to do was to be with me and that he was really upset that everything had not gone the way he'd planned.

And from the sound of his voice, I knew he wasn't lying.

Next morning, I was woken by the sound of pounding on the door. By anyone's standards, it was pretty early to be visiting someone unannounced. But then I guessed it had to be Gilles. He was the only other person I knew, except for Antoine of course, who had the security code for the building. Anyone else would've had to use the buzzer at the entrance. So when I opened the door, I was startled to find the smiling face of Catherine Deneuve greeting me.

Bonjour! You must be Antoine's mother, I said.

My son told you I would make a visit?

No, no. Not at all, but he told me you looked like Catherine Deneuve, and he's right, you really do look like her.

I'll take that as a compliment, she said, combing some stray, pearl-white hairs back behind her right ear with her ring-studded fingers. But I must remind you that Deneuve is five years older than me which makes a very big difference, you know. She paused. So Neve, are you going to invite me inside?

I opened the door wide and let her pass by. She was wearing a pink suit with black trim - classic Chanel. Either that, or an expensive knock-off. I tightened the cord around my cotton kimono as I padded down the hall in Madame Tribolet's wake. She smelt of tuberose and oud with a hint of tobacco. Every inch of her oozed elegance and glamour. And I watched in silence as she surveyed the living room. No doubt checking on my domestic suitability. And making herself right at home too.

Madame had seated herself in the centre of the sofa and with an outstretched arm was indicating that I should sit in one of the tub chairs facing her. She was certainly not lacking in confidence. And I wondered if her haughtiness had been inherited or if her sense of superiority was acquired through years of practice.

My name's Mireille, she said, a fact I already knew. But everybody calls me Mimi, and I think it very good if you do too. Her English was not as good as Antoine's, but her commanding tone made up for any linguistic missteps. At any rate, I was grateful that Antoine had told his mother that my grasp of the French language was only rudimentary.

I won't keep you from your business, she said. Whatever that meant. I just wanted to check on how you are getting along.

I told her I was fine. Just fine.

Ah! You see, my son called me yesterday evening and *en passant* he said he was a little worried about you. Mireille raised her right hand to her face and with a miniscule space between her thumb and forefinger, emphasised the word little.

Somewhat stunned by her audacity, I said nothing. Did this woman have no idea what impression she was making?

But then she smiled. So, I thought it was time for me to meet you. *Et voilà!* Here I am.

I offered to make her a coffee or tea, knowing my own mother would've been proud that I hadn't forgotten my manners.

With a wave of her hand: *Non, merci.* It's very nice of you, but I only dropped by to introduce myself. A forced smile. To meet you and to welcome you. Then suddenly she stood up. I followed suit. Perhaps Antoine will bring you to lunch *chez moi* one Sunday. I would like that very much.

So would I.

Mireille then stepped towards me and took both my hands in her own. I hope to get to know you better. I have a feeling we could be friends. I wasn't so sure about that. But she smiled faintly and nodded. I don't know whether my son told you, but I did not like his last petite amie.

I tried not to look startled.

Oh, Mireille sighed, Clotilde was always accusing Antoine of unfaithfulness, always assuming the worst. She knew how women can be attracted to creative and intelligent men like him. So she was constantly suspicious, sure that he was cheating on her. But so what if he was? It is what men do. And women too – if they want. *Un petit liaison* – it's nothing. *C'est normal.*

I wasn't so sure about that. But Mireille hadn't finished yet. Do you want to know the secret to my successful marriage? She didn't expect a reply, so got none. I always closed my eyes to my husband's occasional infidelities. I loved Bernard and I knew he loved me and really that's the only thing that matters, *n'est-ce pas?*

Who was I to disagree if it worked for her? If I didn't oppose her view, did that make me gutless? The last thing I wanted was to get into some slanging match with Antoine's mother.

Mireille farewelled me with une bise – a brush of her cheek on each of mine - but not before handing me a small white card that she'd taken from her purse. If you need anything, anything at all, just give me a call.

Once I closed the door behind her, I checked out her card. Mireille, correction Mimi, lived just around the corner. She also knew the security code to get into the building. I wasn't sure what to make of this, but then Mimi's entire visit seemed a bit odd to me. Perhaps it was a cultural thing. Anyway, there was no use worrying about it, that was for sure. I had other things on my mind.

Like wanting to hear my own mother's voice. But I'd have to wait until it was morning in Sydney before I could call her. So I decided I'd spend the day setting up the external hard drive I'd brought from Australia and begin reacquainting myself with my novel. But first, I'd take a little wander around St-Germain-des-Prés. Surely Stella would've known the area well, and there was no time like the present to breathe in the magic of Paris's past,

Antoine didn't come home Friday evening as he'd promised. Ever unpredictable, he arrived late Thursday night instead. The weather had been vile all day. I'd gone to bed early and fallen asleep to the sound of a raging storm outside. I hadn't heard him get into bed, but I'd felt the kisses on my shoulder and his expert hand between my thighs next morning.

That first day, we stayed close to home – lingering in bed, cocooned in the warm stupor of love. We also talked a great deal. Mostly about our respective mothers. Over breakfast, I gave Antoine a run-down of Mireille's visit, leaving out the bit about Clotilde. Even so, he seemed irritated by the fact she'd dropped by and insisted he'd never suggested she visit and that he'd given her the building's security code some time ago. For emergency use only.

I suggested that she may have thought meeting me was a matter of some urgency.

Non, non. She's always poking her nose everywhere, he replied. Besides, there's a landline here. If she wanted to meet you, she could've called first. Like a normal person. And she knows it. I'm not going to have her interfering in our lives.

I tried to defend his mother but when I called her Mimi, he really became annoyed, saying he loved her, but she was *une grande manipulatrice*. Oh, he said, she'll make you think you're the greatest of friends, then *boum!* I warn you, don't be deceived by her.

I hadn't expected such an explosive response from this calm and level-headed man, but I did understand these bizarre contradictory feelings that offspring can have for their parents. Loving them one minute and being infuriated by them the next. Anyway, I told him I'd be careful, that I was sure I could handle her, and that he wasn't to worry.

He did calm down and laughed when I told him what Mimi had said about how she dealt with her husband's petits liaisons. Antoine knew all about his father's infidelities and said that having an afternoon tryst before coming home to one's wife was quite common in France. Particularly with his parents' generation. He cleared his throat and added: They call it *le cinq à sept*, but it's something of a cliché today. I promise you Neve, I am not at all like my father.

He stood up then and asked if I'd like a coffee. Before I could respond, he offered an alternative: would I rather see how he's not like his dad. He emphasised the word, not.

I wasn't sure what he was getting at, so just smiled and said: whatever you'd prefer.

That's when he scooped me up in his arms and carried me back into our bedroom.

That night I phoned my mother, or rather, used FaceTime so I could show Rachel around the apartment and introduce her to Antoine, who promptly told her how he hoped she'd visit us soon. Of course, she was delighted and said she'd think about it. When the call was finished, Antoine rang his mother and arranged for us to take her to lunch on Sunday. So I had till then to work out how I was going to tell him what Mimi had told me about Clotilde. And although back in Hanoi we'd made a pact that our relationship would be built on an egalitarian model of honesty and trust, that there'd be no secrets, no silences, nothing but plain dealing, I was a bit worried about how I'd go about raising the subject. Particularly when neither of us had discussed in any detail our previous relationships. In a way, our individual pasts had nothing to do with the two of us in the here and now. But I wanted to see what his response would be to the implication that he'd been unfaithful.

I didn't have to wait long.

In bed next morning, it was Antoine who spoke first. He wanted to talk about how we were going to deal with his future absences from Paris. I'm a little afraid, he said. Because I understand, better than anyone, that most relationships can't sustain such frequent separations and I don't want that to happen to us.

And then he told me the whole sorry story of the disintegration of his relationship with Clotilde. From the beginning, it had been a disaster, even though Antoine believed at the time that he was hopelessly in love with her. But the reality was they weren't well-matched – two very different people with little in common. She would often joke that the only kind of music she liked was what she heard in elevators. She hated when he had to go away, but refused to accompany him, because she worked in real estate and had to be on call, in case a client needed to check out a property or finalise a deal. Well, that was her excuse. But then came the accusations.

She was sure I was unfaithful, he said. And when I denied it, she'd laugh in my face. Said I was stupid, that I should go ahead and do as I please, that it was all the same to her.

He took a deep breath. I waited.

I don't think Clotilde ever really loved me. But finally – thankfully, she left. She was the unfaithful one. She'd fallen in love with one of her clients – a woman, who was selling her apartment. They're now living happily together in Lyon.

Smiling, he shrugged and shook his head. Then continued: I know you must be thinking – that maybe I'm a possessive guy or that I don't trust you, but we have already been apart too long. Those months before you came here were hard, very, very hard for me. I wasn't in top form. I couldn't concentrate for long. It was terrible.

He moved closer and buried his face in my neck.

Don't worry, I said. I'll never lie to you.

So can I be the first person who sees you every single morning? Will you come with me when I go on tour?

Of course I will, silly. I don't know why you're making such a big deal about it.

Then he silenced me with kisses.

A little while later I told him how his mother viewed the breakup of his relationship with Clotilde. He flashed a smile. Then started to laugh. She told you, what? *Mon Dieu, elle est incroyable!* I swear she makes things up to suit herself, then repeats them so often, she's convinced they're true.

After we'd taken Mimi to lunch the following Sunday to La Coupole, one of her favourite restaurants, I was in no doubt that Antoine had never raised the issue with his mother. Because from the minute the three of us stepped into the cab, she was thoroughly charming and animated, more than happy to talk about where they were headed, which was into Montparnasse, Stella Bowen's heartland. When I briefly mentioned my novel, Mimi was genuinely interested and spoke of the hundreds and hundreds of artists' studios that had once occupied the quartier back in the first couple of decades of the twentieth century. So, she said, did this Stella of yours happen to be in Paris in 1927?

Yes, she was.

Well then, she must have gone to La Coupole, because that was the year it opened.

I told her I couldn't recall ever finding any reference to Stella having dined at the iconic brasserie.

Maybe she didn't, but there's a legend that when the restaurant opened, hordes of avant-garde Parisian types partied there so hard one night that things got out of control and the police had to be called.

Oh, I'm not so sure that would've been Stella's scene, I said. She mixed in bohemian, artistic circles but she was in many ways a somewhat conventional person.

But she liked parties, *non?* And even if you have no proof she went to La Coupole, you are writing fiction, are you not?

I laughed. She had a point. But I was glad the taxi had just pulled up outside the restaurant, leaving no time to explain to Mimi why I wanted to keep my fiction true to what was known of Stella's character.

Even though Antoine claimed La Coupole was a little *ringard*, I couldn't help wondering how the massive art-deco dining room with its mosaic tiled floors, wall length mirrors and painted pillars by various art students of people like Leger, Matisse and Vassilieff[6] could be considered out of date. True, its food was neither haute cuisine or on trend, but it was delicious and well-presented, and I swear I could taste the dazzling history of the place.

You know, said Mimi, as a waiter scuttled by holding aloft an enormous platter of fresh shellfish, Camus celebrated his Nobel prize for Literature here.

I was about to tell her that after winning the Tour de France, Cadel Evans celebrated here too. But a single glance at Antoine, who gave me a sly wink, made me think better of it. His mother was enjoying herself, and she'd already changed the subject, wanting to know all about Antoine's plans for the year. Her pride in his abilities and achievements was obvious. And even though I was less than approving of the way she dealt with her husband's philandering, I decided I liked her.

As we took our time over coffee and petits fours, Antoine told

---

6. **Marie Vassilieff:** (1884 – 1957) At the age of 23, this Russian born painter moved to Paris and studied under Henri Matisse, becoming an integral part of the artistic community of Montparnasse. Her artwork was inspired by Cézanne and Cubist in style. She was also known for her decorative furniture pieces and doll portraits.

us about an idea he had for his next project. He'd been thinking a lot about the meaning of liberty in the wake of the Charlie Hebdo attacks and the kosher supermarket siege. He talked about the huge demonstrations that took place across France to honour the victims, the commemorative concert in Strasbourg and the impact of the online slogan *Je suis Charlie*. The graffiti condemning extremism in all its forms and the flowers, flags and messages covering the bronze statue of Marianne, the personification of France, that sits on top of the grand monument at the centre of the Place de la République. Sometimes the conversation slipped into French, and I was heartened to find I could follow most of what was being said.

The meaning of liberty in this country has shifted, said Antoine.

Oui, tu as raison. In the past, said Mimi, it was all about freedom to rebel against an oppressive monarchy.

Exactly, said Antoine, whereas now the focus is on specific freedoms - the freedom of speech and of thought. But as we have seen, this freedom comes at a terrible price.

So what's your idea? I asked.

Well, all I know is I want to compose something on a grand scale, something major, something of epic proportions, something that encompasses all these ideas and emotions I have about what is happening to my country. But I don't want to rush at this. It's too important.

For a moment no-one spoke. All three of us recognised that it was still early days. All Parisians, no matter their religion or ethnicity, had been affected by the actions of these fanatical extremists. Sure, there was a palpable sense of solidarity on the streets, but beneath that, raw emotions raged - like anger, uncertainty, and fear. So while everyone went about their usual lives, heavily armed police guarded every corner of every boulevard and tiny alleyway. Proof that another attack was expected.

Then Mimi said: I think you're being very wise. Best to let grand ideas such as these marinate for a while. Remember, it's still early days. Best to see how things pan out.

Antoine never said he'd taken his mother's advice but as the weeks and months went by, I noticed that he hardly ever mentioned his proposed Charlie Hebdo inspired composition. I believed it was because we were both too busy being happy. It seemed as if neither one of us could get enough of the other. Later, we took to referring to 2015 as our year of unbridled lust. Not that we spent every waking hour together but we both agreed we rather enjoyed the rhythm of our days. Most mornings after breakfast, Antoine would go downstairs to his studio, where he'd remain until late in the afternoon, while I'd tramp the boulevards and streets of Montparnasse in search of Stella's soul. After a light lunch, I usually walked to the library, the Bibliothèque de l'Arsenal in the Marais to continue my research on Ford Madox Ford. And as stimulated as we were with our individual work, our daily routine never seemed to affect our ardour. When together it seemed like we were in a constant state of arousal. Even in those evenings when attendance at recitals, gallery openings and film premieres were hard to avoid, we were often overcome by a sense of urgency to give in to our mutual desire. All it took from either one of us was a surreptitious smile or a nod of the head, and we'd be making sudden but polite excuses so we could head off into the night and into each other. Neither of us was in a hurry to cease this period of sexual excitement and settle into a steady loving domestic relationship.

I guess it'll happen when we're ready, I said one night, but hoping it would never end.

Antoine smiled, placed his hand on my breast and said: I think we're making up for all the time we lost last year when our relationship was conducted remotely, don't you?

But of course, there were plenty of other things we did together in that first year. Like meeting many of Antoine's friends and associates. Ange Morat being one of them. We'd been invited to a cocktail party, the birthday celebration of a Dutch video-artist who wanted to collaborate with Antoine on a musical work with the Orchestre de Paris. When Antoine bought himself a stylish new linen suit for the occasion, I felt a little wary. No matter how often I scoured Vogue, my relationship to high fashion had never been the best. Nevertheless, I decided I owed it to Antoine to make a bit of an effort for this event.

In a quirky little shop not far from Sacré-Coeur, I found what I considered to be a stylish but understated calf-length blue dress, as blue as the cobalt of a Moroccan tiled courtyard wall. I threaded some matching blue ribbon through my hair, which I braided and pinned up creating a bun at the bottom of my head. I was happy with the result, especially when I stood before Antoine that evening and his eyes lit up. I think I'd prefer it if we stay at home, he said, smiling.

The party was held in a vast, loft-like studio somewhere in the outer western reaches of the city. And the first people we ran into were Sacha Durand, Antoine's manager and his partner, Ange. Despite the fact they were dressed in an aggressively flamboyant style like everyone else that night, Ange struck me as down-to-earth and unpretentious. When Antoine introduced her and said she spoke several languages, including Arabic, she'd looked embarrassed for a moment and hurriedly explained that her father, a diplomat, had been born in Lebanon and expected all his children to be fluent in Arabic as well as French and English.

I taught myself Italian later, she said. But that's another story for another day.

I was mesmerised by the way she spoke. With her lips a vivid red and slightly pushed forward in a classic French pout, Ange asked many questions about my curatorial work and my life in Australia, which I was more than happy to answer. Being tall, dark and willowy, I was sure Ange would've made a great catwalk model. But instead, she was a high school teacher of literature. And an enthusiastic one at that. Every time she spoke about her current batch of baccalaureate students, her eyes lit up the room.

What with the lively conversation, the music and dancing, Antoine and I stayed a lot longer than we'd intended. And when we finally decided to leave, Ange handed me her number. Let's have lunch together soon? Just you and me, she said, giving me a wink.

I'd love that, I said. And I wasn't lying. I'd made my first Parisian friend.

In the lead-up to May, Antoine conducted three recitals of his work in the Amphitheatre of the Opera Bastille. After which, we flew down to Cannes for my birthday. Up until then, my only experience of French beaches was when I'd spent a fortnight in France back in the summer of 2008, the year I worked in London. A couple of my gallery friends and I had taken off for the Brittany coast in the hope we might develop a tan by lying around on the sandy beaches of Dinan. But for the entire time we were there, none of us exposed our skin to the sun, mainly because it never appeared.

But not so in Cannes. The weather there was perfect. But the place was crowded. It was after all film festival time, and although Antoine and I had no intention of attending any cinematic events, I had more than a sneaking suspicion that he wanted to be part of the action. Or at least to be seen by everyone there. For we spent a lot of time in the lobby of the legendary Carlton Hotel, where we were staying along with an epic number of movie industry people from across the globe. Many of whom made a beeline to say hello to Antoine. Some of these were seriously famous, others were simply glamorous, and the rest were just a cast of wannabes.

I wasn't surprised by any of this. The art world was just the same. What astonished me was Antoine's response to all this attention. He clearly enjoyed being centre stage - even when he was being surrounded by what he called music entrepreneurs, who looked more like sleazy hard-nosed money men to me. So while he basked in the limelight, I sat back in the shadows thinking about fame and celebrity in general and how success, or the lack of it, could distort a person's ego.

Yet when Antoine showed me the cement slab on the allée des Étoiles, where his signature and imprint of his hands rested in the pavement, I couldn't deny that I was extremely impressed. So much so, I took a photo with my phone and straight away sent it to Rachel without comment because I didn't need to. The photo said it all.

Despite secretly wishing we'd gone instead to Antibes or Juan-les-Pins, where I knew Stella had once visited, I did manage to enjoy myself. I loved everything about the Carlton with its Belle Epoque décor and its imposing exterior. Especially the story I'd heard from the concierge about how the two giant gun-metal grey domes that perched on the hotel's roof were constructed to celebrate the breasts of a famous pre-World War I courtesan. When later I'd told Antoine about it, he'd laughed and said: Surely you don't believe that?

But I don't care if it's true or not, I said, the fact that there's such a myth about these cupolas tells you an awful lot about the French!

Towards the end of our stay, Antoine suggested we spend the summer in a more peaceful environment. Somewhere close to the Rhone, he said. We'll rent a villa and spend our days swimming, relaxing, exploring. I can do some composing, and you can write there too. What do you think? It's a good idea, *non?*

I took this as an apology for bringing me to the chaos of Cannes during the world's most famous film festival.

One afternoon towards the end of May, Antoine asked me to join him in his studio downstairs to listen to his new album, Entre Nous – the one he'd been working on when I arrived in February. It was the first time I'd heard it in its entirety, which opened, surprise, surprise with the piano sonata he'd begun composing in Sydney, 'Reflections of Neve'.

Needless to say, I was incredibly moved by the entire work. It sounded superb. Like a yearning for some of life's most inaccessible truths. I loved the way there was a patterned layering of piano and strings on some of the pieces, while others were quite experimental and incorporated vocals with a whole range of different instruments from carillons and harpsichords, banjos and bouzoukis to bizarre industrial sounds like the heavy clunk-clunking of trains in shunting yards.

Antoine, in his usual modest way, claimed it worked so beautifully because of the clever use of electronic manipulation. But I agreed with the album notes that Sacha had written describing the album as an intensely personal form of sonic poetry. I was also very touched to find a dedication to me on the notes as well.

The album was to be released the following month with a string of concerts to follow. And although Antoine was concerned that it may receive a negative reception, reviews were unanimous. It was another critical success.

As Antoine drove into the courtyard of the elegantly restored 13th century bastide that was to be our home until the end of August, I couldn't help thinking how lucky I was.

Oh my god, this place is beyond beautiful!

I thought you might like it, he said, grinning – clearly pleased with himself.

And while it warmed my heart that he gained pleasure from pleasing me, I felt I had to say that I'd never be able to repay him.

Don't be absurd, he said. I'd be insulted if you even tried. I've worked hard for my money and so I choose to spend it as I wish. And I'm extremely happy to have fallen in love with a woman who can appreciate beauty when she sees it.

Located in the heart of the Alpilles, the property was only a half hour's drive north of Arles. Set in five hectares of stunning landscaped gardens, it also had a huge pool and pétanque and tennis courts. What's more, the property came with its own on-site cook, cleaner and gardener. All a bit Downton Abbey to me. Though by the end of our first week there, I'd become accustomed to the bastide's extravagance.

Around this time, Sacha and Ange joined us. They were on their way to Spain and only intended to stay two nights, but thanks to my urging those two nights turned into two weeks. Together, the four of us explored the region: visiting Arles, Avignon, Les Baux and Orange. And because the evenings were so balmy, we always dined out on the terrace. On one particular night, we'd lingered there, drinking more wine than usual and savouring the Provençal night sky. I started talking about Vincent Van Gogh and how, after mutilating his ear, he'd found solace in an asylum, which was just outside the town of Saint-Rémy.

That's not far from here, said Antoine. We could go tomorrow if you want and check out the Roman ruins of Glanum while we're there.

So it was decided.

We left straight after breakfast next morning and first visited what was left of the ancient city of Glanum. It was all rather impressive, particularly the mausoleum and what was left of the triumphal arch. But I was keen to pay homage to Vincent. And we didn't have far to go. Now a museum, the asylum, which had once been the monastery of St Paul de Mausole, was right next door. We wandered around its beautiful garden and visited the old cloister itself, where Van Gogh had lived in a ground floor cell and where he'd painted some of his most famous works.

I was moved by the loving reconstruction of his room, but none of us were keen on loitering there and so we launched ourselves onto the narrow-cobbled streets of Saint-Rémy's historic centre. That was where Ange and I each bought one of those long and loose fitting, boho style dresses, made from light cotton - perfect for summer. Especially when hanging around the pool. Which was precisely how we intended to spend the following day. Me in my navy floral number, which Ange said complemented my ash blonde hair, and she in her plain white one.

So next morning, when I joined Sacha and Antoine by the pool, neither of them looked up. They'd already been for a dip and were lying on their stomachs, sunbaking, which didn't bother me in the slightest. I wanted to spend the next hour or so re-reading The Good Soldier beneath the shade of the vine-covered pergola a couple of metres away from them.

Not long after I'd made myself comfortable, I looked up from my book and saw Ange walking, head high, down the gravel path towards the pool. Like me, she was wearing the dress she'd bought the day before. But unlike me, she chose not to wear any underwear beneath hers. With the sun so bright, the white cotton was virtually transparent, which was precisely the desired effect. Ange was proud of her body and not afraid to display it. Whereas I knew I didn't have the courage or the self-belief to parade almost nude in front of friends.

Up until then, I hadn't noticed how different Ange and I were. Ever since we'd met, we'd got on extremely well. I'd presumed we were likeminded and shared similar interests and values. But we'd never before spent more than a few hours together at any one time. It was only now I felt that compared to Ange and her audacious free spirit, I was dull and conventional.

When Ange reached Sacha's lounge chair, she tapped him on the shoulder and not looking at all surprised, he sat up and claimed his right of possession by taking hold of her buttocks with both hands and pulling her to him. Ange wriggled free and standing directly in front of him, began to remove her dress. What would you like to do now? she asked him.

Startled, I noticed Antoine now sitting up and struggling not to ogle her. I couldn't blame him. Even I couldn't avert my eyes as Sacha scooped Ange up and threw her in the pool.

Within seconds, Antoine was beside me. Let's leave them to it, he said.

I followed him inside and up to our room and instead of asking him if he'd like me to be more like Ange, I told him how unnerved I was by the poolside performance we'd just witnessed. He laughed and said he couldn't understand why. I tried to explain that the whole thing made me feel unsophisticated and parochial. And to underline my point I asked him to look at me. Just look at me, I said, in this frumpy navy dress. I look more Amish than amorous.

A sudden burst of laughter from Antoine. '*Oh chérie, comme je t'aime!*' he said, embracing me.

We spent the rest of the day in bed.

Even so, I couldn't stop thinking about the incident and my response to Ange's provocative behaviour. Antoine's attitude had been completely different to mine, which made me wonder what my reaction would've been if I'd been French. I was sure I wouldn't have felt as threatened as I had been. But I reasoned that I couldn't really blame my feelings of insecurity on some kind of cultural clash because I knew instinctively that Ange's little striptease wasn't just for Sacha's benefit either. Ange had stage managed the entire performance. I probably should've applauded her. But I'd missed my moment. And perhaps that was for the best.

Next day, it was as if the previous morning had never existed. With only three more days before Ange and Sacha headed south, most of our conversation centred around their travel plans in Spain. The white dress was never mentioned or seen again. Once they'd left, the provençal summer heat became quite oppressive. It reminded me of Australia, especially when accompanied by the furious pitch of cicada song. Which didn't make me feel homesick, just less estranged from my surroundings.

The rest of August passed by with Antoine and I spending our mornings at work: he on the piano, and me on my laptop. Afternoons were lazed away by the pool. And on one particularly sultry afternoon, I told Antoine how cooler I felt when I went barefoot on the stone tiled floors.

If you wore that cotton dress you bought in Saint-Rémy, *sans culotte aussi, peut-être?* he said, you'd probably feel even cooler.

And he was right. The remainder of our stay turned out to be the most languidly sensual time I'd ever had.

Not long after returning to Paris in September, I accompanied Antoine on a concert tour of France. Ten cities in two weeks is no fun in anyone's book. And while I'd been keen to visit Strasbourg, Lyon, Marseille and Bordeaux, I saw very little of note, and the entire trip became a bit of a blur. Worse still was what followed in October - a promotional tour across Europe for Antoine's new album. Because his performances were always powerful, I had come to really enjoy watching from the wings, but on that tour, he was exhausted after most of them. What with rehearsals by day and concerts in the evenings, sight-seeing was out of the question. Not that I ever complained. I'd made a promise and was happy to be with him. Besides, these tours for me were a great introduction into his world. By accompanying him that year, I learnt two things: Antoine knew an awful lot of people and a lot of women found him very attractive.

That second point was made obvious to me by the less than subtle way I was often sized up by his admirers, who clearly regarded themselves as being more worthy of his affections than I'd ever be. In the circles that I had moved in back home, I rarely noticed flagrant flirtation of the kind I witnessed when I was with Antoine. But maybe that was because I'd never been in love before with a man so desirable to others.

But none of this unduly affected me. I could hardly question Antoine's love and support. For despite his deep devotion to his music, the patience and generosity of spirit he showed me was undeniable. He happily listened to all my doubts about my ability to bring Stella Bowen to life in a novel and kept reminding me how much he'd liked what he'd already read of my manuscript.

All creative people suffer from self-doubt from time to time, he said one night as we were strolling back home along the Quai de la Tournelle. You just can't let those doubts defeat you. You're a very capable woman. All you lack is confidence. Deep-down, you know you can do it. Otherwise, why did you start? You must face your fears head-on and finish what you've started. That's how you'll bring Stella back to life again.

That's when he suggested I set myself an achievable deadline and then just go for it.

You make it sound so easy, I said. There's a lot that's unknown about Stella. Even some of her letters were redacted, or worse – destroyed by well-meaning family members. And while I know that facts are malleable when it comes to writing one's own life story, there are far too many gaps and silences for my liking in Stella's memoir – some of which are quite bizarre.

Like what?

Like the Spanish flu. She actually lived through it when a quarter of the British population was hit hard by it. And the worst hit were young adults in her own age-group. Yet she never mentions it.

Perhaps she wasn't affected by it that much.

Maybe. Though I don't know how. Anyway, I have to say I find all the mysterious bits of her life just as compelling as the verifiable truths. So I guess that's what attracted me to her story in the first place – the way she edited her life and curated her narrative to suit her personal agenda.

Well, that explains your obsession with her, and that's why she's the perfect subject for you.

But am I the perfect novelist for her? I mean, I don't even think of myself as a writer.

Why not?

Because silly, I've never had anything published.

That's not true, he countered. What about all your exhibition notes you've written for the gallery?

I laughed and said: That's not the same as writing a novel.

Perhaps not, Neve. But it doesn't matter if you don't have all the information you'd like. You have an empathetic heart, so just make it up. After all, it's fiction you're writing. You should think of the whole thing as an act of love – to Stella.

What could I say to something so incredibly sweet as that?

Then, mid-November, life, as I had come to know it, turned sour. We'd been to a show in the south of the city – in Montparnasse actually – to see Fabrice Luchini give a dramatic recitation of the work of famous French poets. At the same time, a suite of terrorist attacks was being played out across northern Paris, so we couldn't get back home till quite late. It had been hard to get a cab – unusually hard – but once we did, the driver explained why. Like everyone else, he was spooked by the assault on the city and refused to cross the Seine, dropping us off instead near the church of Saint-Sulpice – about a thirty-minute hurried walk to our place.

As soon as we were inside the apartment, Antoine switched on the TV. We both flopped down on the sofa and side by side watched open-mouthed the horror of the night's events unfold: suicide bombers detonating their belts at entrances to the packed Stade de France during a football match between France and Germany; patrons of popular cafés and restaurants fired upon by AK-47 assault rifles; a massacre at the sold-out concert by the American rock band, Eagles of Death Metal in the historic Bataclan theatre. The number count of victims kept rising, rising. Then President Hollande declared a state of emergency, pronouncing the attacks an act of war by Islamic State.

Numbed, we stayed all night glued to the screen, while the eee-aw, eee-aw of police sirens filled the air outside. Then our phones started ringing. First, it was Sacha and Ange. Then Mimi. Were we all right? Antoine told her we hadn't slept but invited her for lunch. I nodded approval for we both could tell by his mother's voice that she was frightened. She only calmed when Antoine assured her that he'd walk around to her apartment to accompany her back to ours.

There were more calls, including a long one from Tamsin. And as soon as we'd finished talking, my phone rang again.

I'm so please you've picked up, said Rachel. I wish you'd called me. I've been worried about you.

I'm sorry. Of course, you must've been worried. I didn't think. It's all a bit of a shock and difficult to process. I should've called, I know.

But Rachel wouldn't hear of it. No, no, she said. You don't need to apologise. I understand. I'm just glad you're ok. Have you had much sleep?

We've been awake all night. It's hard to sleep when you're wondering if it's safe to even go outside. There's hardly anyone out on the streets and except for the occasional sound of choppers and sirens, it's eerily quiet.

But not wanting to worry her unduly about my safety, I told her Mimi was coming for lunch.

That's nice, she said. I'm looking forward to meeting her.

Yes, not long now. Only two months to go and you'll be here with us.

And in this way our conversation shifted to my mother's proposed visit next year. That's when she told me she would come in the warmer months, but she'd only be staying with us a couple of nights, that she didn't want to be a burden.

Before I could protest, Rachel reminded me that she liked her independence. Footloose and fancy-free, she said. I've booked a charming little hotel for the rest of my stay. It's not far from you.

And right at that moment, I couldn't have cared less. As Rachel prattled on about her plans, I glanced at Antoine, who looked pale and haggard. If I hadn't known better, I'd have thought he was badly hungover. So once the call from my mother ended, I offered to make some coffee while he had a quick shower.

Thanks, he said, forcing a smile. I feel sick for my country. Hollande has just called in the army.

For several weeks after the attacks, Antoine spoke of little else. There'd been 130 people murdered but his main concern was centred around the survivors and the loved ones of the victims and of course, the first responders – the police and medical teams, especially those who'd witnessed the carnage at the packed Bataclan. He fretted about the kind of horrors that might visit their sleep each night. He talked about the difficulty they'd have when trying to maintain an emotional distance from the victims. The words trauma and stress punctuated everything he said. Naturally enough, Paris had markedly changed. Domestic security was being ramped up. Police seemed to be everywhere.

It scared me a little but then just before Christmas, Antoine seemed calmer. He told me he'd decided to channel his anxiety into his work, his grand project, the Liberty Suite he'd spoken about when I'd first arrived in Paris. He was certainly happier and more energised, and as his lovemaking was even more vigorous than usual, I felt relieved. Christmas and New Year came and went. I was making progress on my novel, and Antoine's precious project was well underway. Then in April, Tamsin and Finn made a surprise visit.

Prior to leaving Sydney, the pair had been married. They'd told no-one as they'd wanted a no-fuss, stress-free, registry office wedding. There hadn't even been a reception. Their only celebration was to be these two weeks together in Paris where, via Twitter and Instagram, they intended to announce their marriage to family and friends back in Australia.

A bit like an elopement really, said Finn.

Brilliant! I said, meaning it.

Glad you think so, said Tamsin, because Finn and I would like you and Antoine to help us memorialise our marriage here in the City of Love.

I looked at Antoine and just knew he was wondering the same thing as I was: how were we supposed to do that? Then Tamsin explained: she'd brought a wedding gown with her from Australia, and they wanted photos taken of the two of them in all the romantic clichés of Paris. You know, she said, like those pics of couples standing on the steps of Sacré-Coeur at sunset.

Or sipping cocktails in Bar Hemingway at the Ritz, chimed in Finn.

Charmed by their exuberance, we agreed to help them live out their fantasy. So a few days later, all four of us met up by the Champ-de-Mars, that long stretch of lawn and manicured gardens that run from the Ecole Militaire to the Eiffel Tower. After taking some glossy magazine style photos of the smiling bride and groom, Gilles picked us up and chauffeured us around to several other iconic settings for yet more snaps.

By noon, they were done, and so we headed off for a celebratory lunch in a little bistro close to the hotel where Finn and Tamsin were staying. Any apprehension that I had had about Antoine and my Australian friends not getting along was washed away by a great deal of champagne and lively conversation, mainly from Antoine, who spoke at length about his Liberty Suite.

If it's as good as I hope it will be, I'd like to take it on tour, he said.

Would you include Australia in that? asked Finn.

Of course, I'd love to go back there. Antoine's gaze flicked to me. My mouth suddenly went dry. This was news to me. But he read my mind and said: That's if Neve agrees to come with me. I smiled and reaching my fingers across the table to touch his hand, he continued. But this time I'd like to play in smaller, more intimate settings to maximise the emotional impact on the audience. Are there such venues in Australia?

Oh god, yes. I can think of quite a few theatres in Sydney that might interest you, said Finn, looking at Tamsin for support, who dutifully added: there are heaps in Melbourne too.

See, said Finn, you'll be spoilt for choice. All the major cities, even regional ones, would have suitable venues.

Perhaps when the time comes, you might like to help me and my manager, Sacha with this. And with the lighting as well, of course.

It'd be an honour. Finn beamed and raised his glass in a toast.

It was late in the afternoon when we all went our separate ways. The day had been hugely successful. The newlyweds were unquestionably delighted. Once home, Antoine immediately kicked off his shoes and sprawled out on the sofa. I have to say it's been an exceptionally joyful day, he said. Perhaps we could do something similar?

But we don't need to because we live in the City of Love, I said.

Yes, I know. But I'm talking about the idea of eloping. Maybe Venice would be an ideal location for us.

Ask me again when I've finished my novel, I replied.

When I thought about it later, I realised my response that day had been flippant. But I knew if I'd expressed any interest at all in his proposal, the next thing on Antoine's agenda would be for us to have a child. And there was no way I was ready for that. Right then, my life was wonderful - better than I'd ever thought possible. I had no real domestic duties to speak of. And most evenings we ate out. More importantly, I was starting to feel I was getting somewhere with The Only Reality. I had a room of my own and absolutely no constraints on my personal time such as a baby's frequent and indisputable demands. I was no Stella who, after attending to Julie and then helping Ford out on the farm, had very little time left over for herself. But I realised this had more to do with good luck than good management. And the changes in social expectations certainly helped too. But with plenty of child-bearing years still in front of me, I wanted to take advantage of the life I'd been given.

We'd arranged to spend summer in the hinterland north of Cannes not far from the town of Grasse, the perfume capital of the world. But when a lorry driver decided to plough into pedestrians celebrating Bastille Day along the Promenade des Anglais in Nice, killing eighty-four people, Antoine decided Portofino would be safer. We spent August there instead. Even my mother was spooked and postponed her visit to the following year, duly arriving mid-March.

As Rachel's first morning in Paris was quite mild for that time of year, she and I took a stroll arm in arm along the Seine. She wanted her photo taken standing beside one of the more colourful bouquinistes' stalls. You do know, she said, that the Seine has been described as the only river in the world that runs between two bookshelves? I shook my head. I hadn't heard that before. My mother didn't appear to be surprised by my negative response when she added: And I suppose you also don't know that you're living the fairy tale of a flawless life.

I grinned. I hadn't detected the slightest bit of sarcasm in her voice. Perhaps a touch of envy, but that may've been wishful thinking on my part. Because ever since I'd flown out of Sydney, I'd wanted Rachel to see that my decision to follow my heart had been right.

But it was a high price to pay. I didn't get much writing done while she was in France, mainly because I felt obliged to spend a great deal of my time with her. For someone who reckoned she liked her independence and who'd insisted she didn't want to be a burden, my mother seemed to expect an awful lot of attention from me. As it turned out, the 'charming hotel' she'd chosen to stay in was not conveniently close by at all. Sure, it was in the Marais, but way up near Place de la République, which, in anyone's opinion, is a pain in the arse to get to by metro from Île Saint-Louis.

Nevertheless, by stifling my feelings of frustration at having my writing routine impeded, I managed to enjoy Rachel's company. Most of the time. Certainly, the high point of her visit was the two weeks we spent together driving around the Mediterranean coast from Marseille to Monaco. Antoine didn't come with us, because by the time Rachel arrived in Paris, he was totally immersed in orchestrating his Liberty Suite, so nothing could physically drag him away from the studio. Even so, he rang me every morning and evening, something he always did when we were apart.

Besides booking flights and hiring a car, nothing else had been planned for our two weeks on the Riviera. Not even accommodation. Though I did make sure we visited several places Stella had mentioned in her memoir. Overall, we got on so well, it was almost like old times. That is, until the night before we were to fly back to Paris.

We were staying in Toulon, about an hour's drive to Marseille airport and had decided to dine in the hotel's restaurant downstairs. We'd just finished our main course and were enjoying what was left of our wine, when Rachel breathed out slowly. It sounded almost like a sigh. So, she said, is he going to ring you again tonight? Her tone immediately putting me offside.

Of course, I replied, placing my glass back on the table. He said he'd call me around ten.

I see, she said, letting out another long breath. Don't you find all these telephone calls a bit suffocating?

What do you mean?

I hoped that'd be obvious. All these calls, this constant checking up on you – don't you find it rather controlling?

No, I don't. I think Antoine's just being caring. That's all.

Rachel raised her eyebrows. Really? She sounded incredulous.

Jesus, I said, wanting to toss the rest of my wine in her face. But I managed to restrain myself and swallowed the contents of my glass instead.

Look darling, I'm not trying to be difficult. I'm your mother. I care about you. And I do understand. Antoine can be charming, but surely you must've realised by now that your relationship is based on a power imbalance: his age, wealth, fame, and the fact that he's literally supporting you, must make for an unevenness in authority between the two of you.

Please, stop now. Can't you at least try to respect my judgement?

My darling Neve, I've been around a lot longer than you, and it's been my experience that it's often quite difficult to recognise controlling, possessive and emotionally manipulative people – especially someone you're having a relationship with.

If you ask me, it's you who's being all those things. Not Antoine. And I want you to know I'm not going to take it from you, not now or ever. So let's try to enjoy the rest of our meal. OK?

Thankfully the waiter brought our desserts which put an end to our conversation. That's when I realised there'd be no teary farewells next week when my mother flew back to Australia.

Part Four
1923 – 1932
The Only Reality
by
Neve Palmer

drawn back to art

Like the nearby Rothschild estate, Harold Munro's Villa des Oliviers is situated on the chemin des Moulins, a narrow strip of road that runs high along the peninsula, known as Saint-Jean-Cap-Ferrat. But Munro's villa is no sumptuous palace. It's basically a humble dwelling that can only be reached via a rough, old goat track or by mounting a vertiginous set of stone steps.

Nevertheless Ford and Stella, who've now been in France for over two months, aren't at all daunted - even with their considerable luggage. The sun is shining, and the stony ground beneath their feet is dry. Bone dry. There's definitely no mud here. The villa itself might be considered small but there are still five individual rooms – three at the front and two at the back. And despite the primitive cooking facilities with its ghastly cast iron charcoal burner, there's running water and electric lights. Quite luxurious when compared to their cottages back in England. All things considered, 1923 is shaping up to be a truly grand year.

Stella stands within the frame of the front windows that she's thrown open to admit the early morning January light, as well as the heavenly view. The little villa is still asleep. But there before her is the loveliness of the Villefranche harbour and beyond that, Nice. Only ten kilometres west. She drinks it all in – the tiny fishing boats bobbing in their moorings, the stone wall terraces, the swathes of clustered blue-grey olive leaves along the hillside, the old church steeple, a stand of cypress trees and of course, the huddle of houses with their flat tiled roofs that seem to be climbing away from the sea, frightened perhaps by a British man-of-war that's floating on the Ricketts' blue water.

Yes, she must paint all this.

Then suddenly, the scent of eucalyptus. How can that be? She doesn't yet know that these gum trees had been introduced to France almost a century ago. But right now, this smell and this light remind her of home. Of what she's missed. The salty air. The sun. The vast blue sky. A climate that nurtures the soul, that uplifts the spirit and that isn't demoralising. What a country this is – to offer such mild winters.

So far, France has brought them nothing but good fortune. She and Ford spoke of this, along with many other things, on the train from Paris to the Riviera, when they'd sat up all night, unable to sleep. Thankfully, they had a compartment to themselves with enough space for little Julie and her nurse maid, Lucy to lie down on the two bench seats that faced one another, while Stella and Ford took up a position at the end of each bench next to the windows.

And so once the darkness of night entered the carriage, their discussion of all they'd experienced since their arrival in Paris a month ago became a spontaneous act of appraisal of the City of Light. They agreed that it had been an exhilarating time for them both, especially after the news from Duckworth that he intended to publish The Marsden Case. Right away, Ford signed the contracts allowing the publisher to take over his entire future, past and present work. Of course, securing their Montparnasse lodgings on the rue Vavin had also been an incredible stroke of luck, particularly since they were only a two-minute walk away from the Pounds' studio.

Even now in Cap Ferrat, Stella can still see them – Ezra and Dorothy standing on the footpath waving to them, as she and Ford turned the corner of rue Vavin.

'Our place is tucked away just inside here,' Ezra said, smiling as he pushed open the narrowest of entrance doors Stella had ever seen. 'Unless you've been here before, you'd probably walk right past it.'

'That's why we thought it best to wait for you out on the street,' explained Dorothy. Then added, 'Everyone's dying to meet you.'

Ezra led the way across a delightful courtyard bowered by a canopy of leafy tree branches. Dorothy squeezed Stella's arm and whispered:

'It's so good to see you again.' Then arm in arm they'd followed the men. As they did, Stella couldn't help but be alert to the dark-stained façade of the stucco walls that needed a coat of paint. She'd also noticed the weathered wooden shutters of the surrounding studios – some open, some not. And there was a line of dripping undergarments strung up on high and a battered plaster statue with vaguely Greek pretensions standing to one side. She was beguiled by it all.

And she smiles again now at the memory of how tired she and Ford had been after their cross-channel journey. The last thing they'd thought they needed was a party. But the gaiety and conversation inside the Pounds' studio had enlivened them both. Music was playing somewhere in the background as they were introduced to a whirlwind of people, most of whose names Stella was certain she'd never remember beyond that day.

And now looking out from the peninsula, she knows she'd been right. Of course, there was no forgetting James Joyce, who looked pale and sickly, but oh, how he'd showered Ford with gratitude for the wonderful review of his novel, Ulysses that Ford had written.

'Good grief, man,' was Ford's reply, 'there's no need to thank me.'

Only Stella knew otherwise. She was silently grateful to Joyce for being so thoughtful and courteous. She'd witnessed so many times the generous way Ford nurtured and encouraged the efforts of other writers, how he assisted them by sharing his vast knowledge of all the arts. But she understood very well, then and now, that he was in more need of affirmation than anyone realised. There'd been many times she'd witnessed his acute agitation when he perceived even a hint of any unkind criticism of his own work.

She knew it was a matter of personal pride to Ford to give credit where it was due. And Joyce deserved to be told that certain books could change the world, and as far as he was concerned, Ulysses had already done so. 'The way you've presented human consciousness is something I've always strived to do. You've written a masterpiece, James. You truly have.'

Of course Joyce, ever humble, changed the subject and asked about Ford and Stella's plans while in France. They talked of Provence then, and Joyce asked them to bring him back a shell cameo if they happened to get themselves to Menton. That was when Ezra interrupted and whisked Ford and Joyce away leaving Stella to follow in their wake.

And before too long, Ford was holding court – his bulky frame encircled by listeners eager to hear his views on Henry James. Surrounded by disciples, he was in his element. As for Stella, she was content to be an observer that evening. That was until she was introduced to the American wife of some French man of letters.

'Oh Mrs Ford,' said the woman, 'you must give me the rundown on what's happening in the literary world of England.'

And without thinking, Stella replied: 'I'm afraid I'm a bit of a rustic so I really wouldn't have a clue.'

Oh, how she's lived to regret that gaffe!

Later, as they walked back to their lodgings, Ford's rebuke had stung her.

'Good Lord woman, what were you thinking? You might've got away with that kind of ignorance back in England, but you won't be able to do that here. There's not a soul in Paris, who thinks being a numbskull is particularly amusing!' He took a breath, then told her she'd not only let him down, but she'd also let herself down. 'And since you've happily spent quite a pretty penny on elocution lessons in order to rid yourself of what you perceive to be your ghastly Australian accent, why not start thinking about dropping your rubbishy colonial persona of being culturally gauche? Don't you think that would be a grand idea? Because I'm quite sure it won't serve you well in this country.'

The memory of his words still brings tears to her eyes. It was the first time he'd ever shown any anger towards her. But he was right. While she'd never liked being the centre of attention, she had to admit she often tended to play the ignorance card. Not because she was stupid or uninformed. But more from fear she might make an irretrievable error, or worse still, cause pain to others. She knew she wasn't the fount of all cultural knowledge, but she wasn't a philistine either. So why then was she so self-effacing?

When she and Ford talked about it again during that night, as their train steamed down towards the Riviera, they'd both agreed that all in all the Pounds' party had been a very bizarre welcome to Paris. For not an hour after Stella's social blunder, a young woman, whose face looked like a catastrophe, suddenly burst in the door, and announced: 'Marcel Proust est mort!' And then, so was the party. The news had sobered everyone.

The next day, Paris was stricken. Proust's death had cast a gloom over everything. Even waiters in cafés wore black armbands as a show of respect.

'Can you imagine English waiters doing this for Thomas Hardy?' Ford had asked Stella. 'You'd be lucky to find one who'd even heard of him! Such a widespread display of grief for a writer certainly says something about this nation.'

She saw his point and wasn't at all surprised when he decided that as a representative of English letters, he should attend Proust's funeral.

So off they both went.

It was a mammoth affair and beautifully stage-managed in the chapel of Saint-Pierre-de-Chaillot. The entire interior had been draped in black and silver. There were clusters of massed candles, a choir of angelic voices and a profusion of flowers. The organ played Bach. As a knight of the Legion d'honneur, Proust was given military honours by a squadron of officers, which led the funeral procession to the family plot in Père-Lachaise. It had been quite a spectacle.

And as their train sped on through the nocturnal fields of rural France, Ford had leant forward in his seat and took Stella's hands in his. 'I think these last four weeks in Paris have been very well spent, my dear.' His voice was gentle. 'Since Proust's death I've felt a pressing need to take up a serious pen once more. I have this idea, you see. Inspired by Joyce too, of course.'

And then he'd told her, explaining how Pound had his Cantos, Joyce his Ulysses and Proust his great sequence, À la recherche du temps perdu. All works on a grand scale. All in their own way revolutionary. And that's what he now wanted to do - to make the effort to write something ambitious in size and concept that would explore time and consciousness. But in his own way. 'It's not from any rivalry,' he said. 'Nor do I wish to imitate. But the story can only be one I could've written – the story of my own time. The story of my war.'

Ford paused and shifted in his seat. Stella urged him to continue.

'And it's not going to be just about death or even self-sacrifice. Or about fear and the horror of war. But like I said, it will be about my war and the sensation of panic and anxiety. It will be about trauma and loss of memory. Something I hope the world of readers will never tire of.'

So the idea for Parade's End had arrived.

'Oh my darling,' replied Stella. 'It sounds wonderful. Wonderful. You must start right away.'

Then she felt the lightness of his bushy, yellow moustache that crowned his upper lip scrape across her forehead. 'And you must start painting in earnest too, my dear. We should both seize this time together.' That was when he asked her would she be happy to design the dust jacket for The Marsden Case. Of course, it was an honour, and she said as much, and then his mouth found her lips. And after a minute, his hand reached beneath her dress and found the warmth between her thighs.

Later as dawn broke, the light-filled, provençal landscape had exploded outside the window of their compartment. And there beside the train tracks appeared the Rhone River.

Now, looking out over the bay to the tiny port of Villefranche, she understands why this southern part of France is the country of Ford's heart, his very own holy land. Life is so less complicated here. They all feel so much happier.

Julie is quite content to be taken care of by Lucy. And as for Ford, who's always liked a hearty lunch, he's now immensely pleased with just some fresh bread and cheese and fruit. All of which provides Stella with long stretches of free time to do as she pleases. Which, this very morning, will be to make some preliminary sketches of the harbour.

But first she brews a nice pot of tea.

It isn't till the end of February that Stella finally shows Ford her little oil painting of Villefranche harbour.

'Oh, I do like that!' he cries. 'You've captured the blue of the Mediterranean brilliantly and the white-washed stone steps leading down to the quai – just lovely, lovely.'

Stella beams.

Then he adds: 'It's so good, it could easily be a travel poster for the area.'

She wonders if this comment is some kind of veiled criticism. But no. She decides it couldn't be. Ford is nothing if not encouraging of her work as an artist.

And then a letter from Dorothy arrives. The Pounds are touring Italy, and Ezra thinks it's high time Stella sees some real pictures. Dorothy has underlined the word real. So, said the letter, would she like to pop over for a couple of weeks? Join her in Florence? And together they could tour Assisi, Perugia, Siena, Genoa and so on.

Ford insists on her going, convincing her that she deserves it and has absolutely earned it. 'Besides,' he says. 'I'm more than capable of looking after everything here.'

Her trip to Italy is the first time she's been separated from Ford and Julie, and she misses them dreadfully. Despite this, she tells Ford in her letters home that she's having a heavenly time. She loves the way the churches with their paintings and frescoes harmonise with the Italian landscape that contain those same churches and chapels. And she writes of her discovery of Giotto, who speaks to her from down the centuries.

When she returns to Villefranche, her enthusiasm for the paintbrush is reawakened. She's full of ideas about formal composition, linear design, and thin paint.

'I can't begin to tell you how much I learnt about art and about myself in Italy,' she says, as she curls up to Ford in bed on her first night home.

'I don't doubt it, my darling.'

'I mean, I know it's not fashionable to prefer the figurative, but that's my preference and I think it's my strength too. I can't see what the attraction is to abstract art. There's very little of it that's truly beautiful. And beauty is what I want in my life.'

'Then you must trust in your instincts. It's the only way forward.'

'I know you're right, but then you're the only person I can discuss this with. I'm always frightened of saying anything like this to other people.' She holds Ford's gaze. 'I mean, I couldn't even show Dorothy any of the watercolour sketches I did in Perugia or Assisi for fear I'd receive nothing but her scorn. The only thing she believes I should do is to make arbitrary patterns from the natural objects I see. But my eye tells me differently.'

'So then, pay attention to what you see. Not to what you're told.'

onward

They are happy and productive in Cap Ferrat. Life in every aspect seems so much better for them now. At Easter though, when the villa's lease comes to an end, they're obliged to move on.

Ford wants to show Stella more of what he calls le vrai Provence around the Rhône valley and so he chooses the sleepy little town of Tarascon as their base. But not long after they'd settled into the Hotel Terminus, Stella heads off to Paris for two weeks. Her trip to Italy had made her realise she needed to work on her brushwork and learn more about pigments and the mechanics of things in general. To this end, she arranges some lessons in the city with Sonia Lewitska, a painter and printmaker, whose work she admires.

Everything's going well until quite by chance she runs into the Pounds. When she explains why she's in Paris, Ezra can't help himself. He ridicules her interest in Lewitska, saying she's 'old school' and beneath his contempt. Stella is mortified. Her confidence stalls, and she pours out her heart in her letters back to Ford.

As always, he's quick in his response and support of her. He writes reminding her not to pay any attention to his criticisms, that when it comes to aesthetics Pound is utterly ignorant, and as for the prevalence of one type of art over another, that's simply a matter of cycles. But if there is one truth, it's this: good drawing, good colour, good patterning will always bring about an emotional response, which is after all the desired effect all artists wish to produce.

He assures her that she has great gifts and all the makings of an artist. All she lacks is a certain self-confidence. Nevertheless, Pound's words have become an unseen scar within her.

Once she's back in Tarascon in their rooms at the Hotel Terminus, Stella is grateful to be in Ford's arms again. She calls him her 'dearest darling' and tells him how much she loves him. Being apart from him always seems to strengthen her feelings for him. And for little Julie too. It had been a real wrench leaving her to go to Paris, especially when she's growing up so quickly.

But now Stella's determined to pursue her own direction in art and next morning begins work on a series of small, detailed portraits on wood panels. She draws up a weekly roster that also leaves her some time to spend in the local cafe or to explore nearby towns like Arles and Avignon.

Days flow by. Each one more and more idyllic, especially when picnicking on cured seasoned sausage, tiny black olives, and cheap red wine. Or when working en plein air in Avignon, where she starts to paint what will become a sun-drenched scene of the bridge and its river. This will be a bold, severe, and geometric work, and she'll make sure that no one could ever compare 'Bridge at Avignon' to a travel poster.

But there is one false note – a day she'll never forget.

'Must I go?' asks Stella, when Ford tells her that Didier, the local barrister has offered him tickets to Nîmes' first bullfight of the season.

'It's up to you, my dear. But if you're asking my opinion, I do think that one must see these things at least once before dismissing them out of hand.'

And then a few days later, Tarascon and the surrounding districts are transformed by bullfighting fever. Colourful posters promoting the event appear throughout the town. People speak of little else, with excitement reaching its peak when a cavalcade of beribboned, open-topped carriages, conveying the matadors in their glittering costumes, drive through the streets. It reminds Stella of a scene from the opera, Carmen. She decides to go to Nîmes.

Thankfully, their seats in that ancient arena don't face the sun, and while she's fascinated by the theatrics of the spectacle with the picadors on horseback, the wild roar of the crowd, the music and the balletic movements of the matadors, their capes spread wide one minute, then elegantly wrapped around them the next, it's the blood that horrifies her. The senseless stupidity of all that blood makes Stella's stomach muscles heave. They witness the slaying of six bulls that day, two by Manuel Garcia, the great Spanish matador, known as Maera. Even though he dispatches his bulls with cool precision, the cultural significance of the sport eludes her. She's sickened by the whole experience.

By the end of May, Ford is pleased with the progress he's making on Some Do Not, the first part of what will become his tetralogy, Parade's End. But around this time, the annual fair comes to town and sets itself up across the road from the Hotel Terminus. Overnight, a myriad of gaudy lights and caravans and clowns and show-booths appear. There's also an ancient, colourful carousel churning out its mechanical music no matter the hour, which is often overpowered by squeals of pleasure and shrieks of laughter. It becomes all too much for Ford. He can't write. He can't concentrate. He can't sleep. And without a sea breeze, the days are becoming very hot. There's no alternative but to relocate. But where? Didier, of course, comes to the rescue with a suggestion. He recommends the small township of Saint-Agrève, north-west of Tarascon in the area known as the Ardèche.

On their arrival one night in early June, the place is wind-swept and freezing. It reminds Stella of the grim parsonage at Haworth in West Yorkshire, where the Brontë sisters once lived. Ford promptly comes down with an acute bout of bronchitis. But while the furnished rooms are spartan in the little Hôtel de la Poste where they're staying, the meals there are excellent, and Ford's strength gradually returns. When summer finally visits in July, the area is suddenly made beautiful with fields and fields of cheerful flowers. Stella stops cursing Didier, and Ford gets back to Some Do Not. All's right with the world once again.

By the time September arrives, both she and Ford are, for the time being, ready to leave behind provincial France and launch themselves onto Paris.

the transatlantic review

They'd only been there a couple of days when Ford insists they call in at Sylvia Beach's English language bookstore, Shakespeare and Company, up on rue de l'Odeon. Perhaps someone there might know of a reasonable place they could rent. But no. They are met with the same downcast faces, the same shaking of heads and the same negative response they'd been given previously: aren't they aware there's a rental crisis in Paris?

'Let's clear our heads and take a stroll through the Luxembourg Gardens?' suggests Ford, trying desperately to appear upbeat. 'Should be lovely this time of year.'

But they hadn't walked very far when a portly gentleman approaches them from the opposite direction. 'Well, I'll be damned,' he booms. 'Fancy running into you here! After all these years too.'

The two men shake hands vigorously. Looking delighted, Ford turns to Stella, 'So can you guess who this might be?'

'Your brother, Oliver?' And of course, she's right. 'Not that that was difficult to work out. The two of you are the spitting image of one another.'

There are introductions then, and Oliver promptly invites them back to his cottage. 'I'd love you to meet Muriel,' he says. 'She's a novelist you know.' And then looking directly at Stella, 'I think the gods are telling us you both should come.'

And so they set off together, with Oliver talking non-stop: 'Now I need to warn you, our place is not salubrious. Don't, whatever you do, expect something grand. It's a tad down-at-heel, I'm afraid. Muriel prefers to say it has a certain *style rustique* about it.' Stella laughs. She thinks Ford's brother is utterly charming.

And she thinks the cottage is too. It is part of the artists' colony known as the Cité Fleurie on the boulevard Arago, but it's free standing and set back from the thirty or so artist studios, all of which had been constructed chalet-style back in the 1880's using recycled timber. What impresses Ford most are the associations the place has – Gaugin, Rodin, Modigliani had all used the studios here.

Muriel doesn't seem at all surprised when Oliver introduces them. She welcomes them warmly and tells them she's about to go to America. One thing leads to another and before they know it, Ford and Stella agree to rent the cottage for 200 francs a month. Even though there are few creature comforts and certainly no modern conveniences like gas or electricity, it does have its very own walled garden with unruly Virginia creepers and nasturtiums galore.

'Ah!' quips Ford, 'an avant-garden.' The entire complex consists of picturesque little pathways running through a romantic chaos of autumnal trees and shrubs. In the gentle, autumn light that day, it seems a bargain too good to pass up.

Within days, they move in. Without Lucy though. She'd been terribly homesick since they'd left Tarascon, so she'd returned to England. While the September sun is still pouring into the cottage's big French windows, Stella's not overly concerned with the lack of domestic assistance.

'Don't worry, we'll cope,' she says to Ford one morning, as they sit drinking tea in the warmth of their garden with Julie happily drawing pictures at her feet. 'And we'll certainly be able to put to good use the money we save from Lucy's wages.'

'Yes, indeed. Very good, my dear. Very good,' he replies, refilling his teacup. 'But one small thing I believe we should do is to have a little celebration, don't you think? Just the three of us, of course. *Un déjeuner en famille dans un restaurant. Comme les français.* What do you say, Stella? Would you like that?'

And yes, they have much to celebrate. So a few Sundays later, they walk up towards the boulevard du Montparnasse, Julie sometimes skipping along beside her parents. They stop first at a little café where Stella and Ford each order an apéritif and a sirop de fraise for their daughter. Then on to Le Nègre de Toulouse, for their cheap and hearty cassoulet and plenty of vin ordinaire.

Later that afternoon, they dawdle back home. Not because they're inebriated. And not because they're tired either. But because they see no need to rush, what with the sun shining through the plane trees on the boulevard and the sheer wonder of the stream of humanity promenading up and down. Everyone seems contented and at peace. Stella has never felt so happy. Everything has fallen so beautifully into place. And so quickly too.

First, to be living in the cottage in Montparnasse, the most stimulating quarter of the most exciting city in the world and then to have four of her portraits accepted in the prestigious Salon d'Automne – it's absolutely exhilarating. And of course, there's Ford. Dear, darling Ford, now walking tall – his creative powers having finally come back to him. What resilience! What strength of purpose! He's completed *Some Do Not* and his heroine, Valentine Wannup, is his tribute to her. Stella! A priceless gift.

And what's more, he's been offered the editorship of a new monthly literary magazine, to be called the Transatlantic Review. It's to be distributed in America, as well as in Britain and France. So the world will see what he's truly made of. His genius will be recognised at last. Despite a niggling doubt that the financial viability of this proposed magazine is rather shaky, she's thrilled for him and for herself. How lucky she is to be loved by such a unique and brilliant man. To be living with him here, now, in Paris.

Suddenly Ford grabs her hand. She stops in her tracks and turns to face him.

'Let's not go back to England?' he says in a rush.

'I was about to say the exact same thing. And yes, I'd much rather stay here.'

'So shall we sell Bedham then?'

'Fine by me.'

They embrace, and Ford lifts her into the air and twirls her round and round. And not one passer-by bats an eye at this spontaneous affirmation of life.

'Papa, please. My turn now!' Julie is tugging at Ford's coat tails. 'Spin me! Spin me too, papa!'

By the time they get back to the cottage, they've decided that first thing next morning they'll send word to England to sell Bedham. With exchange rates being what they are, they're both confident that the money from the sale will allow them to purchase a small house in Paris, as well as a smaller one in Provence.

It's been a very special day. 'We must do this sort of thing more often,' suggests Ford. 'I'm afraid that now Lucy's not around, it's going to be up to you to keep the home fires burning, my dear, because I may not have much time to help domestically, what with having to set up an office and attend meetings with writers and printers and such. You do understand, don't you?'

Stella nods. It doesn't bother her at all. In fact, she's certain she'll be able to get back to some serious painting by the end of the year. Surely by then, the review will be up and running and they'll be living in their own home and will have found a nanny for Julie as well. Besides all that, she knows she's going to enjoy spending more time with her daughter. Julie's demands are so few. So uncomplicated. All will be well. It's only a matter of time.

She tells Ford not to worry. She'll handle everything. But she does insist they initiate one family outing per week, preferably on a Sunday. Just like any French family. And so, a routine begins – aperitifs at La Closerie des Lilas followed by lunch, invariably at Au Nègre de Toulouse, where they're often joined by friends.

But as autumn grows colder, the grimly damp reality of their cottage, that has no foundations, becomes all too obvious. It's time to move on. Again.

Knowing the money from the sale of their property in England will soon come through, Stella steps up her efforts to find a permanent home. She drags Julie along with her on her daily forays into the outer suburbs of Paris: Meudon, Vaucresson, St Cloud. All she wants is a little house with a garden and a railway station close by. Surely, it's not too much to ask.

Meanwhile Ford is becoming more and more engrossed in setting up his literary periodical. First, he writes a prospectus and then starts frequenting Les Deux Magots and the Café du Dôme. Often with Ezra in tow. And it's not too long before word goes round that the great English writer and critic, who can judge the quality of a manuscript by its smell, is to be the editor of a new periodical, that will surely be a game-changer. For Ford's credo is well known. He isn't one to discriminate by gender, youth, age, or country of origin. Or even literary faction. His stated intention is to publish only good work.

Quality work. All this is creating excitement in the young and talented writers now living in Montparnasse, particularly those from America, who are extremely sure of the greatness of their own literary gifts.

Ford knows that expectations for the new magazine will rise even further once he's managed to secure some office space, so he persuades the independent publisher, Bill Bird, to allow him to set up an office in his premises that was once a huge domed wine-vault. With the ground floor already taken up by Bill's bulky seventeenth century printing press, Ford sets up a birdcage like office on the gallery level. So far so good, but there's still an obstacle to overcome. Without secure financial backing, there'll definitely be no Review.

Then, out of the blue, along comes a patron of the arts and wealthy lawyer from New York, who offers to provide the sum of 40,000 francs. But only if that sum can be matched. Understandably, when this news is presented to Ford in his freshly established editorial office, he's somewhat shaken. Why is everything always so damned complicated? He suddenly wants to bolt and get himself home.

As soon as he enters the cottage, he pours himself a large glass of red wine left over from the night before and sits down with it at the table. Despite Stella's weariness from house-hunting, she takes up a chair opposite him. She senses something's wrong and knows she needs to listen.

'I really don't know what can be done,' Ford says, shivering. 'I might have known it was all too good to be true. At least then, I'd never have invested so much precious time and energy on the bloody thing.'

Stella is silent. She can see how pale and miserable Ford looks as he takes great slurps from his glass. She knows how much this venture means to him. He'd even asked her to design the review's logo for the cover. And now this! The room fills with Ford's pain. And Stella feels it keenly. He deserves better. He's always supported and encouraged her work. Always believed in her. It would be so wonderful if he could have his review. It would be the icing on the cake now that he's restored his creative vigour and been working so hard to get this periodical off the ground.

'I'll never be able to raise that amount of money,' Ford says. 'There's no way round this dilemma, my dear. I simply must abandon the whole thing and…'

'No, no. You mustn't do that! Remember, we have the money from the sale of Bedham.'

'But that's to buy a house, my dear. It's what we'd agreed to do.'

'I know. But we also chose to be a part of this vibrant Left Bank artistic life, so we can change our minds, can't we? And who knows? You may never get another opportunity like this again. We will manage, I know we will. We always have.'

And so it's done. Under its lower-case title, the first transatlantic review appears in December. It's a moment of great pride to Ford. A time for quiet celebration. Or at least a little party for Julie, who's turning three.

As Christmas looms, one of the larger studios in the Cité Fleurie compound is about to become vacant. It's an opportunity too good to miss. They pack up their belongings and move in. It's been quite a momentous year.

plat du jour

So he finishes off the last bit of croissant and, hating the taste of condensed milk, slowly drinks what's left in his bowl of café au lait. Surely the French realise it's no substitute for the real thing. Especially now the war is well and truly over, the transportation and storage of the fresh variety shouldn't still be a problem. But it's no use getting irritable. Besides, it's almost noon, and he'll soon be having lunch.

Outside, on the boulevard, it's snowing again. Light, powdery, fairy-tale white. Inside, thanks to a well-placed cast iron hot water radiator, it's pleasantly warm. He settles back on the banquette. Ah, this is the life! Catching the eye of the waiter, he asks for a vermouth. May as well have an apéritif, while checking out the news of the world.

Well, what do you know! Lenin is reported to have died, and in Chamonix, the inaugural Winter Olympics is about to commence. While on the other side of the world in Australia, the English cricket team is set to lose the Ashes.

So what?

Not the slightest bit interested in any of it, he folds the newspaper firmly and places it on the floor beneath his chair, then takes a sip of the vermouth that has just been brought to him. Needn't rush. Knowing Ezra, there's a good chance he'll be another hour.

Ford begins to flip through Forum, a new American weekly magazine Gertrude Stein[7] has given him. Supposed to be full of criticism and commentary, fiction and poetry. 'Just your sort of thing,' she'd said. 'You must let me know what you think of it.'

Fully intending to do so, he begins to read the first article: '1923 - A Year in Review'.

Good Lord! Harry Houdini has done it again. Freed himself from a straitjacket while suspended upside down in San Francisco. No doubt pickpockets had a field day while the crowd was looking skywards. Are there people who actually care about this nonsense?

He takes another sip of his drink and reads on.

Chaplin's full-length feature film, A Woman in Paris may be a critical success but it's a box-office failure. The audience wanted comedy – a bit of the old slapstick, not the serious drama Chaplin has served up to them. Nobody cares if he's written, directed and produced the damn thing. All they want is a laugh. They want their little Tramp. And so they feel cheated. And at that moment, reading this pathetic tripe in this so-called reputable journal, Ford feels cheated too.

Another mouthful and he drains his glass. Feeling relaxed now, he signals the waiter to bring him another. In for a penny! And there it is. Finally a piece he's mildly interested in: 'Drunkenness on the rise in America'. Speakeasies have been raided across the US, and its citizens arrested in 'bewildering figures'.

Well, well, well. Of course, it's no surprise to Ford. You've only to see the way these Yanks here in Paris put away their liquor. Like

---

7. **Gertrude Stein:** (1874 – 1946) American writer and art collector, she moved to Paris in 1903 and made France her home for the rest of her life. An advocate of the avant-garde and a bold experimenter, she hosted a Paris salon with her life partner and secretary, **Alice B. Toklas** (1877-1967), where the leading figures of modernism in literature and art gathered.

children set free in a sweetshop. The word moderation is not a part of their lexicon. The only thing America's Prohibition has succeeded in doing is to stimulate such a passion for drinking in the people that they can't resist being intoxicated. It's probably the reason so many of 'em have come to Paris in the first place. No ludicrous laws like that here. No siree! The French know how to drink. Not for inebriation. But for pleasure and to be sociable.

The waiter returns and places another vermouth along with a tiny plate of olives on Ford's table just as Ezra appears. 'Hope you haven't been waiting too long,' he says, taking off his gloves and pulling out a seat.

'Not at all. Not at all.'

'Shall we order first, then talk?' Ezra surveys the menu. *'Le plat du jour* looks good.'

'I rather fancy the rabbit,' says Ford.

They place their orders and get down to business. 'So, how's Stella? Painting, I hope?'

'Well, she really has no excuse not to anymore. Especially now we've found Madame Annie to help with Julie. But she doesn't seem to be producing much if that's what you mean.'

'Aha, so how's madame Annie working out?'

'From what I can tell, Julie's becoming quite fond of her. Stella though refers to her as the old battle-axe. I think she finds her a bit intimidating at times. But the woman seems pleasant enough to me.' He fiddles with his fork. 'But then I do try to steer clear of all that domestic nonsense.'

Talk then shifts to the transatlantic review. Pound voices his approval of Ford's inclusion of some poems by e e cummings in the first edition but he stops short of telling his old friend that he ought to drop the pompous, self-congratulatory tone of his editorials. 'There needs to be a lot more unconventional pieces,' is what he says instead.

'Of course, of course,' comes the reply. 'Joyce has agreed to give me a section of his work in progress. That should stir things up a bit. I think a lot of readers may well find it quite perplexing. But it'll make 'em see more clearly though.' Ford laughs. 'And I'm sure I'll get Tristan Tzara on board as well.'

Pound is dismissive. 'Dada will be dead soon – if it isn't already. More of the young Turks – that's what's needed. Remember, if this thing is to survive, you've got to make it new.'

The waiter interrupts with their meals. Pound unfurls his serviette and placing it on his lap says: 'Oh and before I forget. Young Hemingway's back in town. I'd like you to meet him. He's talented, ambitious and very disciplined. I think he'd be a fine sub-editor.'

'Tell me more.'

'Well, he's tall. Good looking. Married to a very nice woman by the name of Hadley. They have a baby son they call Bumby. Or something like that.' Ezra pauses. Children are of little interest to him. 'Gertrude seems to like him. Apparently, she thinks he's got what it takes. As long as he gives up journalism and sticks to writing creative stuff.'

Ford finds this last comment interesting. Such an endorsement wouldn't have come directly from Gertrude. Everyone knows she loathes Ezra. Some time back, he broke her favourite chair, and she's refused to see him ever since. It has to have come from Hemingway himself. Nothing like a bit of self-promotion, thinks Ford and says: 'I look forward to meeting him then.'

Both men fall silent while they eat.

making it new

Every Saturday evening, Gertrude Stein and her life-long companion, Alice B. Toklas, hold their weekly at homes in their sixth arrondissement studio on the rue de Fleurus. And it's in October at one of these soirées that Alice asks Stella to join her and Gertrude for lunch on the following Wednesday. 'It will only be the three of us,' she whispers conspiratorially, making it quite clear that neither Julie, whom they both adore, nor Ford is invited.

It's not the first time Stella has received such an invitation. She likes both women very much and enjoys their company, knowing they enjoy hers too. 'Oh goodie!' she says. 'We can indulge ourselves in a spot of cosy low-brow conversation.'

'Precisely,' says Alice, smiling.

When Stella knocks on the studio's large double door at the appointed time, she isn't expecting Gertrude to open it. But there she is – greeting her with open arms. Although stout, she's an impressive looking woman, who has an air of self-possession that Stella admires and wishes she had more of herself.

'I'm very glad you've come today, Stella. I've been thinking about you ever since I saw you here last Saturday. You looked so sad, so forlorn. Didn't she, Alice?'

'Indeed she did.'

A lot of people underestimate Alice, but Stella isn't one of them. The minute she met the two women she knew instinctively it was Alice who wielded the power. She may play the servile minion to Gertrude's genius but if she disapproves of you, soon enough, so will Gertrude.

'I didn't think my misery was that obvious,' says Stella.

'Oh, I doubt anyone else would've noticed. But you know Alice. She has a gift for this sort of thing and naturally she alerted me.' Smiling, she takes a breath. 'Now, we don't wish to pry. Not at all. But we do hope everything's all right, my dear. Nothing wrong with Julie, we hope?'

'No, no, she's fine. It's just that… Stella pauses. They've moved into the parlour, and Alice gestures her to take a seat. But she remains standing. 'It's just that… well, I'm worried about Ford.'

'Ah-ha! I thought as much!' Gertrude sounds pleased with herself. 'You don't have to say another word about it unless you want to. And if you don't, we won't think less of you, you know.' Stella smiles weakly. She suddenly wants to tell them everything. But Gertrude continues: 'So why don't we eat as we talk? Alice has prepared a delightful lunch for us. And we shouldn't upset Alice, should we now?'

Even Alice laughs at this. In the centre of the room is a small, low-lying table spread with a feast set out on two large platters – one containing mouth-sized vol-au-vents, quiches and open sandwiches and the other filled with cold meats and cheeses and fruit. The three women sit down with Gertrude taking up her usual position beneath her portrait that Picasso had painted of her twenty-five years ago.

'Help yourselves,' Alice says.

Gertrude piles her plate with food and begins to eat with her considerable gusto, in contrast to the more diminutive Alice, who eats daintily, like a tiny exotic bird.

'Do try my *vin de cassis*. I think you'll like it,' Alice says, handing Stella a glass of colourless liquid.

Stella takes a sip and glances up at the surrounding walls that are plastered from eye level to the ceiling in watercolours and oils by the likes of Cézanne, Matisse, Gauguin, Renoir. It's like lunching inside a museum. The wine is liquid warmth in her mouth and it loosens her tongue. 'As I was saying, I'm worried about Ford.' And then in a rush: 'He's depressed. I've known him too long not to be able to read the signs that others may not see. He's a great bluffer, you know.'

'Which is part of his charm.'

'I'm glad you think so, Gertrude. Not everybody does though.'

'Who cares about everybody? I certainly don't!'

'I know. But you're different. I'm worried that he might not be able to spring back from this, from what others are saying about him. I know he's never been any good with finances. But he really has done everything he possibly could to keep his precious transatlantic review afloat. So now that it's about to be wound up, he's absolutely demoralised, and I'm sure he's anxious about his reputation, not to mention his lasting legacy as well.'

Alice refills their glasses, while Stella speaks. 'Maybe it's true what some people are saying – that from the very beginning the magazine was doomed, and that Ford and I've been foolish to sink so much of our own money into the venture.'

'Now, now…no good will come from thinking that way. That's the past and the past is the past is the past and what's done is done.' Gertrude pauses momentarily and leaning across to Stella, pats her hand. 'What you and he must remember is that the review was a grand idea, and I'm certain that one day, it will be regarded as being visionary. As for Ford himself, when it comes to discovering and nurturing new talent, he has no equal.'

'I wish Hemingway thought like that. He's blaming Ford entirely for the failure of the review, which is indefensible really, considering the way he's been churlish and aggressive towards Ford, showing him absolutely no respect.' Stella closes her eyes for a moment and exhales. She understands how a young ambitious writer might view Ford as passé, a representative of all the outmoded aesthetic traditions he's rebelling against. But Hemingway's nasty. 'You know, I once overheard him referring to Ford as the golden walrus.' She pauses again. She feels pain even saying these words out loud. 'Don't get me wrong, I really like Hadley and consider her a good friend, but Ernest – well, I should've realised earlier. From the time he started working at the review, when he used to sit at Ford's feet and praise him, that was when we should've been suspicious about his intentions because that was just the beginning of his campaign to undermine Ford.'

Stella can feel her face burning with indignation, but she's not about to stop. Besides, her audience is transfixed, silently waiting for her to continue. Which she does.

'I mean, when Ford was forced to go to New York to find backers who'd help bail out the magazine, he entrusted Ernest to edit the August edition while he was away. But what did Ernest do?' She hesitates a moment then: 'He wilfully violated the internationalist principles of the review by making it a predominantly American edition.'

Gertrude raises her eyebrows. 'Remember, Stella, I was in that edition.' Her voice is gentle, teasing.

'Yes, I know, but your piece doesn't really count because it had been serialised since the April edition. And just in case you think I've forgotten, I'm also fully aware that you're both wonderful godparents to Bumby.' She smiles at both women and is instantly comforted that neither of them appears upset by a word she's said. All three of them have remained in that genial zone of women having lunch together. 'I suppose what I'm trying to say is that I know Ford is not without fault. And despite him making a great show of doing things efficiently, it's all been smoke and mirrors. But Hemingway hasn't helped. He's precipitated the review's end with his blatant sabotage.'

There! She's said it. And what a relief it is! She's aired her grievances to these two friends, friends she knows she can trust. But she's not sure what Ford would think about her doing so. She bites into a little quiche and lets its gooey centre slide down her throat. Then pops the rest into her mouth, while the weight of the studio's silence settles itself on her.

Gertrude places her empty plate on the table and turns her head to face Stella. 'Well, it's very nice to know that you feel at ease in confiding in us.'

'Indeed,' says Alice, sniffing. 'But you should know, my dear, that I, unlike some, have never been taken in by Mr Hemingway.'

Gertrude clears her throat. 'Yes, that's true, and everyone knows I have a weakness for him. But lately I've become suspicious of his motives. I'm sure he's been playing me off against Ford. But that's of no great matter. What you must realise now is that he's like so many of these young Americans who served in the war. They drink too much. They are intellectually lazy and they have no respect for anything or anyone. They're our lost generation.' Gertrude knows only too well what Hemingway has been saying about Ford – that he's a pompous, lying windbag and a washed-out, washed-up barrel of social pretension. But she's certainly not going to upset Stella any more than she is already. The poor girl doesn't deserve it. So she continues: 'Ernest is to be pitied. He doesn't understand irony, especially when it's Ford who's delivering it.'

'Irony isn't the only thing Ernest doesn't seem to understand.'

'Oh, I'm sure of that. It irks him that Ford sees literary tradition as a work in progress, that it's continually being revitalised by a variety of talents and voices. Hemingway just doesn't get that. But the way I see it, Stella – Hemingway's real problem is his male ego.'

'You mean Ernest thinks Ford patronises him?'

'Of course, he does. He can't see beyond Ford's gentlemanly ways, which he despises. To him, Ford represents the old-world order that should be done away with.'

'But if he hates him so much, why then does he keep attending our parties and dances?'

'A good question,' says Alice, putting some cheese and grapes on Stella's plate and then on Gertrude's.

'So you can see why I'm worried about Ford's peace of mind, not to mention his self-esteem, which is fragile even at the best of times. He might appear impervious to criticism, but it's sheer pretence, as you both know.' She sighs. 'And I bet the Latin Quarter rumour mill is working overtime right now. Unfair and vicious personal attacks on him may well leave Ford a nervous wreck. And I'm not sure I'll be able to cope with that again.'

'Oh, you'll cope my dear because you must,' says Alice.

'And you also must understand that Hemingway is annoyed by Ford because he recognises himself in him. Perhaps only subconsciously, but they do both play roles. Ford likes to play the wise and helpful father figure. While Ernest likes being seen as tough and manly. That's why he's fascinated by all that staged violence like bullfighting and boxing and hunting. It's all about virility and machismo.'

Stella is taken aback. 'Do you really think so?'

'I know so. When he first came to Paris, he showed me some of his short stories. I liked them. Except for one. Which I'll never forget. It was called Up in Michigan. And I told him what I thought of it, that it was salacious and inappropriate and that it told me more about him and his ego than I wanted to know. He was insulted and said I was a nineteenth century prude. Me – of all people – being called a nineteenth century prude by a man like him! A man, who'd written a story about a woman who's sexually violated by a man with an over-sized penis! It took my breath away.'

'Oh dear,' says Alice, 'that's news to me!'

'Don't worry. It was in a chapbook and only had a small print run. McAlmon[8] published it, and I doubt it will ever be published again.' Gertrude sounds emphatic.

Stella isn't sure what to make of Gertrude's disclosure. What she does know is that the only way she can have an opinion about Hemingway's story is to read it herself. Nevertheless, Gertrude has given her a lot to think about and for that she is grateful.

Alice brings in tea and hand-made chocolates, which signals that the lunch will soon be at an end. Stella doesn't mind in the least. She's given voice to her worries and has been soothed by the couple's response. She feels stronger and less fearful now and hopes she might be able to return to her easel this afternoon and get some painting done before she goes to meet Ford for dinner.

dining at Lavigne's

Even before she rounds the corner and turns into the boulevard du Montparnasse, she knows she's going to be late. She'd had words with madame Annie yet again. The woman is always grumbling about something. This time she'd ignored Stella's request to leave Julie's bedroom window ever so slightly ajar at night. And when spoken to about it, she'd taken great umbrage at Stella's remarks. The woman will be the death of her!

As she enters the Nègre de Toulouse, she decides not to mention Madame Annie to Ford tonight. Nor will she tell him too much about her lunch today with Gertrude and Alice. It would only make him more depressed. If that were possible.

---

8. **Robert Menzies McAlmon:** (1895 – 1956) American writer & poet. Founded Contact Editions - a small publishing house in 1920s Paris. He also typed and edited James Joyce's handwritten manuscript of *Ulysees*.

Monsieur Lavigne, the proprietor, greets her with smiles, while gently bowing his head in his usual courteous manner. 'Bonsoir, Madame Ford,' he says and motions her to the rear of his restaurant, where he keeps a private room just for the pair. As far as Lavigne is concerned, the Fords are the most highly esteemed of all his clientele. Thanks to them introducing so many people to his restaurant, his business is now booming. But on this night, the back room is empty, except for Ford, who's seated in the far corner and making short work of one of Lavigne's jugs of *vin ordinaire*. As soon as he sees Stella approach, he awkwardly rises from his chair.

'No, no,' she says. 'Stay where you are.'

Ford flops back down on his seat. He looks even more worn out than he'd been the night before. But is it any wonder? He pours her a glass of the red, and Lavigne re-appears with a basket of fresh bread rolls and the menu, which isn't needed. The good proprietor recommends the *blanquette de veau*. So that's that. They'll have the veal.

Stella begins to explain her lateness, but Ford waves it aside. 'Never mind, my dear. I'm sure it couldn't be helped. I've got some exciting news to tell you,' he says. 'A young writer came to my office today. Her name is Mrs Ella Lenglet, and I think she's quite a find. She brought a manuscript for me to read, and I'm here to tell you that from what I've seen so far, I'm impressed. In fact, I believe she's outstandingly original. But of course, she needs direction. Her writing's raw and frightfully untutored. I mean, it's almost formless. Hardly any punctuation. But there's something instinctively modern about it. If you know what I mean.'

'So what kind of things does she write about?'

'Oh Stella, you can't imagine. It's a bit wild but utterly compelling. Lurid stories set in a world you and I know little about - Parisian lowlife, the demi-monde of street thugs and dangerous petty crooks and the women who live with them.' As Ford speaks, his voice becomes noticeably more buoyant and energetic. She hasn't heard him this animated in weeks. 'For some time now, she's been living on the margins of respectability, you see. I understand that her husband's a bit of a rogue. But by Jove, she's good. And I do believe she's eager to listen and learn. Even though she's quite a shy little thing.'

'So will you publish her?' asks Stella.

'Absolutely. I've told her I will already. Hopefully I'll be able to help her shape and refine something of hers for the December issue. And if that's to be the last edition, it may as well go out with a bang, don't you think?'

Ford looks almost happy.

the blue hour

There's a distinct chill in the air as Stella hurries along the quai. A few stubborn leaves remain on the plane trees. Winter is on its way, and she's glad she'll soon be inside the warmth of the review offices. For some weeks now, she's wanted Ford to put an end to these weekly Thursday afternoon tea parties she helps to set up. They're meant to be for would-be contributors but tend to attract all sorts of freeloaders. They've been a financial outlay the review can ill afford. But Ford was adamant. There'll be no changes to routine until the final edition is rolled out. It's undignified not to do so. And anyway, he said, the whole sorry business will be over by the end of next month. So Stella decided not to waste her breath arguing with him.

When she enters the cavernous space that contains the review offices, she smells the heavy scent of jasmine and roses and heliotrope. It's not unpleasant but it's far too sickly sweet for Stella's tastes.

'At last! You're here,' says Ford, who's rushed to greet her and is puffing slightly. 'There's someone I want you to meet.' He grabs her by the arm and leads her to the other side of the room. He extends his hand towards a waif-like creature sitting in the corner. 'This is the young lady I've been telling you about.' He pauses. 'Stella, I'd like you to meet Jean Rhys…'

Jean remains seated. Ford appears flustered and addresses Jean: 'Oh dear, I'm awfully sorry, perhaps you'd prefer to be introduced as Ella Lenglet…'

'Not at all. Not at all.' She smiles up at Ford and speaks directly to him. 'I've changed my name many times, but I'll be sticking to this new one you've given me. I like it very much and I'm sure it will serve me well.' Her voice is lilting and soft as air. The kind, thought Stella, that needs to be dropped an octave to sound real.

'Well, I'm pleased to meet you. Ford has told me what a talented writer you are.'

'And he's the first man to ever tell me I'm good at something.'

'I'll fetch us some tea,' says Ford and launches himself into the growing laughter and chatter of the room.

Just then Jean rises from her seat. She smiles demurely, and Stella can see how men would find her extremely alluring. She has large, almond-shaped, blue-green eyes and a small Cupid's bow mouth, lipsticked red. She looks fragile and a little lost, dressed as she is in a flimsy, black lace, sack-like garment – more appropriate for evening cocktails or a *bal musette* than for afternoon tea in a publishing warehouse. But despite this and the assault on her olfactory nerves, Stella thinks it best to get to know Ford's new protégée. She asks her the name of her perfume.

'It's *L'Heure Bleu*e by Guerlain. It reminds me of twilight, my favourite time of the day.'

'Well, it's lovely – the fragrance and that time of day,' says Stella, sitting on one of the nearby chairs. Jean sits down beside her. 'Ford tells me you originally came from Dominica.'

'Yes. I was born there and I spent the first sixteen years of my life there. Do you know much about the place?'

'I know it's a volcanic island in the Caribbean and very lush and beautiful. And I vaguely remember that it's a British colony too.'

'Yes, it's all those things. And it's where my woes began. I had a very lonely childhood.'

Stella relaxes a little. She and this girl have a few things in common then. 'So, you're an exile like me and wanted to leave as soon as you could?'

Jean trills a laugh. 'Where are you from?'

'Australia. You can imagine the comments I've had to endure from certain people about my accent.'

A flicker of understanding flashes between them. 'I wouldn't worry too much about people like that. They're just crazy scared that you might prove to be better than they are.'

Ford has come and gone with tea and cake, leaving the pair to get to know one another. Jean does most of the talking, sweeping through the major plot points of her life like an island tornado: her Welsh doctor father, whom she adored; her harassed and exhausted mother of six children; Meta, her Creole nanny, who despised little Jean and fed her terrifying tales of voodoo and zombies; her escape into reading; her time in a convent boarding school and then at sixteen being packed off to England to finish her schooling; a short time at drama school, where she was deemed a failure, which led to her working as a chorus girl, touring small towns in Britain.

Here she abruptly stops. 'That's enough for one night,' she says.

And in some ways, it is. Stella is stunned. She's done the sums. Jean might look and act like she's only twenty years old but from the dates she's just mentioned, she has to be older than Stella by at least three or four years. There's also something innately sad about her. Nevertheless, she warms to Jean. 'Do you feel like a drink? A real drink?' Jean blinks and nods. 'Let's find Ford then and get out of here? I bet there's not a single person in this place right now who's bought a copy of the review.'

bal musette

Ford had looked pleased when Stella invited Jean to dine with them the following night at Lavigne's. She'd felt sorry for the poor girl, not just because she looked in need of a hearty meal or two, but she'd also been abandoned by her husband, a dubious character, who was on the run from the police, leaving her with barely a franc to her name.

When they'd left the review offices, Ford had suggested a tiny bar near the Pont de la Tournelle. The place was smoke-filled, warm and welcoming and over a couple of drinks, Jean had poured her heart out to them both. She told them how she hated England and all its grey gloominess and that she never, ever wanted to go back there. She spoke briefly of her baby son, who'd died of pneumonia three weeks after he was born. And of her daughter, Maryvonne, whom she'd placed in a clinic because she could no longer take care of her. It was an inventory of despair. Jean needed saving.

Stella looks across at Ford and knows exactly what he's thinking. She's often heard him quote the advice that his grandfather, Ford Madox Brown had given him as a young man: 'Beggar yourself rather than refuse assistance to anyone whose genius you think shows promise of being greater than your own.' But it's one thing to nurture the emergence of a talented new writer and altogether something else being a good Samaritan. Particularly when the Samaritan himself is in financial straits.

Stella watches Ford reach over to place a reassuring, protective hand on Jean's shoulder. She also witnesses the grateful smile Jean gives him in return and realises that with the impending demise of the transatlantic review, promoting this girl's development as a writer could be Ford's consolation. All Stella can do is support him in this. A little kindness costs her nothing. After all, compared to Jean's situation, she and Ford lead lives of luxury.

'You simply must join us for dinner tomorrow evening.' She scribbles down the name and address of the Négre de Toulouse on a scrap of paper she's retrieved from her handbag and passes it to Jean. 'Meet us here at 7 p.m.'

'And after we've eaten,' chips in Ford, 'we'd love you to be our guest at our very own bal musette.'

'Oh, I'd like that very much,' says Jean. 'I always enjoy listening to accordion music. I've been to quite a few bals up around Montmartre.'

'I think you'll find our Bal du Printemps is somewhat different to those establishments.' Stella hopes she doesn't sound too judgemental but like most people in Paris, she knows that the dance halls and cabarets in the northern reaches of the city are mainly frequented by racketeers, washed-up artists, prostitutes and pimps. They're largely unsavoury places. Whereas their bal musette is only a stone's throw from the Panthéon. It's a café by day and a dance hall by night and has always been closed on Fridays. Until Ford convinced the proprietor to open it for him every Friday night, when he and Stella could guarantee a lively clientele.

'I can assure you,' says Ford to Jean, with a paternal pat on her shoulder, 'you'll meet some wonderful people there. And they'll want to meet you too. Especially once they've read your work.'

It's still a little early when they arrive at the Bal du Printemps. The place is not yet full, but the proprietor doesn't seem to care. The accordionist is already seated up on the small, elevated platform above the dance floor. A half-smoked cigarette dangles from his lips. He's wearing his usual expression of boredom yet is playing a frenzied tune while beating time with his right foot that has several bands of tiny, jingling bells strapped around his ankle.

More than a dozen couples are swirling about on the brightly lit dance floor. Several young men, with shirt sleeves rolled up past their elbows, lean against the long zinc bar drinking beer and surveying the scene. Occasional raucous laughter punctures the air. Stella's eyes drift towards the nearby banks of long, wooden tables, all painted scarlet and she sees Claudine, the proprietor's daughter scurrying from one chattering nest of people to another as she distributes drinks.

There's a flurry of greetings, and it seems to Jean that Ford and Stella know everyone that is anyone in Montparnasse. They introduce her to some painters whose names she instantly forgets and to a writer called Scott Fitzgerald, who's talking in a huddle with Ernest and Hadley Hemingway, both of whom she's already met in the review offices but like this evening, has barely spoken to. And then there's an astonishing looking woman with piercing sea blue eyes, called Nancy.

Stella and Ford move on to another table and motion Jean to follow them and take a seat. Happy not to be in the limelight, Jean obeys and removes her crushed velvet coat, placing it on the back of her chair. That's when Stella tells her that the Nancy she's just met is the heiress to the Cunard shipping fortune. Her childlike smile tells Stella she's impressed.

Without sitting down, Ford says he'll get some drinks and lumbers away from their table. He's not gone long before he returns, exclaiming: 'Look who I found holding up the bar!' Then directly to Jean: 'I'd like you to meet a very good friend of mine.' And after a short theatrical pause. 'This is Mr James Joyce, the greatest living wordsmith in the world today.' And then to his friend: 'And this is Jean Rhys, the girl I was telling you about.'

'Pleased to meet you.' Joyce gives a quick but courteous bow of his head. 'Ford here's been telling me that you're quite the talented writer, Miss Rhys.'

'Oh, I wouldn't say that,' she purrs, feeling a little shaky. If only she had a drink. She knows that would settle her nerves. She lifts her eyes towards Ford. 'My writing needs a lot of work.'

'Well, you can thank God you found your way to Fordie then,' comes Joyce's reply.

The hall has filled with people now. And there's a sudden noisy round of applause as the music stops. Claudine appears bearing several bottles of house champagne that Ford has ordered in his recklessly generous way. Corks are duly popped, and the cheapest of bubbly wine is poured liberally. The accordion strikes up once more what sounds to Jean like 'Everybody Loves My Baby', and there's a scramble for the dance floor.

Jean sips at her third glass of champagne and sees that Stella is up dancing. She's good, very good. Much better than her partner, who seems not to have any rhythm at all. But nobody seems to care. Least of all Ford, who's in deep conversation with Mr Joyce, whoever he is.

Jean has never heard of him but that doesn't stop her from observing the two men.

She notices the way this so-called world's greatest living writer strokes his little toothbrush moustache whenever Ford is speaking, as if he's considering every word Ford utters. And she feels a rush of warmth for Ford, a gentle giant of a man, who is also so full of praise for her abilities. And in public too. He actually believes she is talented!

The two men suddenly turn her way and catch her watching them. She smiles back at the pair but sees Joyce whispering something to Ford, who appears to be nodding his head, as if in time with some music. What with all the noise in the hall and the distance she is from them, Jean has no way of hearing that Joyce is in fact singing a little verse he's just composed to the tune of a well-known, traditional Irish jig:

'Oh! Father O'Ford you've a masterful way wid you,
Maid, wife and widow are wild to make hay wid you…
Blond and brunette turn-about run away wid you,
You've such a way wid you, Father O'Ford.'

She sees Ford laughing uproariously and knows whatever has been said must have been extremely amusing. But she can't help wondering if Mr Joyce has made some kind of joke at her expense. Has he been making fun of her? And if that's true, the thought that Ford finds it so hilarious is quite disconcerting.

She drains her glass and reaches for the bottle to refill it. No, she can't imagine Ford ever doing that. He's far too refined. But just in case, she decides to feign nonchalance and think about it later. She lets her eyes roam the room.

The decor is not to her taste. The walls are lined with pink framed mirrors. Everywhere she looks there are garlands of drooping artificial flowers, as well as hordes of well-dressed and loud Americans. She thinks this bal musette of Ford's is quite absurd – a pathetic, bourgeois imitation of the real thing. Nevertheless, it is exhilarating to be amongst all these gifted people.

'Would you care to dance, my dear?' It's Ford.

Jean stands up and takes his hand. And at that moment, she decides she'd follow him anywhere.

Once on the dance floor he begins to shuffle and sway happily in and out of time with the music like a well-fed circus bear. Jean thinks him endearing. He's fatherly. And he's a gentleman. With him, she feels safe and protected and she suddenly wishes that he'd draw her closer to him. She wants to feel his beating heart.

Then she thinks of Stella.

The music stops for a moment and then restarts with even a faster tune. Taking her hand, Ford guides her back to their seats. Stella is nowhere to be seen. He refills their glasses and raises his in a toast. 'Here's to you, Jean Rhys,' he says, 'and to your glorious literary future.' As the music swells, he tells her she has the face of an angel and then she feels his hand on her right knee. She opens her mouth to speak but he's started to stroke her stockinged thigh.

She looks around her. Of course, no one is taking any notice. There's nothing to see. It's all conveniently happening beneath the scarlet painted table.

'No, no. Please Ford, no…not here…not in public. Show me some respect.'

Ford does as he's told. 'Anything you say, my dear. Anything you say.'

Stella downs her third *fine* for the evening and feels the warmth of it bloom in her cheeks. She only knows about half the people here but oh, how she loves these Friday nights at the Bal du Printemps. There's nothing like a good party to bolster one's flagging spirits. And she can always count on a party being an instant success if some of her livelier artist friends are in attendance. And thankfully, they are tonight. Of course, dancing helps too. Nights like these are what makes Montparnasse so exciting.

Her eyes glance down towards Ford. She can see he's in his element again – holding forth to Jean, his latest literary find. He's always been generous with his time and advice. Ever since she's known him, she's seen how he's fed on fostering new writers. And with this one, he's even given her a new name.

But it's near closing time. The accordionist is down off his perch and is packing up to go. They ought to be heading home as well.

Seeing Stella approaching them, Ford stands up and helps Jean into her coat. 'I'll go out now and hail a taxicab for Jean,' he says to Stella. 'Follow me when you're ready. We must make sure she gets home safely.'

Stella nods. She understands. Jean is living in some cheap, fleapit of a boarding house near the Gare Montparnasse. A dangerous area for anybody out walking late at night.

A blast of cold air greets the two women as they step out onto the footpath. Winter's definitely on its way. There's no time for excessive goodbyes. Ford's holding open the back door of the taxi. Jean hops in, waves, and is gone.

'A very successful night I feel, my dear,' says Ford.

'Yes, I thought so too.' She links arms with him then.

'Happy to walk home? Or shall I hail another?'

'Let's walk,' she says, knowing full well that Ford would've already blown their household budget for the rest of the month on Jean's taxi fare alone. 'The exercise will do us both good.'

'And we have a bit of padding too.' He taps his belly. 'So we shan't feel the cold. Not like that poor girl.' He's striding forward now. 'She's such a frail, delicate little thing, I'm sure if she were caught in a howling wind along one of Hausmann's sprawling boulevards she'd be blown clean away.'

an uninvited guest

Finally, the year 1924 is coming to an end and so is Ford's grand experiment. In the last issue of the transatlantic review, he introduces Jean Rhys to the literary world by publishing the episode 'Vienne' from her novel Triple Sec, which he has also renamed. Meanwhile, no one has seen much of Jean.

Ford and Stella are concerned about her welfare when they hear some talk that her Dutch husband, Lenglet had turned up again. But as the lease on their boulevard Arago studio is up at the end of the month, they have plenty of other things to think about. Like installing Julia and the uncooperative madame Annie into the old stone labourer's cottage they've rented in Guermantes, which is an hour's train ride east of the city. And after that, when they aren't visiting Julia, they'll really need to find a more suitable studio in Paris than the one they'd been forced to secure due to a complete lack of choice.

Much of this domestic re-organisation has fallen on Stella's shoulders, as Ford is too busy trying to finish No More Parades, the second volume in his planned tetralogy. As usual she doesn't complain. Because she knows Ford can be selfish and exasperating but at least life with him is never ever boring. As far as Stella is concerned, such use of her time and energy is a small price to pay. And besides, Julie adores him.

What Stella is more perturbed about is the fact that Ford is teetering on the edge of serious depression and that simply will not do. Especially at this time when they all seem to be coming down with the flu which only makes Madame Annie even more ill-tempered than she normally is.

One evening, Ford declares there's nothing else to be done but to cough their way through Christmas and try to make the most of it. 'The packing cases can wait,' he says, presenting Julie with a tired looking tree. 'Let's invite a few friends over to help us decorate this thing. And we shall all feel better in no time. Especially if I mix up a batch of my great-uncle Tristram's punch.'

So it's settled.

Once the guests have arrived and the tree garnished with colourful bows and gilded ornaments to everyone's satisfaction, it's time to make the punch. Ford, in his usual theatrical manner, gathers everyone around him by declaring they're in for a treat.

'I'll have you all know this recipe was once the delight of Brummel and the Regent,' he says. Everyone laughs. They're all used to Ford's way of embellishing his stories. As long as you don't take him too seriously, he can be enormous fun. So they happily drink in his grandiose exaggerations, while he pours a bottle of Jamaican rum into a huge, pre-prepared soup pot, then half a bottle of French brandy, a bottle of port wine, six bottles of hock and six of cider, six syphons of soda water, a quarter bottle of maraschino, the peel of a dozen fresh limes, and the juice of a dozen small lemons into the pot.

He serves it warm. And a very jolly Christmas is had by all.

On the night before New Year's Eve, madame Annie and Julie go to bed straight after supper, as is their habit. Ford returns to his desk to continue his writing, while Stella decides to remain in the warmth of the kitchen, at least until she's answered the letter her brother recently sent her from Adelaide.

Except for the rustling of trees in the wind outside, the steady ticking of the clock on the mantlepiece is her only company. But a sudden pounding on the door puts an end to that. Rushing to silence it, she's surprised to find Jean, coatless and carrying a small cardboard suitcase. She's shivering with cold and looks dishevelled and a little drunk. Her kohl-stained cheeks make it clear she's been crying.

'Come in, come in,' says Stella. And no sooner has Jean stepped over the doorstep, she begins to sob in Stella's arms.

'What's happened? What's the matter?'

'It's my husband. He's been arrested. And I don't know what to do. I don't know where to go.' She's inconsolable.

Undaunted, Stella swings into action and guides Jean towards the divan in the parlour. 'Now you sit down here where it's warm and cosy while I fetch you a blanket.' Jean complies. Moments later, Stella re-appears and places a tartan rug around her guest's shoulders. 'You know, things always seem worse in the dead of night.'

'I'm not so sure about that,' says Jean.

Stella sits down beside her and after offering her a cigarette pours them both a hefty nip of the left-over Christmas brandy. Stella sips at her drink and waits while Jean wipes her eyes with her fingers and then picks up her glass and empties it in one mouthful. Feeling the sudden heat of the brandy warm her from inside out, she turns to face Stella and asks her for another. 'I feel like I've been thrown overboard and I'm drowning in seaweed,' she says flatly.

Stella hands her the brandy bottle. 'You can tell me what happened. I'm very discreet.'

Without further encouragement, Jean does just that. 'He's been charged for embezzlement and is being detained in Santé prison just down the road until his trial in February.'

'Oh dear, that's rather serious.' Stella gets up and refills Jean's glass.

'Yes, and it's all my fault. You see, he was desperate to see me. He'd been hiding out for a while and he thought it would be safe to return to Paris, just to visit me. But no,' she bites at her bottom lip, 'that was a mistake. The *flics* were waiting for him.'

'The police were only doing their duty, Jean.'

'Oh, I know. I know,' taking several sips of brandy. 'I still love him, you see. He's not a hypocrite or an English bourgeois. He's an outsider, like me and he's also my daughter's father. We've been through a lot together.'

'I don't doubt it in the slightest.' Stella is trying hard not to sound contemptuous, which is difficult knowing Lenglet is a disreputable character with what seems like an extremely shady past.

'I'm so very afraid. I have no money. And nowhere to live and I really don't know what to do…' Jean, looking defeated, takes a long drag of her cigarette.

The two women sit in silence for some minutes until Stella sneezes and blows her nose. 'I just can't seem to shake this cold,' she says and sips again at her brandy. 'But I'm sure there are solutions to all these problems. I know it may sound like an empty platitude, but everything will seem better in the morning.' She stifles a yawn.

'Oh no, I'm keeping you up, aren't I?' Jean sounds distressed. 'I'm so sorry, Stella. I really am. I should never have come here. I'm nothing but trouble with a capital T. You'll rue the day you ever met me.'

Smiling, Stella shakes her head and puts her hand on Jean's. 'Don't be silly. You're no bother at all. You must stay here the night, and we can talk about all this tomorrow.'

'But I don't want to impose on you and Ford.' She takes another puff of her cigarette.

'Rubbish!' booms Ford, suddenly appearing like a boulder in the doorway of the parlour. 'Stella wouldn't have asked you if she thought you were taking advantage of us. No, you must stay, and we shall discuss this tomorrow.' Making a quick about-turn, he leaves the room.

'The master has spoken,' says Stella, laughing. 'Do you think you'll be comfortable here on the divan?'

'Oh yes, thank you. Very comfortable.'

Part Five

2018

Once my mother returned to Sydney, I spent most of my waking moments focused on my novel, which meant I spent a lot of time contemplating Stella's artistic development, while dealing with my own. Thanks to Antoine's support and encouragement, my self-confidence as a writer had grown but I seemed to be worrying more about the creative choices I was making. Was I being fair to my characters? I was sure I was with Stella, but what about Ford? Young Julie? Even Hemingway?

It wasn't until the following year though that I began to have problems sleeping. No matter what time of night I went to bed, I'd often find myself wide awake around 3am. I'd be incredibly tired, but my mind would be racing faster than the fleeting dreams I'd just woken from, incoherent dreams of Stella, her painting practice and the Montparnasse of the 1920s. I'd then toss and turn for a while, but fearing I might wake Antoine, I'd take my dressing gown, pillows, and overactive brain to the welcoming coziness of the lounge room sofa. Somehow, this move seemed to work. My mind stilled, and I either fell asleep or was able to solve the problem I'd been wrestling with.

Antoine wasn't really happy about it, telling me he didn't like waking up without me lying beside him and that he feared it might become a habit. I assured him it wouldn't. But neither he nor I believed me for a second.

And one morning a couple of weeks later I was sound asleep on the sofa when I heard him making such a racket in the kitchen, I knew it was intentional. He wanted to wake me. He wanted to talk. I could smell the coffee beans he'd just ground and I listened to him filling his beloved Italian espresso machine. That's when I called out to him: I hope you're making some for me.

And suddenly there he was, standing before me, all smiles and ruffled hair. We could go back to bed, he whispered.

I'd like a coffee first if you wouldn't mind.

Not at all. One minute, he said.

When he brought out the two coffees, I was sitting cross-legged on one of the armchairs and had already opened two sets of shutters so that the room glowed with early morning light. Antoine sat down opposite me, and we sipped our coffee in silence until I spoke. He deserved an explanation for my nocturnal wanderings. It's the novel, I said. It's stalled.

I thought as much. What's causing the problem?

Jean Rhys, of course. She's inhabiting my dreams and I wake up all flustered and can't get back to sleep. So I lie there – re-writing in my head the paragraph I wrote about her that day. But it never seems good enough, so I write another. And another. If I stay in our bed, I become restless and uncomfortable. I'd rather be out here because at least here I can finally fall asleep. But next day, when I start again on my laptop it's just same-same – every day a repeat of the last, and I'm making absolutely no progress.

Hm, said Antoine, but how is Jean to blame for this?

That was just a throw-away line. She's the one I'm currently writing about. Or trying to, I said. It's hard to explain, but I'm conflicted about her. When I told Ange about it, she suggested I re-read Wide Sargasso Sea, which I did. But that only made matters worse.

How so? He seemed a little surprised, and I wondered if he may have been a little put out that I'd spoken to Ange about it before discussing it with him.

Well, for starters, it's an extraordinary work – poetic and powerful – awfully clever. I truly admire her as a writer. Sure, she was unconventional, but she was also a very troubled soul. Her behaviour was abominable at times.

In what way?

I then told him about an essay I'd read that suggested Jean may have had a borderline personality disorder that was exacerbated by poverty and heavy drinking. She was often paranoid, I said, especially in later life and would lash out at any perceived threat or imagined insult. Because of the way she behaved even the local kids in the

Devon village where she lived believed she was a witch. All very sad really.

Antoine said nothing for several seconds, then offered: I guess like most of us, she was a complex human being?

I nodded. I find her fascinating too, I said. But I wouldn't want my readers to think I was treating her unfairly.

Well, I wouldn't worry too much. She's not your main character.

No, but she's a pretty pivotal one. Stella's life changed dramatically once Jean appeared on the scene. And what gets me, Stella's extremely reticent about Jean in her memoir. She barely mentions the whole affair and doesn't even name Jean. It's like she wants to erase her completely from her memory.

But don't we all do that to some extent? Don't we select the beautiful memories we want to keep and try our hardest to eradicate the events we don't like? He waited a moment for a response but there was none, so he continued: Or perhaps your Stella simply wanted to keep her private life private?

I remember at this point looking directly into Antoine's eyes and giving him a half smile. You're probably right, I said. She did emphasise some things and omitted others. Whether conscious or not, her memoir was an act of reconstruction.

I think all autobiographical writing is. In that way, it's a bit like spin.

We both laughed at this. Antoine placed his cup on the coffee table and added: But I do believe if Jean acted badly, you must write that.

Yes, but that's my dilemma. You see, from everything I've read, I'm sure there was some terrible incident, some devastating event involving Jean, which became the point of no return for the three of them. There must've been. As far as I'm concerned, the silence on Stella's part says it all. Besides, my narrative needs a turning point, so I've got to invent a couple of dramatic scenes, loosely based on what I know and I'm afraid Jean may not look so good.

Oh ma chérie, stop worrying about what others might think. You can't control that, no matter what you do, there'll always be people who won't like what you write. And anyway, as you know, everyone has an opinion these days about everything. Just stay focused on the fact that you're making fiction out of what you understand to be Stella's life. Because no one, and I mean no one, really knows what that was truly like.

I went to Antoine then and sitting on his knee, kissed him tenderly on the cheek.

Let's face it, he said, Stella represented her life in her memoir as she wanted it to be seen. And Jean plundered her life to make fiction. Both shaped their own reality as they saw fit. You can only do the same.

Part Six
1925 – 1932
The Only Reality
by
Neve Palmer

posing

Jean convinces Ford and Stella that all she wants to do is to escape from the city and her troubles. 'Just for a little while,' she tells them. 'I'm too upset to stay in Paris right now. I need to get away from all my problems. I need to think and clear my head.'

So with their help, she spends the first few weeks of the new year in Cros-de-Cagnes, a small seaside fishing village on the Mediterranean Sea not far from Nice. And when she returns, the Fords agree she can stay in their cottage in Guermantes. She has nowhere else to go and besides, she seems so much more relaxed, so less distressed than before.

But only after a few days there, she manages to shock Stella by telling her that she only came back from the south because she'd been frightened by her surroundings. 'Do you know,' she said, 'the only room I could find in Cros-de-Cagnes was in a bordello?'

A few weeks later, Lenglet is finally sentenced to eight months imprisonment. He'd already advised Jean that it was in her best interests to take up the Fords' offer to live with them on a more permanent basis. But she does feel obligated to them and tells Stella she'll help out in any way she can and promptly offers to sit for her.

Stella's delighted. At last, a willing model of her own. She'll start by painting her portrait. But first some preliminary drawings. Wearing her artist's smock, she begins to sketch. Her round, brown eyes move back and forward, back and forward between Jean and her easel. And soon, the two women find themselves enjoying one another's company.

On one particular day, after sharing their stories of childbirth, Jean says: 'To be perfectly honest with you, I deplore the biological functions of my body. There's nothing that's pleasant about any of it.'

Stella laughs in recognition. 'Oh, I agree,' she says.

'But nevertheless, I must admit, I'm proud of my body and I'd be more than happy to pose naked for you, if you'd like me to.'

'Why thank you. But for the time being, I'd like to focus on portraiture.' While saying this, she notices something feline about Jean that she hadn't observed before. Not sure of what to make of it, she smiles and adds, 'but in the future anything is possible.'

A domestic routine is soon established. Each morning, no matter if they're staying in the dingy studio apartment on the avenue de l'Observatoire, as they do most weekdays, or if they're spending a weekend with young Julie in Guermantes, Jean serves coffee to Stella and then to Ford, who is often hiding behind a newspaper. 'It's the least I can do,' she says. 'You're both so kind and generous. I'll never be able to repay you.'

After breakfast, Stella might mend some of Jean's clothes or make new ones for her, while Ford reads aloud Jean's latest piece of writing. Whenever he sees fit, he bellows at the room: 'Cliché! Cliché!' And although at times Jean finds this humiliating, she says nothing because later he will take the time to show her how to shape a story and cut any melodramatic ending. He also guides her in her reading. But best of all, he shows her that he believes in her. In the afternoons, they all tend to go their separate ways – Ford and Jean to their writing and Stella to shop and cook. And if time permits, she takes to her easel.

Late at night though, Ford often finds himself standing at the foot of Jean's bed. He likes to watch her sleep. He knows he's being idiotic, like some lovesick adolescent boy, but he can't help himself. She's becoming an addiction. This child-like woman is so lovely, so fragile and vulnerable. He knows he's falling in love with her. Because he wants her badly. Very badly.

One night in the early hours of the morning, Ford is standing in his usual spot beside Jean's bed. The room itself is dark, but he can still see well what he's come to see. A shaft of light from the street below beams in through a narrow gap between the window's curtains that hadn't been completely drawn.

When Jean rolls over, Ford catches a glimpse of her arm's pale white skin. He smells the sweetness of her perfume and hears her murmur in her sleep. He wants to touch her but doesn't dare. Instead, he touches himself.

With a sudden movement, Jean sits upright. Throwing off the bedcovers, she whispers: 'Well, well, I was wondering when you'd get around to visiting me.' She holds out her hand beckoning him to sit beside her. He does as she suggests. 'Don't make a sound,' she says. 'We wouldn't want to wake Stella.' And then she sinks to the floor to bury her head between his legs.

The following week, Stella shows Jean the portrait she's done of her. 'What do you think?'

'I like it. But you've made me look sad.'

'You were sad when you first started posing for me.'

'Well, I'll have to sit for you again and this time I'll be happy because I am. Because I've made some decisions.'

'That's wonderful!' Stella means what she says but is a little surprised by Jean's sudden good humour. She wonders if she'd visited Lenglet in Fresnes prison eleven miles away, when she and Ford spent the weekend with Julie in Guermantes. Perhaps that would explain her change of mood. So, she asks her straight out.

'Good God, no! I'm trying to forget all about him. I'd like to put aside my past. Besides Fresnes is too far away. I haven't got time to go there. I need to write so I can build a new life for myself. I might even be able to get my daughter back.' Jean dabs at her nose with her handkerchief and then adds: 'Ford keeps telling me that I need to be strong and focussed, less reckless. And I want to show him that I can do it.'

'Anything's possible if you try hard enough.'

'And what about you? How is your art going? Do you feel your work is progressing?'

Stella feels a little uneasy. She's detected an underlying hostility to these questions and can't help feeling she's on unsteady ground. 'Actually, I'm working on a couple of portraits of Ford and have done a few preliminary sketches of the sculptor, Yvonne Serruys. Perhaps when I've finished them, one will be good enough to be exhibited this summer at the Société National des Beaux Arts.'

'Then you must be ready to paint me in the nude.' Jean has begun to undress. 'I've been told many times that my body is quite beautiful.'

Stella hasn't seen this coming. She wonders if she's being mocked or set up in some way. She can feel her neck and face heating up but keeps her eyes fixed on Jean's head. When she blinks, she lowers her gaze, telling herself to stop being ridiculous.

Jean stands stock still, perfectly relaxed in her nakedness. 'So, what do you think?'

'Lovely,' answers Stella. 'Shall we start next week?'

When she tells Ford later, he guffaws. 'I trust you've taken her up on this very kind offer?'

'Of course, I have.' But Stella feels the need to explain. 'It's just that I thought it a little odd that a person one hardly knows and who's normally extremely shy in company, should make such a proposal in such a manner.'

'Granted. I'm sure there'd be people who'd consider her behaviour somewhat unconventional, but I find it rather refreshing, don't you?'

In fact, as winter begins to turn to spring, Ford finds Jean more and more exhilarating. He's started to believe she's rejuvenating him. He's writing now with great vigour. Everything about her excites him. Especially her unpredictability. He can't get enough of her.

Only the other night, they were sitting side by side at the *bal musette*. Stella was up dancing and although the place was packed with many of Stella and Ford's friends, Jean reached down beneath the bench table and rested her hand on the crotch of his trousers. Ford managed to maintain his composure and stared straight ahead. She leant closer to him and whispered in his ear: 'Do you think Stella suspects yet that we've fallen in love?'

Ford's eyes widened and his mouth drooped open. 'She soon will if you don't remove your hand immediately.' Naturally, he wanted her to continue but instead willed himself not to become aroused by shuffling along the bench seat away from her.

Later in the darkness of her bedroom, he told her she must refrain from such public displays of impropriety and stressed that they needed to be discreet. He called her his little minx. And she pleaded with him then to take her. Which he did.

Afterwards, he told her he loved her. 'But how is that possible?' she cried. 'If you truly did, you wouldn't treat me so badly?'

'Whatever do you mean? I worship the ground you walk on. You know that.'

'But I don't believe it for a second. How can I when you come to me in secret? When everyone sees me as just a member of your entourage?' Jean sat up and with her arms wrapped round her knees, she rested her head on the brass bedhead.

Ford lay on his side. 'Now you're being ridiculous.'

'Am I? Well, tell me why the only role you allow me to have in public is that of the acolyte to your benevolent master? It's such hypocrisy, and I feel ever-so demeaned by it. We must be the talk of the town.'

'My dear girl, people don't even know. Nor do they have any right to know. That's why I'd like it to be kept that way.' Ford was emphatic. 'It's nobody's business but yours and mine.'

'What about Stella? Shouldn't she know we're in love? After all, she's being deceived by us both.'

'I can't see why she needs to know. Everything is perfect. She's happy. We're happy. Why upset the old apple cart?'

'It's just that I don't like living in the shadows.' Jean's lips trembled and she began to weep. 'I want so much to be happy. And I do feel at peace with you. We understand each other. We may be full of contradictions, but we are two of a kind. Both of us are too sensitive for our own good. That's why we're different from other people. And it's also why I want you all to myself. I don't want to share you and I don't want to be miserable anymore.'

'Oh, my precious, precious darling.'

Jean took his left hand and placed it on her right breast. 'See how ready I am for you! Whenever you're near me, I'm like this, and I'm so afraid that I'm going to be dreadfully hurt for loving you. Because I know I'll go completely crazy if you're ever cruel to me.'

'That's not going to happen, my darling. I will never hurt you.' Ford removed his hand and began to stroke her cheek instead. Whenever he touched her in this way, she felt warm and protected. His voice was calm and soothing. 'We shouldn't do anything rash. Please remember I have Julie to consider. And as for Stella – well, you know there's been no intimacy between us for some time, and we tend to go our separate ways now. But you must understand that in the past she's been an incredible source of strength to me, and she's always supported everything I've ever wanted to do.' Then he took Jean's hands in his. 'So please believe me my love, when I say I want to make you happy and that I'm determined to do that no matter what you may say.'

He then kissed away her tears and hoped they'd never speak of this again.

may day

There's something different about Jean that Stella can't quite fathom. She knows Jean's a sharply intelligent and attractive, thirty-four-year-old woman, who has a certain kind of emotional honesty about her. Especially when she starts bragging about having lived in the more poverty-stricken, disreputable parts of Montparnasse and then, for added effect, admits to being sexually experienced. One thing's clear. Jean's a survivor. But why play the helpless ingenue? It's a curious contradiction that Stella finds bewildering.

She's not sure Jean can be trusted. Worse still, she's begun to wonder if Ford's become a little too enthralled by her. She must stay on her guard and look for signs. But even having made this decision, Stella still takes quite a while to comprehend the full extent of Ford's duplicity. It's only after dining with the Bradleys does she start to realise how precarious her relationship with Ford has become.

It was Stella who'd suggested they invite the couple to dine with them at Lavigne's. She'd become very fond of Jenny, who was French, bilingual and a great conversationalist. And William or Bie, as Jenny liked to call him, was a charming and extremely cultivated man, who'd been Ford's literary agent ever since the pair had moved to Paris.

As soon as the Bradleys arrived at the restaurant, Jenny presented Stella with a pot of *muguet*. 'I hope this lily-of-the-valley brings you happiness all the year long,' she said.

Stella breathed in the flowers' scent. 'How lovely! I'll plant it in the garden in Guermantes when I go there next week. But I'll have to make some sketches of it first. I think it will make a very fine painting.'

'I'm glad you like it,' Jenny said. 'We, French call it u*n porte-bonheur,* a good luck charm, that we give friends on the first of May. I think it's one of our more beautiful traditions that started way back centuries ago, when King Charles IX was given some *muguet* as a gift. And because he very much liked these spring flowers, he decreed they be given each year to the ladies of the court.'

'That's what I love about this country,' declared Ford, 'it's ability to revolutionise a king's order and recast it in such an egalitarian fashion that the thing becomes even more delightful than the princely original.' Everybody laughed and so began a leisurely lunch that extended well into the late afternoon.

After finishing dessert, William raised his glass and proposed a toast. 'We need to celebrate Ford's completion of No More Parades.' He looked at Ford. 'I know, my friend, that you're worried that some people may think the book's altogether too gloomy but it's my firm belief that you've written a masterpiece!'

With that said, Ford in an expansive mood, paid the bill and promptly invited the Bradleys back to their studio apartment. 'You must come and have a look at Stella's recent work. I think you'll both be quite impressed.'

Stella blushed. In actual fact, her cheeks were burning. It'd been a while since he'd paid her a compliment. She felt a bit tipsy and supposed the others did too. They'd all consumed a great deal of wine. More than was usual.

Once back at the apartment, Stella showed the Bradleys the portraits she'd been working on. When Ford suggested the two she'd done of him were a little severe, William and Jenny said nothing. Their combined silence conveyed their opinion. She fetched a bottle of port from the dresser and poured some into four glasses.

'I think you ought to show them the nude you've done of Jean,' said Ford. Then facing the Bradleys added: 'It's really quite superb.'

Stella brought out the painting from behind a screen and placed it on the mantlepiece to allow William and Jenny a close-up view. The couple stared transfixed. At only 12 X 18 inches, it seemed to produce a visceral thrill in the observer. William spoke first and thought the work was extremely accomplished.

Jenny called it stunning. 'I know you've told me before Stella that you did lots of nudes in charcoal when you were at art school in London. But you must have been experimenting with oils for quite a while to create such luminosity in this one.'

'It's all to do with the layering of paint,' explained Stella, who'd already finished her glass of port. 'It's only my second reclining nude.'

'Well, she's magnificent,' said William. 'You've done yourself proud.'

Stella noticed a smile crossing Ford's face. Her stomach churned. She thought she was about to be sick.

'I love how you've framed her body,' added Jenny, turning to her friend, 'with the lushness of the forest green velvet quilt.'

'So where is your sitter tonight then?' asked William, addressing Ford. 'I thought she still lived here with both of you.'

'Oh, she does. She does, but the poor girl suffers from some sort of nervous anxiety, which is dreadfully debilitating…makes her lethargic, you see, and the only thing she can do is to stay in bed until it's passed. Quite sad really, for one so gifted.'

Something in the way Ford spoke proved to Stella what she most feared – he was in love with Jean. But she was sure his perception of her was just a fantasy – his dreaming mind's creation. In reality, Jean was nothing like what he imagined her to be. Nevertheless, Stella couldn't look at him. Instead, she focused her gaze on the mantlepiece, on the painted nude, on her rival. She kept telling herself to remain calm, stay cool-headed and fight the urge to flee the room. She stood up and felt herself swaying. 'I think I'm going to be sick,' she said and tottered towards the parlour door.

'I told her not to order the *coquilles Saint-Jacques,*' said Ford.

A few weeks later, Ford puts forward the idea to Stella that he and Jean should go to Guermantes without her. He explained that he needed to put the finishing touches to the study he'd been creating for himself in the rickety annexe next to their cottage. 'And when you come down later in the week, we can be a normal family again and spend the entire weekend with our Julie.'

'And what's Miss Rhys going to do while you're playing carpenter?'

'Apart from getting some fresh country air, which she sorely needs, I'm going to get her to translate four of her stories into French – the ones that I believe need work on syntax and grammar. That way, she'll soon see I'm right about what she needs to do to improve her craft and perhaps finally understand why I hold that view. I think that'll keep her more than occupied!'

Stella, aware that her rival had restored Ford's ego and replenished his creative powers, now knows that Ford thought so too. She passed no comment. It was better that way. And she told herself that they wouldn't be able to get up to too much, what with Madame Annie always noseying about.

a break away

On the train to Guermantes, they sit facing one another. Like an old married couple, thinks Jean. Ford was able to convince her to accompany him by saying she didn't look well, that a change in environment would do her good, and that they'd be able to stay together all night, every night they were away. That was when she'd thrown her arms around his neck. At that moment, she'd never been so happy. Five long days without Stella's hovering presence would be a gift from the gods. And of course, she knew what a relief it would be not to burn up with jealousy every time Ford left her bed to tippy toe back to Stella's before daybreak.

But then, there in that carriage, she suddenly feels guilty about Stella who, she must admit, has been very kind to her. Chillingly so, come to think of it. Surely by now Stella must realise that she and Ford are intimate and that their domestic situation has become a farce. She couldn't possibly be so naïve to think Ford's still in love with her. Maybe it's all part of some perverse game the two of them are playing, and she's their innocent pawn.

She looks across at Ford, who's engrossed in his book. He's such a gentle, sensitive rock of a man with his big shoulders and quiet voice. How lucky she is to have found him. He understands her. He takes her seriously. She feels aroused just looking at him and can't wait to get to Guermantes.

But then, what guarantee is there that all will be well there? They'll have little Julie and the dreaded Madame Annie to contend with. And as for their sleeping arrangements – well, who knows what they might be?

'A penny for them?' asks Ford, shutting his book. 'You look worried, my dear.'

'Well, yes. I was thinking about Stella and feeling rather guilty.'

'Oh, for heaven's sake, let's not spoil things.'

'It's just that I don't think she likes me anymore.'

'What rubbish! Of course, she likes you.'

'But I know she doesn't. And frankly, I couldn't care less. What upsets me is that she goes around pretending she does like me. It's the hypocrisy that galls me.'

'Well, I think you're wrong about Stella. You're doing her an injustice.'

'Oh really? Do you think so? Well, I'll tell you one thing I know to be true and that is she doesn't like living in a harem. And I know that because neither do I.'

'Good grief, Jean. Now, you're really being ridiculous,' he says with some force. 'I can't bear it when you carry on like this. I truly can't.' Then Ford turns away from her and stares out the window. An awkward silence settles into the compartment. A few minutes later he startles her: 'Look!' he says. 'We're almost there.'

An old hansom cab is waiting to meet them when they step from the station. It's almost evening. The village is slowing down, preparing for the night. Jean feels calmed by the stillness of the street and the comforting sound of the horse's hooves as it makes its way to Ford's cottage.

When the cab pulls up outside, the first thing she notices is the light already shining from the window. Madame Annie opens the door and greets Ford quite warmly. Then in rapid-fire French informs him that Julie is already asleep upstairs and that she intends to follow as soon as possible. She also wants monsieur Ford to know that as requested she's prepared a meal for them both and what's more, has taken it upon herself to set the table for their supper. She then stands back and casting her eyes over Jean, as if this were the first time she'd seen her, says that as she'd not been told where madame Rhys intended to sleep, she has made up all the available beds, including the one in monsieur's study.

'*C'est très gentil. Très gentil, madame. Merci,*' says Ford, laying his praise thick onto the woman's retreating back. Madame Annie says nothing else. As far as she's concerned, she's made her position clear. She's now off duty.

Ford and Jean watch in silence as she mounts the narrow staircase. Once she's disappeared and is heard moving about upstairs, Jean rushes into Ford's arms. 'Oh my God! Why on earth do you put up with that old dragon?'

'Well, for starters, my dear, as a widow in her forties, I'd say madame Annie is not as old as you think. And I put up with her because she's devoted to Julie and is a completely different person when she's around her.'

'But she's so incredibly rude and overbearing.'

'She's even worse with Stella, but she's wonderful with Julie, which is all that matters.' He pauses and gently releases Jean from their embrace. 'But do let's have some supper and I'll explain everything while we eat. Shall I open a bottle of burgundy?'

'Oh yes, please,' says Jean.

It's Ford's view that madame Annie's only source of happiness is Julie. The child loves her, while no-one else does. 'She's to be pitied really,' he says, shaking his head, then taking another mouthful of wine. 'I think she's a possessive woman and feels threatened by Stella and me. Whenever we're around, and she sees Julie enjoying our company, the look of jealousy on her face is a sobering sight.'

'She obviously thinks she runs this place,' says Jean.

'I suppose she does. But right now, that suits me just fine. She knows I'm here to work.'

'And I think she's got a fair idea why I might be here.'

'No doubt. But that's no matter to us.'

'What do you mean?'

'After what she said tonight, I wager she'll be avoiding us for most of our stay. After all, it's in her best interests.'

'And ours?'

'Precisely,' says Ford, as he opens another bottle of wine.

It seemed a natural choice for Jean and Ford to install themselves in the annexe. It was where he'd set up his study and as it wasn't an extension of the cottage itself, it provided them with a degree of privacy neither of them had experienced since their relationship began. And so, over the next three days a domestic pattern evolved that seemed to suit everyone. For Ford's prediction had been correct.

Under Madame Annie's watchful eye, Julie kept well away from her father's study. It was where he did his work. It was where he wrote and where he needed peace and quiet. Besides, madame had a routine with the child to uphold. There were dogs to be walked, shopping to be done, wildflowers to be picked and neighbouring children to visit.

As for Ford, very little work of his own is done, and he's certainly not picked up a paintbrush or hammer. Except for meals in the cottage and a few hours each day spent with Julie, most of his time is taken up in giving advice to Jean about her writing. Or making love to her.

On Wednesday evening, madame Annie announces that tomorrow is Ascension Day and that after morning mass, there's to be a grand fête in a nearby village. And having secured transport with a local family, she and Julie will be gone for the entire day. Naturally, the child is keen to go. There'll be music and dancing and games, she tells her father. It's a fait accompli.

After farewelling his daughter at the gate next morning, Ford goes back to the annexe. He needs to catch up on his correspondence, so Jean offers to prepare a late lunch. Perhaps outdoors if it's warm enough, she says. A proposal Ford finds most appealing. He's feeling a little jaded from the activities of the last few days and hopes a nap in the afternoon will also eventuate.

It's well after one o'clock when Ford finally lumbers up the slight incline behind the annexe. There at the start of the old orchard beneath an apple tree still in bloom, is a colourful patchwork rug with a large wicker basket beside it on the grass. Jean is nowhere to be seen. She's obviously forgotten something and has returned to the cottage kitchen. But no sooner does he set himself down with his back resting against the tree trunk than she appears. Looking extremely pleased with herself, she brandishes a bottle of champagne in each of her hands. 'Look what I found hidden away in the pantry,' she cries. 'It's just a perfect day for it, dear Fordie. Don't you think so?'

Her joy is infectious. 'Where are the glasses?' he says and takes a bottle from her and proceeds to open it.

Jean sits down beside him and watches him pour the sparkling liquid into two champagne saucers. 'Down the hatch!' she says and empties her glass. Ford laughs and follows suit. Then refills both glasses. She really is quite adorable, he thinks. Especially when she's like this – full of youthful exuberance. He's definitely done the right thing bringing her with him to Guermantes. It's restored his vitality as well as hers. And of course, she's such a beauty, especially now in one of Stella's old, loose-fitting, white muslin dresses.

Before too long the second bottle of champagne is opened. 'I'm getting a tad peckish, my dear. Is there anything to eat?'

'I was wondering when you'd ask me that. Perhaps you'd like to start with an hors d'oeuvre, monsieur.' And before he responds, she jumps up and standing at his feet, lifts her dress over her head. Completely naked now, she lets her dress dangle from one hand, while the other she rests casually on her hip. She smiles down at him. And although this well-rehearsed tableau reminds Ford of a scene from some cheap, backstreet music hall, he can't help feeling aroused by it. She leans over him then and unbuttons his flies. Within seconds, she straddles him.

'My God! Have you no shame?' At the first sound of Stella's voice, Ford and Jean spring apart. But Stella doesn't wait to witness the effect her words have made. She simply turns and with as much dignity as she can muster walks back towards the cottage.

'I must go after her,' says Ford, scrambling to his feet.

'Why? And just leave me here? Like this?'

Ford sighs. 'Oh, for heavens' sake, Jean, have some self-respect and get yourself dressed.'

'Is that an order? Am I to be bossed around like some servant girl, who can only be made love to when the mistress of the house is not around? Is that all I am to you?' Tears are streaming down her cheeks.

'I beg you, please, don't do this. Not right now.' Ford's face is ashen, and it crosses Jean's mind that he's suddenly looking incredibly old. 'It's all a terrible mess, and I'm just as unhappy as you are. Surely you know how much I love you, but I really must go to Stella. She deserves an explanation. I owe her that. At least.'

'And what do you intend to say? That it was the sun? The champagne? That it was the first time and it'll never happen again? So that then we can all carry on as before - with me, living with the two of you. Do you really think that's going to work?'

'I don't see why not.'

Stella's head is swimming. This wasn't the proof she'd been looking for. She feels terribly, terribly betrayed, but she also feels quite stupid. She can't understand why she's so shocked. She'd not allowed herself to imagine such a reality. But why? All the signs were there. She knew Ford had fallen in love with Jean – she'd even seen him flirting with her once or twice but, instead of allowing alarm bells to ring, she'd dismissed the idea of anything serious by telling herself that it was nothing more than a bit of harmless fun. After all, Ford is charming to all women. And it seemed impossible to believe any feelings he had for Jean were anything more than a fleeting fantasy on his part.

It was only recently that she'd started having doubts about Jean's motives. She'd observed how skilled she was with her fawning and fluttering of eyelashes. A woman old enough to know better playing the weak and powerless, little-girl-lost routine. What a charade! There was certainly no sign of innocence or fragility in the orchard this afternoon. But she wasn't about to lay all the blame at Jean's feet. She reminds herself it takes two to fox-trot.

As Stella enters the cottage, her heart begins to pound. She wants to cry and wail but she knows she needs to control these urges. Once in the parlour though, she can't stop shaking. Where had she gone wrong? Hadn't she been enough for him? She'd always stood by him like a loving and faithful spouse should. She'd devoted herself to him for the sake of his Art. So how could he hurt her like this?

Admittedly, their relationship had lost much of its carnal exuberance, but their emotional life had remained strong, buoyed by their love for their darling daughter. Having moved in liberal and artistic circles for some time now, she knew Ford needed an occasional erotic spark to inspire his work. Surely, he must realise she'd understand if he indulged in the odd discreet affair. But this association with Jean could hardly be described as discreet. Which Stella finds baffling.

She opens the old French dresser and pours herself a glass of gin. Straight. Then sitting down on the nearest armchair, she steadies herself and starts thinking about everything she stands to lose if Ford decides to leave her. She'd always assumed that she'd grow old by his side. Well, she isn't about to let Jean Rhys rob her of her future as well as her past.

One thing she knows for certain about Ford – he'll soon come to her, full of excuses and begging forgiveness. He'll not want a scene. So she must prepare her response. Now. And quickly. She sees no good reason to remind him that without her regular income from Australia, they'd be destitute. But to suggest he take money into consideration when choosing her over Jean would be foolish indeed. And ultimately, extremely painful. Particularly if that were the sole reason he decided to stay with her. No, she tells herself, she must stay focused on what is truly important to them both: Julie.

Yes, she will fight for him. But not by throwing tantrums. Nor by creating vile public scandals which were so unsuccessful in poor Violet's case. And she'll definitely not be making any unreasonable ultimatums either. Because she knows this isn't going to be a regular battle for supremacy. Oh, no. This will be civilised. More like a war of attrition. And she's utterly determined to set the rules of engagement.

It will start here, within the hour. But she must prepare herself for the possibility that the battle may not be won for quite some time. Perhaps even months. But whatever happens, she needs to maintain her composure at all costs. The day is not yet over. And the battle of wits has not yet commenced.

Right at this moment Ford, somewhat out of breath, comes bustling through the door. Is it any wonder? thinks Stella, who's sitting straight-backed and ready.

'Can I get you a top up?' he asks, seeing the empty glass she's still holding.

She nods and watches in silence as he quickly pours himself a drink, then comes towards her and splashes more gin into her glass. He sets the bottle down on the floor and pulls up a chair facing hers. 'Now I'd like to explain…'

'Please Ford, no explanations needed. I have eyes. I saw quite clearly what was going on. Or should I say, what had been going on.'

Ford's bottom lip is hanging open more than usual. Looking sheepish, he says nothing.

Stella continues: 'You know I love you and probably always will. That's a given. However, I don't wish to live in a *ménage à trois*, nor do I think it's proper for our daughter to be witness to that fact. She may be only four years old but as you know, she's a smart, perceptive child. Jean, on the other hand, is impetuous and completely irresponsible. She's a wild and selfish creature, who knows no boundaries.'

'That's somewhat harsh, my dear.'

'Well, I don't think so. The only person Jean was thinking of this afternoon was herself and her own gratification.' She takes a deep breath. 'And there you both were, in broad daylight, exposing yourselves to the elements.'

'Look, I'm sorry, Stella. I truly am. You weren't supposed to be here till tomorrow.'

'I'd made real headway on two of my portraits, so I thought I'd surprise you but instead I...' She looks down at her lap. The vision of Jean and Ford together under that damn apple tree keeps replaying in her head. She must get the conversation back on track. 'What if someone else had dropped by and caught you both at it? What if madame Annie had seen you? Or worse still, Julie? What would she have made of it?'

He looks shamefaced. 'You must forgive me, Stella. I wasn't thinking.'

'Look Ford, let's face a few facts.' She lowers her voice now, as if they were in church. 'Jean's life may have been terrible, but I don't see why ours should be. Would you agree?'

'Of course. But I'm not sure what you expect me to do about it though.'

'Neither do I!' It's Jean. She's wearing an ankle length green silk robe that's cinched on her left hip by an embroidered rosette that allows for a plunging V at her front. She'd entered the room via the backdoor and had then come through the kitchen. 'I think I should be part of this cosy, little conversation.'

'I'm not surprised,' says Stella, still speaking softly, hoping she isn't showing how insecure she's really feeling. 'So tell me. Do you think the three of us can go on living the way we have been doing?'

'I certainly do not!' There's a slight slurring of words. 'Is there any brandy in the house?'

'I'll see what I can find,' says Ford, moving to the dresser and finding a bottle of *eau de vie*. 'Will this do, instead?'

'Of course.' As soon as she has the drink in her hand and Ford has returned to his chair, Jean, who's remained standing, stares down at Stella. 'I know what you think of me so let me tell you what I think of you.'

'I can't wait to hear it,' says Stella.

Jean sways a little. 'I realised a while ago that you'd made some arrangement with Ford about me.'

'What on earth are you talking about?'

'You turned a blind eye to what we've been doing because basically it suited you. You were happy for me to satisfy him, to pleasure him, so that you didn't have to. You think sex is over-rated, you told me so yourself. Whereas I, I love it. I…'

'That's enough!' says Ford. 'You're completely out of line.'

'Well, I disagree! I detest all your bourgeois niceties. And you,' pointing directly at Stella, 'you think you're so bohemian, so avant-garde, but you're nothing of the kind. You care too much about appearances and what others may think. You're nothing but a pathetic, small-town conformist through and through.'

'Will you please lower your voice,' begs Ford.

Stella is near tears and grips the armrest of her chair. 'Get her out of here now,' she says, gritting her teeth, 'before madame Annie and Julie walk through that door.'

When Ford rises from his seat, Jean starts to scream: 'My God! I don't believe it! You're actually going to do what she says!' She throws her glass against the wall then lurches at Ford and with all her strength begins to beat him with clenched fists on his chest. Somehow, he manages to take hold of her wrists, by which time Jean is sobbing.

'I'll take her back to my study,' he says and sees for the first time the fear in Stella's eyes. 'We'll talk later.'

As soon as they are in the annexe, Jean collapses onto the bed. 'My love for you, Fordie, is as big and as wild as the ocean. Do you know that? Do you?'

'I think you should get some sleep.' In case she flares up again, Ford's hoping he doesn't sound too stern.

'I drank too much, Fordie. I drank far too much.' Now she's whining. He can't stand it. But he knows it's pointless to tell her that her behaviour is inexcusable. The last thing he wants is another scene. Besides, he has unfinished business with Stella. 'You get yourself comfortable, and I'll make you a nice pot of tea.'

He plumps up her pillows, and she seems to settle then. Ford looks at his watch. There isn't a lot of time before Julie and madame Annie are due to return. But he puts on the kettle and draws the curtains across the windows. The room's been warmed by the day's sun. Summer is well on its way. He thanks God that there'll be no need for a fire tonight.

By the time the tea is brewed, he's relieved to find Jean making snuffled sleep noises. He puts on his jacket and goes back to Stella.

All evidence of the smashed glass has been thoroughly removed. The brandy and gin bottles have disappeared too. The room is doused in lamplight, which Ford finds comforting.

Stella smiles when she sees him. She knows for certain now that his imagined love for Jean is just that – a fantasy, and there isn't a chance in this world that it'll last.

'She's asleep,' he says. 'I think she judges us by the standards of the terrible life she's led until now.'

'Please don't make excuses for her. Not to me at any rate.' Ford looks desolate. She starts again. 'I'm sorry. I don't wish to be demanding but you're going to have to sort this out. And quickly.'

'But how? You must understand, I do have feelings for her. I'm sorry but I can't help it.'

'I know, but I don't want her living with us anymore, and you heard her yourself, Ford. Neither does she.' She lets her words sink in, then continues: 'So I propose you find her somewhere else to live. And if you choose to see her from time to time, elsewhere of course, I don't want to know about it. Nor should anyone else. So you'll have to be discreet. For Julie's sake, as well as mine.'

'That may be difficult – finding her some place to live, that is. But it's not impossible.' He pauses and takes her hands in his, as he always does when stressing his sincerity. 'Are you absolutely sure about this?'

'Of course, I am. I wouldn't have suggested it if I weren't. You know I love you very much. And Julie adores you. So I really don't see the need for us to destroy her life. We should do everything we can to keep our little family together.'

'You're quite right, quite right, my dear. Jean and I will leave here on the first train tomorrow morning. I'll do my utmost to find accommodation for her before you return to Paris. Just give me a few days.'

a change of heart

When Stella returns to Paris a week later, Jean has moved out of their cramped apartment into a reasonably clean, furnished room in a nearby cheap hotel. At first, Jean is happy enough, for Ford had made it clear it was only a temporary arrangement. Once they have enough money, they'll find more suitable lodgings. In the meantime, he'll visit as often as he could. He also tells her she should continue to join him and Stella on various social occasions. It's only fitting. Proper, in fact. For no one should ever suspect that anything untoward is going on. He concludes by saying that nothing's worse than being the source of malicious gossip.

Despite his reassurances, Jean's insecurity reappears within days. Between visits from Ford, she feels lonely and confined to her room. And she starts to wonder if he might abandon her just like all the other men she'd known had done. Naturally, she blames Stella for her misery and loathes her even more.

When in this state of mind, her thoughts turn to her husband, all alone, locked up in prison and when she finally visits him, she's shocked by his physical deterioration. This is not what she'd imagined at all. He's emaciated and looks anaemic. She hates having to speak to him through bars as if he's a caged animal and when she searches the faces of other visitors there, she only sees looks of quiet desperation. They're the outcasts, the defeated. And she knows she's one of them.

She devises a plan for Lenglet once he's released. He can stay with her until he's deported. When Ford hears of this, he says he won't allow it. That he'll be damned if he shares her with another man!

Nevertheless, Jean is determined. 'That's rich coming from you - you who's quite happy for me to share you with Stella. Only you're forgetting one thing - he's my husband. And I'll do as I please.'

But in late June, when her husband's finally released, he only stays one night with Jean. French authorities have him speedily repatriated to Holland. But not before Lenglet explains that he'll send for her when he can. When he has enough money. That in the meantime, she should try to make a living for herself from her writing.

'That's exactly what I want to do,' she tells him. 'I'm trying to develop my own voice and my own rules for writing. I'm determined to succeed. And Ford has promised to help me find a publisher for my stories.' None of this is a lie.

But Stella is desperate to see the back of Jean. Not long after Lenglet is expelled, she hears by chance about a wealthy and somewhat eccentric American woman, Winifred Hudnut, who lives on the Côte d'Azur and is looking for someone to ghost write a book for her on reincarnation and furniture. When she tells Ford, he thinks it's all a bit of a joke, until he learns that her husband, Richard Hudnut, is the American cosmetics king and although the wage on offer is not that great, it does include full board in the couple's residence in Juan-les-Pins.

What surprises Stella is that Ford doesn't need convincing that this is a marvellous opportunity for Jean. But Ford's feeling trapped, what with Jean's moods, it's hard to get cracking on the third part of his opus. As for her sexual appetite, she seems to be in a permanent state of arousal. The girl is damned insatiable!

Both Stella and Ford are surprised when Jean agrees to go, but she does, and within weeks finds herself living in what appears to be a castle, built by Queen Emilia of Saxony sixty odd years ago. Seated above the little Port du Croûton, it had been completely refurbished in extravagant fashion by Richard Hudnut when he purchased it in 1914. Jean gasps when she sees the Hudnuts' bedroom with its black walls and black bed as well as an enormous black bathroom that has black and green facilities with gold-plated, solid silver taps. Even the staff quarters are opulent, and the French gardens exquisite. Jean has only ever seen such luxury in the cinema.

So when Mrs Hudnut informs her that her daughter and her husband, Hollywood idol, Rudolf Valentino would be visiting later that year, Jean is elated. At last, she's escaped from the heartache that is Montparnasse. Her life of destitution is now at an end. She will swim in the blue, blue sea each morning. She will happily take daily dictation from Mrs Hudnut and help her write her preposterous book. She will dine on fine food and optimism. And although she earns very little, she'll save every sou she's given. As long as Ford remains her lover and patron, she knows she'll be happy anywhere.

a better place

As far as Stella is concerned, life has changed for the better after Jean's departure. She and Ford spent most of the summer in Guermantes. Ford became immersed in his writing and Stella even found time to work on a still life of one of Ford's jackets hanging over the back of a cane chair that had a pair of her walking shoes on its seat. She sees it as her personal celebration to mark the renewal of their relationship.

And then in September, as luck would have it, their friend, Nina Hamnett[9] tells them about a glorious studio apartment on the rue Notre-Dame-des-Champs, which Nina can't afford to rent herself. It had been part of an atelier-style art school and although unliveable, with only one electric light and a single water tap over a zinc sink, it's enormous, and Stella sees its potential with its small outside balcony and lovely huge windows that allow for an abundance of light. Even though she knows it could never be considered a home until there's a kitchen and decent plumbing and heating, she grabs it and immediately sets about organising major renovations that include constructing an enclosed gallery to create a bedroom, as well as installing a cabinet de toilette.

---

9. **Nina Hamnett:** (1890 - 1956) Flamboyant and unconventional, this Welsh-born artist and writer became known as *the Queen of Bohemia*.

From time to time throughout autumn, when the weather's warm enough, she and Ford camp there during the week and even occasionally entertain there, inviting friends for afternoon tea or an apéritif, before setting out to dine at a nearby restaurant. It's on one such occasion, that Gertrude and Alice visit along with the Cubist painter, Juan Gris and his wife, Josette. Over drinks, Stella mentions how slowly the renovation work had been progressing. 'Now that winter's approaching,' she says, 'maybe we ought to clear out of here and let the builders complete their work without any interference.'

'The problem though is finding somewhere to stay,' says Ford.

'What about coming down to Toulon?' Josette suggests. 'It's where we always go during winter. It has a beautiful harbour and there are very few tourists.'

'Plus, it's warmer,' adds Juan, 'and so much cheaper than Paris,'

Gertrude smiles. 'That's because it's a naval base,' she says. 'And everyone knows that sailors don't have much money, so it's pointless for merchants to jack up prices.'

Stella and Ford don't need much convincing. What with the devaluation of the franc, they can definitely afford to go. And so, it's settled. They'll leave for Toulon after Christmas.

By December, Jean's job with the Hudnuts had been terminated. Having been intensely happy living in the comfort of a palatial villa in the south of France, she's now miserable being back in Paris, living in yet another cheap hotel room that overlooks the smoke-filled Gare Montparnasse. But her surroundings aren't the only cause of her misery. Ford is not so interested in her anymore. He doesn't visit her as often as he once did, and the more distant he is, the more she wants him. And the more she wants him, the more she drinks. When she's intoxicated, she pleads with him to stay with her, to make love to her. And when he refuses, she accuses him of not loving her anymore.

Usually, he says he does love her. It's just that he doesn't find her alluring when she's been drinking all day long.

But then one afternoon, he tells her she ought to be writing more and drinking less. She becomes abusive and mutters a voodoo curse on him. Rattled, he leaves in a hurry. He can't understand why she can't be satisfied with the situation. Stella is. He is. What's wrong with the girl?

Later though, he wonders if he couldn't have handled things better, but then he's always hated scenes, and these ones with Jean are becoming all too frequent. It's now plain to him that he's got himself in too deep. He feels trapped and just a little bit guilty as well. After all, she's so delicate, so fragile and she obviously really needs him.

He decides to call on her one morning just before he goes down south. Surely, she'd like to know that he's about to send a couple of her stories to Edward Garnett, a highly respected reader for publishers in London. That should brighten her spirits, he reasons. And if she takes that news well, he'll invite her to join him, Stella, and some other friends at Lavigne's that very night.

Ford finds her naked and spread-eagled on the bed. Cigarette smoke hangs in the air. The room is a mess with over-flowing ashtrays and several glasses, some with drink still in them, are on the corner table. An over-turned chair as well as various empty bottles are scattered about on the floor. Jean has been entertaining guests.

'What are you doing here? Stella not accommodating all your needs?' She props herself up on her elbows, aware she's slurring her words.

'You need to pull yourself together,' he says.

She sees his look of cold contempt and hears the slam of the door on his way out.

It takes two days by train to reach Toulon – a not so pleasant journey for Stella, Ford, Julie, madame Annie and their poorly house-trained Alsatian dog, Toulouse – a gift to Ford from monsieur Lavigne. But the rooms in the Hôtel Victoria that Juan and Josette had found for them are perfect and incredibly cheap.

Stella falls instantly in love with Toulon. Her artist's eye is charmed by its harbour, packed with all sorts of seacraft, and the tiny, cobbled backstreets, with their small squares and ornate fountains, many of which are covered in moss. It's like an enormous stage set with the natural fortress of Mount Faron as its backdrop looming high above the city. And then beneath the fat, plane trees in the Cours Lafayette, there's the colourful market, which delights her too. In fact, the whole, vibrant, work-a-day busyness of the place thrills her.

But more than this, she and Ford are mixing in a very different circle. Whether in a dance hall or café, they are surrounded by painters like Othon Friesz,[10] who introduces them to the writer and art critic, Francis Carco.[11] The talk is often centred around art and Stella revels in the conversation. She's also painting a great deal. And when she visits Othon in his studio in the attic of an old warehouse on the quai, he tells her about a similar space below his that's available for only ten pounds a year. She snaffles it up. It's structurally primitive and has no electricity or water, but it has a sublime view of the harbour.

And with Othon close by, she's able to view first-hand the methods he's developed over many years - some of which she's been struggling with for some time. He takes her seriously and doesn't regard her as a wife and mother who occasionally dabbles with a palette and paints.

So Provence yet again works its magic on Stella. Its sunlight and sweet-smelling air, its simplicity of life and thought helps cleanse her heart. Her fear of losing Ford fades. 'I truly understand now why you consider Provence to be your spiritual home,' she tells him one night as they lie together in bed.

Ford edges closer to her and takes her hand. 'Well, if we both love it so much, why don't we make an offer on that old mas we saw up on Cap Brun? You know, the one with that shady terraced garden, not far from Othon's place?'

---

10. [Achille-Emile] **Othon Friesz:** (1879 - 1949) Born in Le Havre and known as a founding member of the Fauves, who later returned to a more traditional, looser style of painting. His work is represented in numerous major collections across the globe.

11 . **Francis Carco:** (1886 - 1958) French poet, novelist, dramatist and art critic, born in New Caledonia. Known for his works depicting the street life of Montmartre and for having had an affair with the New Zealand writer, Katherine Mansfield.

'Oh yes, that would be lovely,' she says and presses herself to him.

However, when their offer is rejected, Stella is quietly relieved. The review had depleted most of their finances. For now, owning property is out of the question. But she hadn't pointed that fact out to Ford on the previous night because she really didn't want to curb Ford's enthusiasm for the idea, nor did she desire to dampen his renewed ardour for her.

Instead, they set off on a little trip to Rapallo. The Pounds had moved there months ago, and Ford wanted to speak with Ezra about accompanying him on a working tour of America. Some Do Not had been quite a success in the States, and there is every indication that No More Parades would do even better there. A speaking tour, or something like it, would surely assist in the publicity of both his and Pound's work. But Pound will have none of it. Italy is his future. Mussolini, he argues, will raise all artists out of poverty, unlike leaders of Socialist regimes, who are strategically selective in artists they support.

Unconvinced, Ford and Stella return to Toulon. And by Easter, they begin to head back to Paris, breaking their journey with a little excursion to Castelnaudary, for a feast of the famous local cassoulet. After a very pleasant lunch and the lucky purchase of some antique furniture at bargain prices, Stella is happy to return to Paris and their renovated studio apartment on the rue Notre-Dame-des-Champs.

back in Montparnasse

When Stella and Ford fled Paris, Jean spent most of January trawling the dives of Montparnasse. She roamed from one bar to another. Day after day. A drink here. A drink there. Until she managed to anaesthetise the pain of abandonment she felt or until she was asked to leave by some waiter who had no time for women who drank alone. That's when she'd return to her hotel room to rage at the coldness of men's hearts. And when she'd done with that, she'd take a draught of Veronal to put her to sleep.

Ford had written to say he'd be back in Paris after Easter, but it is almost May before he gets round to visiting Jean. And even on these visits, he's flustered and full of excuses: how he can't stay but will be back as soon as he can; that he has to sign some contract or see his agent, but she must come to dinner to meet so-and-so next week. Later, he tells her there are problems with his American publishers, and he isn't being paid his royalties and he might very well have to go to New York to sort it out.

Of course, Jean can't bear it. Sometimes she taunts him, screaming. Twice she physically attacks him. Other times, tired of arguing, she barely says a word. But once he's gone, she takes to the bottle. What else is there to do in this hotel bedroom in hell?

One morning, she wakes quite late with a frightful headache and an absolute certainty that her hunger for love is in fact the true curse of Eve. She begins to think that maybe, given time, she'll probably come to terms with Ford's rejection of her. She'll surely find another lover one day and that will be it. But what still terrifies her is the idea of an existence without Ford as her mentor. She thinks she'll never be able to find a replacement, who'll provide the kind of support she knows she needs, whose intelligence and knowledge she respects and whose advice she trusts.

She spends the rest of the day in her room, wrestling with her thoughts. Her pride tells her that Ford must have some strong feelings for her still. Everyone knows he's encouraged lots of other female writers, but it's only her, a little nobody from Dominica, whom he'd singled out. He'd told her that she was like no one he'd ever met before; that she was 'his girl'; that in fact she was a genius. And to prove his belief in her, he'd given her a nom de plume, a new identity and shown her a new way to live. All of that surely amounted to something. And if he really didn't care for her why on earth was he still paying for her lodgings?

No, it wasn't Ford setting her adrift. It was Stella, the great manipulator. She was the one who was keeping him at bay. Well, she'd show her!

Next day, with a clearer head, Jean decides to follow the last piece of advice Ford had given her and that was to write more and drink less. And she'd also write from her experience just as he'd taught her to. At the very least, it'll be a way of venting her spleen.

a lost soul

Stella looks at herself in the mirror and hears herself exhale. For quite a few months, she's been awfully unhappy. But when Ford takes her in his arms, he's able to reassure her that nothing will ever upset them again. And at these moments, she feels a sudden lightness come over her. Like an unbearable weight is being lifted and that her nightmare is over.

She thinks of Hadley then and wonders how she's faring down in Pamplona with Ernest and that despicable Pfeiffer[12] woman, who's inveigled herself into joining them. What is it about monogamy that men like Ford and Hemingway, find so difficult? Is fidelity just too much to expect from them?

Stella shakes her head and picks up her brush and starts combing her hair back from her forehead. She's worn it like this for years knowing some people thought it a bit severe, but she likes it this way. It makes her feel confident and self-assured. It also accentuates her eyes, especially when she wears a felt cloche. But she won't be wearing a hat like that anytime soon. It's only a matter of days before she and Ford will be in Avignon again – just the two of them for the entire month of August. And the only hat she'll be wearing down there will be a lovely broad-brimmed straw one.

She smiles at her reflection and moves her face closer to the mirror to better apply some kohl around the rims of her eyes. A dash of rouge

---

12. **Pauline 'Fife' Pfeiffer:** (1895 - 1951) American journalist, who became Ernest Hemingway's second wife.

to the cheeks and a little lipstick will finish the job. Not that she's in any rush. Everything's prepared for tonight's party. Having organised several platters of various cold cuts and cheeses, as well as two huge bowls of salad, she's laid the table for their dozen guests, while Ford has gone to fetch an enormous tarte aux pommes from their local patisserie, as well as enough fresh loaves of bread to feed a small village.

Since returning from Toulon in April, sunshine has been pouring through their studio apartment windows with the promise of some early summer warmth. They'd hosted a couple of informal parties, and everyone seemed to agree that now, with the renovations all but completed, it was the ideal place for social gatherings, especially ones that included dancing. But this one tonight was to be a little different. They'd consciously limited the number of guests.

It had been Ford's idea. One afternoon last month, he'd returned home extremely agitated. He'd visited Jean to inform her that from here on in their relationship would be purely professional. 'She attacked me, Stella,' he said, 'she actually physically attacked me.' He'd turned his head towards her, making visible several raw scratch marks that spread from his jaw down his neck to the top of his shirt collar. 'I couldn't calm her. She was like a wild cat, kicking and screeching.'

'Good lord! Whatever next?'

'Precisely,' said Ford, dropping himself onto the divan. 'I want no more of it. No more dramas, no more madness. And I'm telling you now, I'm done with her. It's over. Finished. Kaput.'

Stella sat herself beside him, stifling a desire to cry out with joy. She'd prayed for this moment and now she knew the wait had been worth it. But she also knew better than to parade her triumph. Much wiser to keep her immediate reaction muted. For the time being at least. 'Well, I suppose our lives have been rather messy and chaotic of late.'

'Quite so. Quite so,' he'd replied. 'And I must say, I do think it's time we take more care in our choice of friends. Don't you?'

Stella nodded, wondering if Jean had made any other threats of violence.

'Very good.' Ford had sounded relieved. 'So, what I propose is that we strive to be a little more selective in the guests we invite to parties.'

'How so?'

'I mean, let's only invite people we know well and who are fun to be with, who are sociable, that sort of thing.'

'I like the sound of that very much.' And she really did.

In keeping with this agreement, they'd drawn up a small list of possible guests for that night's party, which was to celebrate Ford's completion of the first draft of his novel, A Man Could Stand Up, the third of what was now referred to as the Tietjens series. Only a week ago, he'd given a draft copy to William Bradley, who'd promptly declared that he and Jenny were taking the two of them to lunch in the restaurant in the Parc Montsouris.

So naturally the Bradleys were the first to be invited, along with some publishing friends of theirs. And dear Marguerite and Ramon Guthrie[13] were on the list, as was Bill Bullitt[14] and his wife, Louise Bryant.[15] With guests like that, there was every indication that the evening would be a great success.

Suddenly Ford appears behind her. 'You look lovely, my dear,' he says, placing his hands on her shoulders. 'What say we have some piano music playing on the gramophone as our friends arrive?'

Over dinner, there's a great deal of laughter and lively conversation. Everyone's enjoying themselves. And not long after the tarte aux pommes is demolished, the table's pushed back against the far wall.

---

13. **Ramon Guthrie:** (1896 - 1973) Poet, novelist, essayist, critic, painter, and professor of French and comparative literature, born in New York City. He was in the middle of the literary ferment following WW1 & of expatriate Paris in the 1920s.

14. [William Christian Bullitt Jr.] **Bill Bullitt:** (1891 - 1967) American diplomat, journalist, and novelist. First US ambassador to the Soviet Union and later ambassador to France during WWII. Considered a radical in his youth, but later became an outspoken anti-communist.

15. **Louise Bryant:** (1885 - 1936) American feminist, political activist and author of *Six Red Months in Russia*. Bill Bullitt was her third husband. Her previous marriage was to John Reed, a journalist and communist activist, who was the focus of Warren Beatty's film, *Reds*.

Someone ramps up the gramophone with 'If You Knew Susie, Like I Know Susie' and Natalie Barney[16] swings into action. She grabs Ford by the arm and the two of them take to the floor. Everyone starts to clap and sing along as Ford shuffles about, enormous beside the short and plump Natalie, all flowing feathers and fringes. It's quite a sight.

Yes, thinks Stella, as she joins the other dancers, this is our way for the future.

A little later, Bradley, who's been standing at one of the windows that looks down upon the street, signals for Ford to join him. 'Take a look at this,' he says, pointing to a woman squatting on her haunches beneath the lamplight directly across the road. She isn't wearing bloomers and with her skirt up around her waist, it's clear for all to see that she's urinating into the gutter.

'I don't believe this is happening.' Ford can feel his heart pounding in his chest. He must do something. Say something. 'I've got to help her. Will you come with me?'

'Of course,' says Bradley.

'Just follow me then,' he says, closing the window's shutters. 'And I'll explain everything to you.' He turns around and sees Stella standing by the gramophone, about to rewind it for the next record. As he makes his way to the door, he calls across the room to her: 'Bradley and I are just going to find some more champagne. We shan't be long.'

By the time the two men are out on the street, the woman is on her feet trying to steady herself with the help of the lamp post. 'That's her alright,' says Ford, as he crosses the road.

'Well, what do you know? Never expected you to come a'calling.' As Jean speaks, she steps off the pavement, trips and falls. Smash. The sound of breaking glass.

'Jesus,' murmurs Bradley, 'do be careful.'

---

16. **Natalie Clifford Barney:** (1876 - 1972) American literary figure, who lived as an expatriate in Paris, where she held a weekly salon for over 60 years and strove to shed light on female writers and their work. Unusual for a woman of her time, she was open and proud of her lesbianism and was inspiration for Radcliffe Hall's character, Valerie Seymour, in her novel, *The Well of Loneliness*.

'Fuck you!' yells Jean, holding up the top half of a broken wine bottle. 'Look what you made me do.'

Ford goes straight to her and, firmly taking hold of her arm, manages to get her to release what's left of the bottle from her grip. Jean staggers away from him but takes only a few steps before she turns back towards him, screaming: 'Just you wait! One of these days I'm going to kill you!' She takes a swing at him, loses her balance, and falls onto the footpath, narrowly avoiding a well-dressed couple, who quicken their step and hurry away.

'For God's sake, Bradley, can you try and find us a cab? We really ought to get her home.'

'Of course, of course.' And William strides off down the street.

Jean starts to groan. Apart from two badly grazed knees, she appears to have no other injuries. Ford's able to get her to sit up and can't help noticing that none of the passers-by stop to help him. Even when she grabs at his crotch and offers herself to him. 'You know you want to,' she wails. But then he sees the headlights of a new Citroen taxi.

Within a minute or two, he and Bradley have bundled Jean into the back of the cab. Ford gives the driver the address, and the taxi pulls away from the curb.

A half an hour later, the two men are back. Bradley pays the driver and adds a substantial tip. 'It's the least we can do,' he says to Ford. 'The poor fellow's going to have to remove the stench of piss from his vehicle.'

'I need a stiff drink,' says Ford, shaking his head. 'What do you say, we find a bar? There's a little one around the corner. Should still be open.'

When they finally return to the apartment, the party is over. Only Jenny remains and she's sitting on the sofa comforting Stella.

'Where on earth have you two been?' asks Jenny. Bradley pulls up two chairs and places them opposite the two women. He sits down in the one facing his wife.

Ford remains standing, his eyes skip between Jenny and Stella and the floor. 'I can explain everything,' he says, looking and sounding contrite.

'I'm sure you can,' Stella says, rather snappily. 'But please no more of your lies. No more deception.' She's had enough of his embellishments and emotional confusions.

'My dear, I can assure you, I fully intend on telling you the truth.'

'Well, that's good. Very good,' Jenny says, 'because we all saw what was happening. Every single one of us.'

'Good God, no!' Ford drops himself down on the spare chair that William had placed beside him. 'How did that happen? I thought I'd closed the shutters.'

Stella looks at him wearily. 'Yes, you did close them on one window, but there are two others, remember? And Louise happened to look out and called us all over to watch the show.'

Ford's face flushes red. 'Well, all I can say is, the way she drinks, she should be the last person to pass any judgement on others.'

'She wasn't doing that,' cuts in Jenny. 'Nobody here was.'

'But having our friends witness that scene tonight and by implication, what that says about our relationship and yours with Jean, is what I find so humiliating.'

'And so do I, Stella, so do I.' And then he starts to explain how he and Bradley had come to see Jean in a most terrible state. Because he, Ford, had felt compelled to assist her; that he could never turn his back on anyone he knew, who was that inebriated, that degraded. It went against everything he stood for as a gentleman and a human being. And finally, how he'd forever be in his friend and agent's debt for helping him get Jean safely back to her hotel.

'The hardest part was getting her into the cab,' interrupts Bradley. 'Thankfully, she passed out once she was inside, so then all we really had to do was carry her up to her room and put her to bed. But we both needed a strong drink when we'd got ourselves back here. And I suppose we lost track of the time…'

'I can promise you, Stella. Nothing untoward took place,' Ford adds.

'I should hope not. Because I don't want anything more to do with that woman.'

'As God is my witness, neither do I.' Ford looks straight into Stella's eyes, pleading for forgiveness. They both know he's got himself into a deplorable sexual tangle with Jean. And after tonight's drama, so do quite a few of their friends. Surely Stella would be the first to realise how he hated his life to be so unruly and that the association he had with Jean could not and would not continue. What he needs and wants now is Stella's understanding that men end up suffering for their desires too.

He sighs and leans forward. 'When I looked out our window tonight and saw the appalling state she was in, I knew I had an obligation to do something, to help her, to get her back home. I felt I owed her that much, but she's a woman possessed, a vampire Carmen, intent on self-destruction. And I can't take any more of her drunken rages, no matter how much I pity her. I just can't!' Ford looks as if he's about to cry. And when Bradley pats his shoulder, he manages to say: 'I'm afraid Ella Lenglet is a lost soul. I'm done with her, Stella. I truly am.'

A week later, Ford sends Jean a short letter from Avignon. He informs her that as he and Stella don't wish her to be destitute, they've decided to pay her a small stipend until she's able to support herself. And with that end in mind, he would continue to assist her in any way he could so that she can make a living through her writing. Furthermore, he writes that he'd be more than happy to provide a preface for her first book, The Left Bank and Other Stories that would be published soon. And then in a post-script, he suggests she should read Francis Carco's novel, Perversité, describing it as a sordid, psychological thriller set in the slums and underworld of Paris. Finally, he tells her if she's interested in translating it into English, she must let him know, as he's sure he can find her an interested publisher.

an ocean apart

The month of sunshine in Avignon is a healing balm for Stella and Ford. As a couple and as individuals, they each find peace of mind in the steady, predictable rhythm of their days in the south. Ford spends his mornings writing, while Stella paints and sketches, which leaves afternoons free for family leisure time. Together with Julie, they explore nearby villages or go for shady walks and refreshing dips in the chilly waters of the Rhône. Even madame Annie is, on occasion, enticed to join them.

And this summer break also helps to stanch the bitter wound Stella suffered when Ford's affair with Jean had been exposed. Even though she'd been humiliated, she knows she still loves him. She had reasoned that if forgiveness was the embodiment of love, that's what she'd do. So when Ford admitted he'd been foolish to allow a harmless flirtation get out of hand and swore he regretted it more than he could say, she accepted it. Particularly when he gave his word that he'd completely extricated himself from this entanglement with Jean.

In Avignon, both she and Ford are happy, proving to Stella that their union between Art and Love is truly possible. She starts to feel optimistic again about their combined futures. So when they return to Paris in September, they devise a plan for the rest of the year. As Julie is to begin school at the start of the academic year that month, Guermantes would have to go. Stella is confident they'll find someone else to take over the lease, but they needn't worry too much about that until they've settled into the lovely little attic flat she'd already found. It's on the fifth floor of a seventeenth century building, directly opposite the Palais de Luxembourg on the rue de Vaugiraud. The rent is extremely reasonable and luxury of luxuries, they'll finally be able to afford to put in a bath! It will be a perfect week-day home, just a fifteen-minute stroll to their studio apartment, which they'll now use for work and of course, to entertain.

And then of course, there are Ford's travel arrangements to New York to organise. His American publishers have scheduled a ten-week lecture tour for him to help promote A Man Could Stand Up. Knowing that he's not the greatest of public speakers, what with his chronic wheezing, Ford, at first, is reluctant to go. But at Stella's urging, she convinces him it's in their long-term financial interest for him to make the trip. Especially if he's able to secure a new contract more lucrative than the last, as Bradley suggests. All in all, it's a very busy time for them both.

The night before he leaves, he asks Stella if she wouldn't mind getting rid of the paintings and sketches she'd done of Jean.

'Of course, I don't mind. I should've thought of it myself.'

'It's just that I'd rather have no trace of her on my return here. I really don't wish to see her ever again, you know.'

She's thrilled to hear these words, said with such intensity of feeling that there's no denying he's truly finished with Jean Rhys. 'Don't worry. I'd be happy to destroy them.'

He puts his arms around her, then adds: 'But you do understand, my darling, that we still must make a small monthly payment to her. Just enough for her to live on and keep her away from our door - but only until she's able to support herself. The sooner she has a publishing contract the better for us all. And when I'm in America, I promise you now, I shall be doing everything in my power to make that happen.'

At the end of October, the Savoie carrying Ford arrives in New York. In his first few letters to Stella, he tells her how delighted he had been to see a pack of reporters on the docks to greet him when he disembarked, and that at least four newspapers next day reported his arrival. America considers him a celebrity. He's being feted. In one afternoon alone, he'd been interviewed sixteen times. He says he's exhausted but is in good humour. After all, he'd been invited to lunches and dinners so wants her to know that all the hard work she'd done, making his clothing presentable before he left Paris, had been more than worth it.

A week later, when Stella reads this, she isn't so sure. From the moment Ford left, she missed him. Dreadfully. She now wishes he was back in Paris. With her. Where he belongs. But she fears that if she dwells too much on his absence, it might just bring her undone. After a night spent in tears, she decides she must keep herself busy until he returns.

She begins work on a couple of portraits of friends and then tackles something more ambitious – a triptych, a project she'd been thinking about since she'd visited Italy with Dorothy Pound, but never seemed to have the time to commit to. While maintaining her love of figurative art, this group portrait will be her nod to Giotto and the work of other Italian primitives she'd seen in Assisi and Arezzo and Siena. Flouting the current trend towards abstraction doesn't bother her. She wants to follow her heart and be true to her own aesthetic principles. Just as Ford says she should.

After doing some preliminary drawings, she begins work on the composition, preparing the three panels with a gold background. The portrait of monsieur and madame Lavigne takes up the larger central panel, with four of their restaurant's waitresses surrounding them like a choir of angels in each of the side panels. In honour of their favourite Parisian restaurant, Stella names the painting Au Nègre de Toulouse.

She keeps Ford informed of the painting's progress as well as detailing all her social engagements. And they are many and frequent. To blunt the pain of separation, she accepts every invitation she receives. She meets the dancer, Isadora Duncan, whom she doesn't much like. Her old friend, Mary Butts, pays her a visit and she frequently dines with Jenny Bradley, as well as having lunches with Olga Rudge[17] and her musician friends. She attends concerts and recitals and sees the latest film by Man Ray. Through Alice and Gertrude, she meets some Russian painters, who all love to dance.

And then there's Hadley Hemingway who, in her usual calm and level-headed way, confides in Stella that she's dreadfully sad about Ernest wanting a divorce so he can marry Fife, who's a Catholic. Despite the anger and hurt she must be feeling, Hadley maintains her dignity, which Stella greatly admires. As for Hemingway – well, he probably can't help himself. She tells all this to Ford in her letters to him, saying she finds it confronting to be reminded of the transitory nature of happiness.

---

17. **Olga Rudge:** (1895 - 1996) American born concert violinist, now mainly remembered as the long-time mistress, muse and champion of the poet Ezra Pound, by whom she had a daughter, Mary.

The truth is no matter how busy Stella tries to be; life without him is dull. She simply can't stop thinking about him. Especially when dealing with workmen installing a bath in their new flat, which she wants ready for Ford's return. Or hearing that the cost of living in France is worsening every week. Then there's madame Annie's pettiness and peculiarities to deal with and what with the havoc caused by Toulouse with his incessant barking and snapping at Julie's friends, well, if it weren't for Ford's correspondence, she'd be seriously depressed. But any news from him uplifts her spirits. For she worries about his health and hopes upon hope that he's remaining chaste. Another betrayal would be just too much! She tells him in her letters that she loves him more than ever and that although she may appear to be gadding about and enjoying herself, her life is truly impoverished without him by her side. And always she mentions Julie, often providing him with a little anecdote about her.

Ford's letters are frequent and no less loving. He answers Stella's questions and encourages her in her work. He gives a running commentary on the people he's been meeting and everything he's doing, including being deluged by the press. He mentions the release of Violet's memoirs in the US which, he fears, may well attract adverse publicity for him. He also tells Stella that no one in New York is a patch on her and that he loves her with all his heart. And when signing off his letters, he always adds kisses for Julie, the 'petit fruit de nos amours', even though he writes to his daughter regularly in French.

So with the success of Ford's American tour, a change in their financial circumstances looks on the cards. Stella feels certain that their future life together will only get better. Especially after she takes Gertrude's strict advice and gives madame Annie her notice. And before she and Julie leave for London to spend Christmas with the Coles in Oxford, she manages to off-load Toulouse. All's right with the world.

Early in the new year, Ford sends Stella a copy of his tribute to her, to be published as a special introduction to the latest American edition of The Good Soldier. He writes it as a 'Dedicatory Letter to Stella Ford'. Naturally, she is moved by its contents but being uncomfortable in the limelight, she's fearful of such overt publicity, so she asks if it were possible to leave out the 'Stella Ford' and just use Stella on its own or the initials of her birth name – Esther Gwendolyn Bowen, arguing that many women artists now stick to their own names.

But Ford dismisses her plea and explains that he very much wants the world to know how devoted and grateful he is to her. And despite her misgivings, he decides to have it published as he first intended. In the same letter, he also tells her that payments to Jean Rhys can now cease as he's secured a publisher for her short stories and another for her translation of Carco's novel.

Meanwhile, Stella is preparing for Ford's return and has finally got around to reading Hemingway's novel, The Sun Also Rises, which has already caused a stir in literary circles. She writes to tell Ford she didn't mind his hard, unadorned style, until it became tiring. And she also didn't like the way he'd betrayed his friends. Understandably, she was hurt by the way he'd portrayed her as a loud, socially gauche woman.

Now she can't help wondering if others see her like that. She wishes she knew more painters than she did writers.

back again

Ford puts down his pen. With only one more day to go before his ship docks in Montreal, he's managed to finish Last Post, his final volume of Parade's End. He knows from experience that it's always a good idea to have a completed manuscript to hand to publishers interested in offering a contract. And now he's glad that Stella had convinced him to book a sleeper on the overnight train to New York. Hopefully he'll get some much-needed rest before he gets there, for he's exhausted. But not unhappy.

The last six months back in France had been good. Very good, in fact. They'd spent most of spring in Toulon and then all of August in Villeneuve-les-Avignon, which had pleased him greatly. Of course, Julie had been an absolute delight. And just observing Stella immersed in her art had made his heart sing. The entire time spent with them both had all been about finding joy in the simple pleasures of life, which had turned out to be the perfect antidote to the drunken stupefaction he'd experienced at so many parties in the States – thanks to the strength of the unavoidable bootleg liquor there.

The only blemish in the last six months that he could recall had happened in his first week back in Paris. Natalie Barney wanted to discuss with him a talk she'd asked him to give at one of her salons. The topic she'd proposed was American Women of Letters. They agreed to meet for lunch at the Rotonde.

As he made his way along the boulevard du Montparnasse, busy and noisy as usual, he hadn't noticed he was being followed. He'd been in a far too jolly mood to even consider such things occurring. All he could remember later was that when he entered the restaurant, Natalie was already there and had ordered him a vermouth, his apéritif of choice. He was just about to raise his glass when out of nowhere, Jean appeared and before he had time to think, she'd slapped him across the face. Hard. Rearing back in his chair, his drink had splashed everywhere.

'I despise you!' she hissed. 'You'll rue the day we ever met, Fordie!' And that was it. She turned around and was gone. In all her shabby glory.

Even now, at the mere thought of the incident, he shuts his eyes. Natalie had been magnificent. He'd been about to explain, to make excuses and concoct some cock and bull story (though he still couldn't fathom what this may have been), when she'd raised her hand. No need. She shrugged her shoulders as if to say, it's of no consequence. And then called the waiter to take their order. Bless her.

And damn Jean! He'd heard she'd left France soon after – gone to Holland to meet up again with Lenglet. Ford fervently hoped he'd never set eyes on her again. All he wanted was a peaceful life. As long as he occasionally felt the admiration and regard that only a woman can provide – a gentle touch, a tender word, a warm embrace, a flirtatious eye, he'd be happy.

He smiles now and moves to the mirror to adjust his tie. It will soon be the hour for dinner. This evening he can relax. New York is beckoning. And so is the lovely Mrs Wright. She's promised she'll be there to greet him on his arrival.

With this in mind, he knows loneliness won't plague him this time round. He closes the door of his cabin and with a jaunty spring in his step, proceeds along the corridor towards the dining room.

drawing away

Snug in their bed, with Ford snoring lightly beside her, Stella lets her mind replay the day, particularly the moment Ford suggested that he ought to go back to New York to secure the best possible publishing deal for Last Post. It hadn't come as a huge surprise to Stella because she saw the sense in his proposal. She knows Ford's work is well regarded there, for the Americans had wined and dined and courted him last time. So the probability of him being offered a lucrative contract is fairly high. And it's not like they don't need the money. That's why she'd made no objection.

But now revisiting their conversation in her head, she feels uneasy. She's detected an eagerness in him. It isn't anything specific he'd said, it's more the way he'd presented the idea to her. His justifications for returning to the States after only six months are in hindsight so complex and elaborate, Stella is suspicious. What is he trying to hide?

She can't help thinking he may have met someone else over there. Not that she has any proof of course. On the contrary, since his return, their relationship has never seemed so strong, - they'd all had such a good time together again in the south of France. But now she wonders if it had been an illusion, that it was only what she'd wanted to see; what she'd wanted to believe. Certainly last year, Ford had been full of remorse over his tumultuous affair with Jean. Her own self-confidence had taken a pounding and perhaps out of sheer desperation, she'd been driven to search for any confirmation of his love for her. She only had to look at the desperate way she'd clung to the words of tribute he'd written about her for the dedication of the new edition of The Good Soldier.

And this thought reminds her how, years ago, there'd been a particular passage in that novel that had resonated with her at the time. It had come somewhere in the middle of the book and it was about what a man most desired in a woman. She now can't recall the exact words, but with her curiosity piqued, she feels compelled to go in search of her old copy.

Locating the book, she quickly finds the passage, thanks to the pencilled lines in the margin, and then decides to re-read the surrounding pages. She's mystified how her youthful, naïve self had directed all her attention on just a couple of sentences. Why hadn't she zeroed in on the preceding statements concerning the impermanence of love? And how on earth had she not taken note of the two paragraphs that then followed – now appearing so obvious and powerful? Especially these few lines:

For every man there comes at last a time of life when the woman who then sets her seal upon his imagination has set her seal for good. He will travel over no more horizons; he will never again set the knapsack over his shoulders; he will retire from these scenes. He will have gone out of the business.[18]

Had it been ignorance or vanity that made her think she was the one who'd make Ford cease his philandering? When they first decided to be together, she'd believed that he'd reached that time of life when he was ready to settle down for good. But as time passed, she'd become complacent so that when she wasn't looking, Jean had set her seal upon Ford's imagination and offered him a fantasy so seductive he couldn't refuse. But all that had ended badly. The fantasy hadn't been workable.

So maybe, with an ocean between them, Ford could've become lonely in America. With his ego needing some feminine reassurance, he may well have looked for a woman who could offer him what he'd described as a new horizon to explore.

---

18 . *The Good Soldier:* Novel by Ford Madox Ford, Penguin Books, 1988 p.109.

The mantle clock in the living room strikes the hour - one o'clock. Stella yawns and replaces the book on the shelf. Although convinced she's now facing a night of troubled sleep; she takes herself back to bed. Ford is awake. 'Are you all right?' he asks.

'Yes, yes.'

'Well, get under the covers then or you'll freeze yourself to death.' He pauses, catching his breath. 'Because I couldn't bear to lose you, you know.'

He turns off the lamp as she climbs back into bed. And as they often do, they fold themselves together beneath the blankets.

The following morning, everything seems so much clearer. Ford is up and already in the kitchen, preparing breakfast. With no need to rush, she lingers in bed a little longer than is usual. Stella's midnight torment is over. There's no point in doubting Ford's love for her. By his actions last night, he'd made it quite clear that he would always love her. Worrying about whether he's interested in some other woman now seems pointless. Because even if he were, she knows he would ultimately come to his senses. Once he's done with his wanderings, that is.

And she'll wait it out. She isn't going to make the mistake poor Hadley made. She gave Ernest an ultimatum and a deadline. Under pressure, Hemingway chose Fife. No, Stella would not be doing that. On the contrary. She knows she can't control what happens in the future, but she can make damn sure she'll never again suffer the way she'd done with Jean. This time she'll make no demands and will ask very few questions. She'll give him the freedom to do as he sees fit. No coercion. No constraints. And no expectations on her part either.

Two days later, Ford tells her he's purchased a ticket on the Canadian liner, the S.S. Minnedosa. 'And I can assure you,' he says, placing his arms around her waist, 'it will only be the shortest of trips this time round, as I truly can't imagine being away from you and Julie for another Christmas.'

'Well of course, we'd love you to be home for Christmas, but unforeseen things can happen, and I want you to know that I do appreciate how negotiations for contracts with publishers can become complex and drawn-out affairs. So if you have to stay longer, I will understand. I really will.' Smiling, she moves closer to him because she wants to touch him. And when she places her hand on his cheek, she says, 'I want you to feel free in every possible way. So please don't feel restrained. I'm sure, my darling, you'll know when it's right to come home.'

A month after Ford's departure, Stella finds a new nanny for Julie. Without a moment of fuss, mademoiselle Renée makes domestic life both easy and a pleasure for Stella, who can now channel the devotion she'd always given to Ford into her work. Most days are spent in her studio, completing five portraits, one of which is of Edith Sitwell[19]. She'd been introduced to her by Gertrude and the Russian artist, Pavel Tchelitchew, who's taken over the lease of Guermantes.

There'd been an instant rapport between them, with Edith happily agreeing to sit for lengthy periods, while Stella experimented with the portrait's composition, using a mirrored image to reflect the back of Edith's head. She also loved painting her marvellous hands. With their elongated fingers adorned with her large, extravagant rings, she was able to convey her queen-like strength, despite her hunched shoulders. And as the conversation flowed easily between them, they quickly became good friends. Edith, for one, is glad to have found an empathetic soul in Stella, someone she can trust to keep her heart's secrets, especially about her all-consuming love for Pavel.

Then in October, Stella has six of her drawings exhibited at the American Women's Club. For the first time in a long while, she is fully immersed in her art. All day, she paints alone in her studio. Sometimes she breaks to read one of Ford's letters from across the Atlantic – all full of gossip, boasts and evasions. His encouraging words about her work please her but his endearments seem shallow and don't ring true. She goes back to work to sketch and compose another picture. Only then

---

19 . **Edith Sitwell:** (1887 - 1964) British poet and critic, eldest of the three literary Sitwells. Much of her early poetry was abstract & set to music. She actively encouraged modernist writers and artists, and was famous for her formidable personality, her eccentric opinions & her theatrical dress.

does she take up her pen to reply to him. She responds with dignity, her emotions muted, and her word choice guarded. Then back again: to paint and brush, to express herself, nobody else, and so to capture likeness. In this way, she hardens her heart and starts to frame up an independent life away from Ford. Which, to her mind, is a very good thing. Especially when he doesn't come home for Christmas.

getting to the point

With her elbow resting on the mantlepiece, Stella watches Ford as he uncorks the bottle and pours the wine into two large glasses. Having placed them on opposite sides of the table, he sits down beside one of them and takes his first sip. Stella pulls out a chair from under the table and sits facing him.

'So how do you feel about being back?'

'Well, it's certainly wonderful seeing my darling Julie again. I missed her terribly, you know.'

Stella nods. Of course, she knows this. His two other daughters had rejected him outright, and that had hurt him deeply, so he's determined never to allow that to happen with Julie. But Stella also knows he's stalling because he hates any form of confrontation, even a civilised one, so she simply says, 'She missed you too.'

'Don't you worry, I've already begun to remedy that.' He takes another sip of his wine. 'And I'm pleased she sees nothing amiss between you and me, which I'm most grateful for.' A silence then falls between them.

Stella feels like screaming from the tension. She wants him to get to the point. Whatever that is. He was the one who'd initiated this meeting, saying he wanted to discuss something important with her. She wishes he'd just get on with it. So she says: 'I know you've only been back three days, but I haven't asked you if you're happy with this flat. Do you find it comfortable?'

She had done what he'd requested and rented the small attic flat next to her much larger one in the rue de Vaugiraud. She'd fitted it out as best she could prior to his return, for it was to be his own little place – where he could live and work while remaining in close proximity to Julie.

'No, no. Everything's fine, thank you.'

'Oh good. I think it's the perfect arrangement. We're separated but still conveniently nearby.' She smiles and waits for a response, but none is forthcoming. She ploughs on. 'I realised from your letters that the intimacy we once shared can't continue. But I see no problem in us remaining friends and sharing our lives, for the time being at any rate.'

'Well, that's all very well, but what I'd like to know,' says Ford, gathering his thoughts and brushing some hair away from his forehead, 'is just what it was in my letters that suggested to you our sexual relations were at an end?'

And so she tells him. 'It was the letter you wrote just before Christmas. You'd started by declaring your deep admiration and respect for me and everything I stood for. Your words were carefully chosen. Every one of them pragmatic and bloodless. They had no warmth, no real tenderness. It was like something you'd say to a colleague, signalling a closure of some sort. I was sure then and still am that it was your cowardly way of breaking it off.'

Ford stares at her, trapping her eyes in his gaze. 'Really? Is that it?' he sounds incredulous.

'No. I was also upset when you wrote that you thought it was your duty to become involved in the re-establishment of the transatlantic review in America. You knew I was fearful of the financial impact your involvement in such a venture may have on us personally. Yet you completely disregarded my opinion, while knowing full well how much we'd lost last time round.'

She chooses not to remind him that he has no filter for possible disaster and absolutely no sense when it comes to money. Because there's no point in doing that. But she does say that she and Julie had been bitterly disappointed he hadn't come back to Paris for Christmas as he'd promised and then put off his return until February. 'When I read that you not only intended maintaining a *pied à terre* in New York but were also thinking of taking a holiday in Bermuda, well, that was the last straw. That's when I realised, you'd found someone else.'

'That will never happen.' But she sees that he's looking down into his glass when he says this.

'Really? Well, look me straight in the eye and tell me you haven't entangled yourself with another woman?'

He looks up and blinks several times. 'Well, yes, I have. That's the reason I wanted to speak with you tonight. It's really the first chance we've had since my return to discuss it with you.'

'What's her name?' She had thought she'd prepared herself, but a little cancer of jealousy surfaces around Stella's heart. 'Tell me about her.'

'Her name is Rene Wright.'

'Oh, and I bet she's just right in a myriad of ways.'

'Sarcasm doesn't suit you, my dear.' Ford smiles weakly and continues. 'For your information, Rene is 48 years old. She's married but is in the process of getting a divorce.' He pauses to top up their glasses. 'Anyway, all that's beside the point.'

'And what exactly is the point?'

'Well, I still want to be with you and Julie. You're my family and I really can't see why we must separate.' Seeing that Stella is about to interrupt him, he holds up his hand. 'Please hear me out,' he says. 'Now that I have a certain reputation to uphold in America, it's highly likely that I will continue to travel between here and New York for some time. And as we both hold one another in high esteem, I'm proposing that we continue to cohabit together with Julie here in Paris for half the year and that I spend the other six months in the States.'

'With Mrs Wright.'

'Well, yes.'

'And I say no.' Stella stands up. She can't believe he's made such an absurd proposal. 'I don't think that's possible. I really don't.'

'Why not? Won't you at least think about it?' He's by her side now, walking her to the door. His voice is gentle, soothing. 'We can discuss it further tomorrow or the next day if you prefer?'

She surrenders. 'No, make it Saturday. Saturday evening.'

'Very well. I'll book a table at Lavigne's. For just the two of us.'

In a confusion of emotions, Stella walks back along the hall to her apartment. How could he have even asked her to consider such an outrageous proposition? Who on earth would benefit from such an arrangement? She only had to think of Ezra, with Dorothy living in one house and poor Olga in another further up the hill in Rapallo, to know the answer to that one. No, she's having none of it. She swings around and knocks on Ford's door.

Once again inside and sitting down, Stella unleashes her pain. 'I'm not going to let you do this to me or to Julie. I think I've suffered enough, don't you?'

'It's all right. It's all right,' says Ford, still standing.

'What do you mean by it's all right? None of this is all right. What's the matter with you?' Tears are running down her face. She's worn out by the strain of dealing with him. Ever unpredictable. Always erratic. 'I've had enough. I've just had enough! I can't believe how cruel you are and how you expect so much of me. I've done everything I could for you. I've allowed you to be the centre of my emotional life. I've lived with you as man and wife, knowing you were married, and I've given birth to our illegitimate child.'

'May I say something?'

'Yes.' She wipes her tears away with her fingers. 'But you need to hear me out first.'

Ford takes a handkerchief from his pocket and hands it to her. 'Very well,' he says as he sits back down at the table and pours himself another glass of wine.

Stella gets up from the divan and takes a seat at the table opposite him as before. 'I have devoted all my time and energy to you and your career because I loved you unconditionally and I recognised your genius. I wanted to help you achieve all the success that you deserved.'

'And don't you think I've appreciated everything you've done for me? For mercy's sake, woman, haven't I made my indebtedness to you public enough?'

'Of course, you have. I've never doubted that. Never.' She reaches for his hand and squeezes it. 'And you must know that I don't regret a thing because I've been happy, so very happy with you. But your betrayals now have made happiness impossible for us. We can't continue as we have done for the last nine years or so. I just cannot and will not accept the conditions you're offering.'

He tells her then to ignore what he's said before; that he'd had second thoughts the moment she agreed to meet him in Lavigne's on Saturday and that that's exactly what he was going to tell her - that he realised what he'd been proposing wasn't such a good idea after all. 'So, I'm sorry. And I apologise for even mentioning it.'

'Apology accepted.'

'Well, am I right in thinking that what you want is a divorce?'

'We're not married, remember, so I hardly think divorce is the appropriate word. All our friends know the truth. It's ridiculous to use that term. But yes, I want a separation.'

'I don't want to argue over semantics with you Stella, but I've always thought of us as being married, and we let plenty of other people think that too. I believe that divorce is separation, and parting is divorce. And if that's what you want, so be it. But I do think it best, for obvious reasons, that we use the word divorce with Julie and Mademoiselle Renée, as well as everyone else not in our immediate circle. Don't you?'

Stella agrees. A decision has been made. They stare blankly at each other for some time without saying a word. Ford breaks the silence, wanting to know what they should tell their friends if they're asked why they're separating.

'Again, let's not veer too far from the truth. Surely, it's obvious to everyone that you've shifted your interests to America. And you can say I've asked for my freedom, which is the case and, if you like, you can add that I've become impossibly independent. I think people will accept that.'

'As long as we remain dignified and discreet and always keep Julie's best interests at heart, I'll be happy,' says Ford.

Stella stands up to go. 'I hope we can still see one another from time to time. And please let's not be the fodder for gossips, Ford. I want you to know that I have no intention of playing the victim like Violet did, nor the deserted wife like Hadley, because I really don't wish to be pitied or judged by anyone. You understand?'

'Of course.' Ford smiles weakly. 'I'd like very much for us to remain friends.'

'I certainly hope so.' She realises then that his mind is still in tune with hers, that he's noticed she's not mentioned she won't be creating any appalling public scenes like Jean had done.

They embrace one another lightly, and as he pulls away from her, she blurts: 'I hope you know that I'll never, ever stop loving you.'

Ford says nothing but gently closes the door behind her.

letting go

It takes Stella quite some time to adjust to the realities of breaking free from Ford. At first, she spends a few miserable weeks away in Bandol with Jenny Bradley. The idea of being by the sea with a dear friend had seemed like an excellent way to come to terms with the fact she'd never again enjoy Ford's good-natured companionship, not to mention his superior intelligence. But the azure waters of the Mediterranean only make her daydream of other summers spent with Ford.

One early evening, the two women are sitting out on the hotel's balcony taking in the view of the little port with its flotilla of fishing boats returning with their afternoon's catch. Jenny can no longer bear the weight of her friend's sadness.

'You can't hide it from me, Stella. I know how unhappy you must be, but cradling your memories is not going to improve things.'

'I know.'

'So what do you intend doing about it?'

'If I knew that, I wouldn't be feeling so miserable. It's just that I can't stop thinking about the past and what I've lost.'

'Well, I'm no expert in these matters, but you might have to train your mind to do the opposite and remind it why your relationship failed in the first place.'

'But I don't want to apportion any blame or…'

'I wasn't suggesting that. You just need to be a little more hard-headed and less dewy-eyed about the life you had with Ford. All those syrupy nostalgic thoughts of yours are getting you nowhere fast.'

Later, when alone, Stella thinks about what Jenny had said. She has to admit she did tend to be overly sentimental and she really must stop wallowing in self-pity. It isn't good for her or anyone around her. But it is so hard. Ford's infidelities had bruised her heart, as well as her ego. What she needs to remember is how their unreliable financial situation, which had been a constant throughout the entire time they'd been together, had dominated and undermined everything. And in the end, that's what really destroyed their relationship. Ford's unfaithfulness had only delivered the final blow.

So like a gramophone needle stuck in a record's track, she sets about reminding herself of all the reasons why she and Ford are no longer a couple. Using this method as often as she can, she soon finds that she's managing better. Her main goal then becomes the creation of a calm, secure and stable home life that includes Julie having a positive relationship with her father. For Stella has seen first-hand how Julie's confidence blooms whenever Ford is in her orbit, which makes her wonder if her own lack of self-belief has stemmed from growing up without a father's love.

While Ford's in New York, he and Stella maintain a regular correspondence but once he returns and despite her intentions not to quarrel, awkward disputes inevitably erupt between them – mainly over money and access to Julie. What bothers her most is the issue of religion. Ford insists on Julie being baptised in the Catholic Church and what's more demands she receive regular religious instruction. While the hypocrisy of his edict rankles Stella, she goes along with it. She's had enough of useless squabbling. Besides, Julie doesn't seem to mind one way or the other.

Knowing she can no longer rely on Ford's royalty cheques; Stella finally makes the decision to make a new life for herself by painting her way to independence. So with high hopes of earning a reasonable living as a portrait artist, she sets to work and obtains several commissions for portraits, which pleases her greatly, particularly when she finds she still has plenty of time to pursue her own artistic interests. All this makes her wonder if she can dare to dream of having her own solo exhibition one day. She has already begun work on a series of studies of views from her studio's windows. She'd done another one of Ford's chair - but this time it sits empty beside open French shutters that look out onto a bleak, wintry scene. See, she is saying, I'm coming to terms with his absence.

Next, she paints a self-portrait to keep alive the memory of this time. Using browns and ochre, the mood is sombre, her face stern, unsmiling, almost fierce. Dark shadows huddle beneath her eyes that stare defiantly out from the canvas. It is the face of a woman who's been hurt. But don't worry, it says, I'll survive.

There is also another painting, one that she decides to put aside. She had started it when Ford was in the States, when she'd been trying to harden her heart against him. But because it isn't like anything she'd ever done before, she began to feel uneasy about it. And she still does, whenever she comes back to it.

That all changes though when Francis Carco turns up at her studio with the Bradleys one afternoon. He asks to see what she's been working on. She shows him some of her finished pieces, which he seems to like, until his attention suddenly turns to a couple of paintings that are leaning against the back wall. He points at one of them and asks her who'd painted it.

'It's one of mine,' she says. 'I thought I'd experiment with a self-portrait.'

'C'est très intéressant, Stella.' After peering at it for some time, he urges her to finish it, saying it has the kind of honesty and daring he greatly admires. Such encouragement and validation from someone who knows so much about art delights her. Francis obviously understands what she's trying to do. She returns to it with greater purpose.

She calls it Still Life with Part of Me, playing with the genre of still life painting and the notion of self-portraiture at the same time. It's her attempt to redefine her identity. It's how she now wants to be seen. Not as a muse or consort, but as an artist in the act of preparing to paint. It is an act of self-realisation.

The picture is cropped just above her unsmiling, determined mouth. And the viewer, who's positioned where the canvas should be, sees only her torso and her right-hand thumb firmly grasping a palette that has brushes thrusting out from beneath it. As a headless figure, Stella wears her dark-coloured artist's smock over an open-necked chemise. Its deep V-neck points towards her palette and paints, her tools of trade.

This is me, it says. I am my palette. I am my art.

les crises

On the morning of her vernissage,[20] Stella hurries into the Galerie Barreiro. Having shaken her umbrella outside, she then places it in the bucket by the entrance. She's on time, but she's drenched. There'd been a sudden downpour - a typical occurrence in late spring.

Gaspard, her art dealer, is already there. As usual, he's unshaven but looks as warm and dry as unbuttered toast. 'Ah, at last!' he says with some impatience then tells her where she can find a towel to dry herself off.

When she returns from his office in the gallery's rear, he has already

---

20. **A vernissage:** Traditionally the day before an exhibition when artists can varnish or put the finishing touches to their works. Around 1912, a vernissage came to mark the opening of an exhibition, to which only invited guests could attend.

lit a cigarette and is in the middle of standing her twenty-five paintings on the floor against the blank but grubby walls. 'When you position them like this,' he explains, 'it's easier to see where you'd like to hang them.'

She moves to the middle of the room near where he's standing so she can survey her work as he seems to want her to do. The light is meagre, coming mainly from the gallery's window that faces the grey morning street. Taken together like that, she can't believe how abysmal all her pictures look, especially the ones of interiors, which are views from various windows. Even Le masque, the recent painting she's done of Edith's elegant hands holding the black mask that a friend had brought back for her from Africa, seems lack lustre here.

Stella's heart is pounding. She feels hot and clammy. All she wants to do is slink away and hide where no one can find her. What had she been thinking? How had she ever imagined she was ready for a solo exhibition?

'Ne t'inquiète pas! Don't let your nerves get the better of you.' Gaspard's gravelly voice breaks through her panic. 'It's normal to feel a little anxious before your big night.'

Stella steadies her breathing. She doesn't believe him but helps him hang her paintings anyway.

Despite her fears, she enjoys the opening immensely. All her friends turn up that evening. She's given flowers and praise. Even Phyllis and her new husband, Aylmer,[21] come over from London especially to be there. They bring champagne. But the focus of everyone's attention is Stella's faceless self-portrait that she's renamed La Palette. Several of her more experienced artist friends critique it without giving offence or resorting to empty flattery. They comment on her clarity of line, her ability to

---

21. [Gerald] **Aylmer Valence:** (1892-1955) Scottish born newspaper editor who, as editor of London's *News Chronicle* in the 1930s, took it in a more radical direction, investigating and critically reporting on the British Union of Fascists.

capture a likeness and her technique of layering paint to create texture and luminosity. Wanting to relish this moment, she parties late into the night.

By the end of the exhibition, Stella manages to sell a good third of her work. She's thankful and somewhat relieved because she's in serious debt. At least now she'll be able to make another payment to the architect, who'd overseen the necessary improvements to her new studio apartment. All things considered, the last three years had been tough since she and Ford had gone their separate ways back in February 1928. First of all, mademoiselle Renée severely injured her back and could no longer complete the most menial of tasks, so returned to Dijon to live with her parents. Then Stella was given notice to quit her old studio on the rue Notre-Dame-des-Champs. The building was to be demolished.

All this, while the Australian pound reached an all-time low. Everyone in Paris was talking about *la crise financière*. Prices were soaring. Even when Ford signed the British rights to his books over to her, only a trickle of money was forthcoming. Meanwhile, what little he made from his U.S. royalties, he spent. He was still sailing back and forth across the Atlantic, not because of Mrs Wright, who'd already left him, but because of his continuing problems with his American publishers. It had become all too clear that neither of them could justify keeping the two flats in the rue Vaugiraud.

Desperate to find a place for her and Julie to live, Stella had signed a long lease on two adjoining studios on the rue Boissonade. One was larger than the other. Both were in poor condition but could be made habitable if converted into one interconnecting apartment. But mid-renovation, disaster struck. The world's major stock markets came crashing down. And the costs of the remodelling spiralled out of control, so that when she and Julie moved in, Stella carried with her a debt she had no means of paying.

But the most painful experience of that time was one Stella could barely bring herself to talk about. Jean's novel of revenge about her relationship with Ford was published both in the U.K. and the States. While a few critics claimed Quartet was brilliant but flawed, Ford was outraged and called it libellous. When Stella finally read it, she thought it a nasty, dishonest little book.

She had always considered Jean to be a very sad person, someone who was depressed by all the traumas she'd experienced in her life. And she could sympathise, having suffered herself from the dark despair caused by rejection and betrayal. But what she could never condone was Jean's destructive behaviour. She was someone who shifted the blame away from herself, always preferring to play life's victim. As far as Stella was concerned, she hoped Jean would take her howling rage and stew in her own volatile juices for the rest of the century.

plus ça change

Not long after her solo exhibition, Stella receives a note from Ford, who has recently returned from the States. She opens it with some trepidation, wondering how he is going to bother her now, but she's surprised to find it contains nothing unpleasant. He has written to inform her that his luck has changed, that he'd fallen in love with a young American painter of Polish origin, named Janice Biala. He wants Stella to meet her – to approve their union and give them her blessing. Stella smiles – his choice of words so typical of Ford. And on top of that, he implies that her support will be in everyone's interests. But such entreaties make no difference. She's already intrigued and wants to meet this Janice Biala, so she arranges a meeting for the following day.

When Stella goes to answer the door, she finds a small, fresh-faced woman with deep-set brown eyes and dark hair, parted in the centre. 'I thought it best to come alone,' she says, still standing on the landing. 'I want to get to know you for myself. I hope you don't mind.'

'Of course not. I think it's a grand idea. Do come in.'

After admiring the studio apartment in all its warm, July morning light, Janice asks to see some of Stella's paintings. 'Your work's so different to mine. Mine is a bit more abstract, but I like yours very much.'

Stella believes her. There's something very direct and candid about Janice that makes her feel relaxed in her company. 'I think it's time for a cup of tea,' she says.

While waiting for the water to boil, they talk together about art and discover they both admire Cezanne. Engrossed in their conversation, they at first drink their tea standing. And then, as the clock strikes the hour, they settle themselves into the low, striped-satin Victorian chairs that Jenny Bradley had unearthed in some Parisian flea market.

'I should tell you that Julie will be back soon. She was invited to spend the morning with one of her school friends,' says Stella.

'Oh lovely. You know, I'm really looking forward to meeting her. Ford has told me so much about her.'

'Yes, and she'll be pleased to see him too. She adores her father.'

Janice nods. 'Well, all I can say is she must have very good taste because I adore him too.' For a moment she's lost in her thoughts, then says: 'I'd like you to know that I'll never, ever leave him.'

'I don't doubt you for a minute.'

They look at one another and smile. 'I have this feeling that you and I have an intuitive understanding of one another. I mean, we are two artists – both of us were drawn to Ford because I think we know he's a genius, and that's what attracted us to him.'

'You mean neither of us cared about his potbelly?'

'Precisely!' And they both laugh at the truth of it.

'When he and I first met last year, I was only twenty-six. So we started out knowing there was a significant difference in our ages, which in itself doesn't bother either of us. What does concern us is that there's no time to waste.'

'I think that's wonderful. I'm truly happy for you both.'

'Thank you, I appreciate you saying that. Ford is right. He told me we'd get on.' She swallows and takes a breath. 'That's why I really didn't want him to come along today. I wanted our first meeting to just be the two of us, where we can establish some kind of accord without him getting in the way. And I think we've done that.'

'I do too.' And suddenly in through the door bursts Julie, pigtails flying. She throws her arms around her mother's neck. 'There's someone very special here who'd like to meet you, my darling,' says Stella.

After introductions are completed, Julie holds out her hand to Janice and gives a dainty little curtsey. 'I shall get more tea,' says Stella, 'while you two get to know one another.'

Another hour passes before Janice makes a move to go. 'Your father will be wondering where I am,' she tells Julie.

'*S'il vous plaît, donnez-lui cent bisous de ma part.*'

'I'll do better than that and give him two hundred kisses from you.' The child seems pleased and leaves the two women to say their own good-byes at the door.

'I'm sure we'll be seeing each other soon,' says Stella.

'I hope so. I do hope you know that Ford holds you in high esteem.'

'Of course, and please tell him I'll never do anything to harm his relationship with Julie. For her sake, I want that to continue to flourish and grow.'

'Thanks for the tea and the conversation. I've enjoyed myself immensely.' The two embrace. 'And when Ford asks me what I thought of you today, I shall tell him that I now have even more respect for him knowing he'd had a woman like you in his life.'

Months go by and while summer turns to autumn, rumours of war and fear of financial ruin stalk Stella's world. Still in debt, and with commissions for portraits drying up, she sees no alternative. To save money, she sub-lets her apartment and takes up Ford and Janice's offer to spend the winter with Julie at the Villa Paul, a ramshackle residence they'd leased on Cap Brun about ten kilometres along the coast from Toulon.

The garden and stone terrace with its fountain are delightful. And the views that look out across the harbour to Saint-Mandrier are spectacular. But the entire domestic set-up is beyond being primitive, it's appalling, particularly if you're forced to remain indoors when the weather finally breaks in October. Several windows are already broken and let in draughts. And only half of the electric lights are in working order. There's just a single charcoal burner for cooking and no cooking utensils or household linen and very limited crockery.

Depressed and feeling defeated, Stella spends the first night in tears. Is this to be her lot? A life of grinding poverty? It feels like she's been thrown back to Red Ford. Except that back then, she'd been in love, and domestic discomforts hadn't mattered much. Especially when the love of her life was a genius. And look where that got her! At least now she has realised how that kind of foolish thinking has led her into surrendering most of her inheritance to furnish Ford's dreams. And now, what little of it is left, isn't even earning enough interest to keep her out of debt.

Nevertheless, she manages to stick it out until the end of winter. When they finally leave the Villa Paul and return to Paris, Stella is fearful. She knows only too well how exceedingly expensive the city has become and that most of the painters she knows are starving. Her only hope for a brighter future comes in a proposition that her old friend, Ramon Guthrie put to her in a letter. He simply asked her how many commissioned portraits at three hundred dollars each would make a trip to the States worth her while.

Her answer is three.

When a telegram finally arrives with news that work, amounting to $1,000 is waiting for her in New York, she jumps at the chance. With Ford and Janice offering to take care of Julie until she returns, she sublets her studio and with money lent to her by Peggy Guggenheim[22], she purchases a one-way fare and sails off to New York.

---

22. [Marguerite] **'Peggy' Guggenheim:** (1898 – 1979) A self-confessed 'Art Addict', she was born into a wealthy, well-known and powerful family. As an art collector, bohemian and socialite, she amassed a huge collection of modern art, which is exhibited in the museum that used to be her home on the Grand Canal in Venice, Italy.

Part Seven

September 2019

When I completed my novel in the dying days of 2018, I was extremely pleased with myself. I'd achieved what I'd set out to do five years ago, which I felt was an accomplishment. Not that The Only Reality was ready for publication right away. I knew it needed some fine tuning and some careful revision before I could send it out into the world of publishers, so I left it to marinate for a few months before looking at it again with a cold, objective eye. Well, that had been the plan. Until I suddenly became extremely busy. Antoine had started receiving a great deal of media attention and general fanfare after launching his symphonic Liberté Suite to the packed auditorium of Opéra Bastille on November 13 last year – the third anniversary of the Bataclan attacks.

From the gentle opening notes of the prelude, he had shaped his composition to reignite memories of the horror of that night by cleverly punctuating the octave leaps of string and wind instruments with sudden silences and heartbeats, taped laughter and babbling restaurant chatter, jarring heavy metal guitar riffs, bursts of gunfire, wailing sirens of police and ambulances. Ultimately, Antoine had managed to capture the emotional pain and grief that had swept the country and what's more, by using the harp as an expression of hope and healing and merging it with the familiar strains of parts of the Marseillaise, he'd evoked the nation's determination not to bend in the face of brutism.

The critical reviews next morning were rhapsodic. For days Sacha's phone didn't stop ringing. Everyone wanted to interview Antoine. The concert had been recorded and an album produced. Just in time for Christmas.

And then in the New Year, I ran into Harper, an old friend and colleague from my internship days in London, who was now managing a prestigious independent gallery not far from the Musée Picasso in the Marais. She offered me a job. It was only a part-time position. Three days a week, most weeks. I'd be working on an exhibition of Indigenous Australian art. And although it sounded too good to be true, I accepted the offer and within days was relishing the work. What's more, over the next seven months, I was able to stop obsessing about fertilisation. Which is why I decided to visit the fountain again.

It was Antoine who'd first taken me there – in another September, not unlike this one, but back in my first year of living in Paris. On that day, we'd strolled around the perimeter of the long rectangular pond and stopped close to the monumental faux grotto that Marie de Medici, widow of Henri IV and mother of Louis XIII, had dreamt up in the seventeenth century. I can remember being surprised to see so few people about. But then the Fontaine Médici is not what you'd call a tourist hot spot, especially on a grey sky morning such as that one, and besides, the fountain is well-hidden by a grove of leafy trees within the Jardin de Luxembourg. Not easy to find. And although the fountain itself is in drastic need of a clean, it remains my favourite place in Paris.

Antoine pulled up two green metal park chairs and after sitting down, he began to explain how the original sculpture of Venus in her bath had been replaced when the fountain was restored back in 1866. This one might be a little, how you say, over the top, he said, but all in all, it's an extraordinary piece of architecture, don't you think?

I'd agreed it was quite startling, then pointing at the giant bronze cyclops who was spying on a pair of white marble lovers, I added: I'm a bit baffled though. I mean, the central focus of the entire grotto is this sculpture, which I guess represents some ancient myth or other. But it's one I don't know, so its meaning and relevance are completely lost on me.

As Greek myths go, it is one of the more obscure ones, said Antoine. Basically, it's about the one-eyed Polyphemus, Poseidon's son, who's madly in love with Galatea, a beautiful sea nymph, and when he tries to woo her with love songs, she rejects him because of his hideous physical appearance. But that only makes him more lovesick. So, when he finds a naked Galatea in the arms of Acis, a mere mortal, he slays his rival.

Oh, that's terrible!

Of course, it is. But what Auguste Ottin, the sculptor is representing here is the turning point of the story - that pivotal moment of discovery when in an instant Polyphemus will make a decision that changes the lives of all three characters forever. This is what's important, Ottin is saying. Not the beginning or the outcome of the tale. But that moment. Polyphemus had free will. He had a choice. He could vent his rage, or he could control it. The decision was his. Passion versus reason.

And fate or destiny played no part?

Well, it doesn't really matter, said Antoine. The result is the same.

So, nobody wins because of the absurdity of jealousy?

Exactement. And then Antoine put his arm loosely around my waist. We should get going, he said.

As we had a reservation for lunch in a nearby restaurant, we made our way to the garden's exit.

Ever since that day, I've thought a lot about Polyphemus and how he chose to deal with jealousy. Was he really exercising his free will when he murdered Acis? His response was so immediate – a knee-jerk, unthinking reaction. Wasn't it possible that his brain wasn't able to regulate such intense emotion? Particularly after Galatea's flagrantly cruel rejection of him? And then to see her in the arms of her lover – his rage was no doubt fuelled by the injustice and humiliation he was feeling. Still, the crime of passion defence is often used to excuse men of violence against women. A defence I cannot tolerate. Nevertheless, it gave me considerable food for thought.

Especially when it came time to write about Stella's response to Ford's betrayal and the consequent break-up. I'd never found any real evidence of Stella witnessing Ford and Jean's in flagrante delicto and the more I learnt about Jean and Stella's character, I was certain that something had happened, a terrible incident that forced Stella to reconsider her belief that her relationship with Ford, a serial philanderer, was repairable. So based on this hunch, I had invented the garden scene at Guermantes and as Stella was no Polyphemus, I made sure she didn't act like a wilful child. Sure, she suffered deeply from Ford's duplicity, but she would never indulge her fury. Of that, I was certain.

So, I took myself back to the fountain again today and sat on another green metal park chair, to be calmed by the soothing sound of the gentle falling waters there - a perfect place for quiet contemplation. Especially this year with all the turmoil and strife that had engulfed the country. Starting in April, the entire population watched unbelieving as Notre-Dame Cathedral caught fire. And while the rest of the world perceived France, with its Paris Agreement, to be a global leader on climate change, domestically things weren't good. There were still random terrorist attacks across the nation. And the weekly peaceful protests by the Yellow Vests Movement demanding economic justice had morphed into civil disobedience, rioting and looting.

Maybe bringing a baby into this troubled world wasn't such a good idea, I thought. Not that I'd had much success with that. I knew my body needed time to adjust from not taking the pill. But my menstrual cycle now seemed normal. So why hadn't I fallen pregnant? Thankfully, Antoine isn't concerned. He's convinced that I worry too much. That I need to relax more and be patient. It will happen, he keeps saying, I'm sure of it. But we need to be a bit more spontaneous – a bit less clinical.

I was taken aback when he'd said that. I'd thought he'd wanted a child even more than I did. But I realised it was easier for him to chill out, what with his composer's mind constantly full of all sorts of sounds, melodies and motifs. I had to admit I'd become hung-up on predicting when I was ovulating. I needed to lighten up a bit and focus my overactive brain on something else. A more structured routine on my days off would probably help. I'd loved being lost in Stella's world, which made me think that maybe I needed to step back into it and start editing my manuscript now rather than in a few months' time.

Suddenly, beneath the lushness of the canopy of yellowing leaves on the other side of the long rectangular pond, a handbag sized dog started yapping at its owner's feet, punctuating the distant rush and dash of the city's traffic beyond the garden's fence. But none of it bothered me. I was thinking about Stella and her pregnancy. She'd embraced the idea of having Ford's child without first fully exploring her ambition to paint. And while Ford was no Antoine, love would have motivated her, as well as that old biological, ancestral imperative which we're all hard-wired to perform. I could relate well to that craving!

Nevertheless, I still thought there was something a little naïve about Stella's decision. She'd often referred to herself as a 'half-baked colonial'. So it was conceivable she imagined that a bucolic existence with Ford would be idyllic. He would write. She would paint, and together they'd grow potatoes and raise pigs – as well as a child. She hadn't factored in the impact a child's demands would have on her time and energy. Particularly given her historical context. Then the thought crossed my mind that having Ford's child was a way to seal herself to him forever. And it had definitely done that.

That's when I picked up my bag. I'd made up my mind. I'd pull my manuscript out of my desk drawer and I'd also throw away my ovulation calculator. I made a pact with myself that I'd try to worry less by enjoying sex more. And perhaps I'd come to the fountain a little more often too. At least until April next year, when I'd be leaving with Antoine on his Liberté tour of Australia.

Part Eight
1933 – 1947
The Only Reality
by
Neve Palmer

marvellous friends

The night Stella crosses the Channel from Dunkerque to Folkestone, she lies awake in her third-class women's cabin, listening to the ferry's creaking boards. It's her fortieth birthday, and her spirits are at an all-time low.

Six months ago, when she'd returned to France from the States, she'd felt reasonably optimistic. She'd not only made enough money over there to repay all her debts, she'd also sharpened her skills as a portrait painter and increased her confidence in her own abilities. But all too soon, she discovered that the market for portraiture in Paris had dried up. Especially for foreign female artists. Without a viable alternative, she'd decided to head to London, where the few pounds she had left were still worth something.

Leaving Paris though had been difficult. For starters, Julie had kicked up an enormous fuss. Desperate to finish the school year with all her friends, she'd pleaded with Stella to allow her to stay. Because it was only for two months, Stella reluctantly agreed. But then there was a scramble to organise the right kind of accommodation for Julie in a *pension de famille*. Thankfully, this gave Stella very little time to fret about her impending separation from her daughter.

On the day of her departure, saying good-bye yet again to Julie was gut wrenching. And just thinking about it now on her bunkbed makes her teary. She sighs and rolls onto her back. She knows she's often plagued by melancholy whenever she's at sea, but this time it's different. This time she's leaving behind a place she truly loves, and the possibility of returning was highly unlikely. London may be offering her a better future, but it won't ever hold a candle to Paris – with its glorious golden light. Its physical loveliness had fed her soul. Paris had panache and leisurely Sunday lunches and conversations with friends.

It had taken her into its arms and taught her how to live and to love. It guided her eyes to see beauty and appreciate the importance of proportion and harmony.

Becalmed by these memories, she finally drifts off to sleep.

London is as she'd expected. The weather's foul, and the food is appalling. But her friends are marvellous. They rally around her – all of them supportive, kind and true. Especially her two oldest and dearest friends. With them, she can be completely herself. They help her settle in by finding her accommodation and offers of work. But most of all, they each provide a sympathetic ear. The morning she arrives, Phyllis insists she stay at her place for as long as she wants. And it's like old times when Mop drops by the following day.

'Now I don't want to see a single crumb left on either one of your plates,' says Phyllis, passing around a platter of corned beef and pickle sandwiches.

'I don't think I'll find that too hard to achieve,' says Stella.

'No problems here either,' says Mop, 'but then I'm eager to hear how Ford reacted to the news of you moving to England. I bet he didn't like the idea.'

Phyllis pours more tea while Stella swallows the last of her sandwich. 'Oh my God, you should've seen the performance he put on. He started by saying he never would've agreed to a separation if he'd known I'd take Julie away from him.'

Phyllis looks at Mop and rolls her eyes.

'Of course I told him I'd never intended to leave France, but I simply couldn't afford to stay in Paris anymore. I also promised him I'd do everything in my power to make sure he and Julie remained close. But he took absolutely no notice. He stormed and raged and paced the room, claiming Julie would forget her French and that I was cruel to uproot a child from a school she loved, a school where she was thriving, to plant her in some third-rate Protestant institution in London.'

She pauses. Her friends look shocked. Phyllis breaks the silence. 'I can't believe he said that!'

'Well, he did. But he didn't finish there. He then asked me if I realised how rudimentary Julie's understanding of English truly was and how awfully difficult it was going to be for her to adjust socially and educationally.' She takes a sip of her tea. 'Thankfully, I was able to stay calm because I'd already spent a lot of time torturing myself about the effects this move might have on Julie, without him pouring on more guilt.'

'Good for you!' cries Mop.

'Yes, but I still thought it best to let him air all his grievances without interruption. And up until that point, I could see why he said those things. What came next though was entirely different. He said he'd never suspected me of being cunning and conniving, but that he should have suspected something was amiss when, of all things, I'd cut Julie's hair!'

'What?' Phyllis starts to laugh. 'So what did he mean? That he preferred it long and expected you to ask his permission first?'

'God only knows! But he used that to argue that Julie needed to spend the entire summer break with him to experience reality in Toulon. He then proceeded to launch into a general attack on my negligence as a mother for allowing her to gain weight.' Stella takes another sip of tea. 'You know, he actually implied I'd bullied her into believing she was ugly and clumsy and that's why he thinks she walks with a stoop!'

'What in heaven's name is wrong with the man?' Mop's voice is indignant. But she sees Stella is about to cry so she moves closer to her and takes her hand in her own.

'Don't worry, I ended up giving as good as I got. I told him I was aware that Julie was putting on weight but that I didn't wish to make a fuss about it; that she'd reached that awkward age of adolescence and if it became a problem, I'd see about it. I also reminded him that after years of worry and harrowing financial insecurity, I was determined to build a new life and environment for Julie so that she would become acquainted with family life and with people who had honourable standards of conduct and that in my opinion moving to England would only make that even more possible.'

'Well, that would've put him back in his box!' says Phyllis, cutting three large wedges of Victoria sponge.

'And then I told him he could forget having Julie for the entire summer vacation because I'd like her to spend some of her free time with me as well.'

'That's splendid!' says Mop. 'You weren't aggressive, but you stood up for yourself. I think that's cause for a little celebration, don't you?' And without waiting for a response, she reaches into her handbag and pulls out a bottle of gin.

Over the next few months, Margaret, who was by now very well-connected to the Labour movement, introduces Stella to several notable people, who commission her to paint their portraits, and these in turn lead to other commissions, as was the case in America. At the same time, thanks to Phyllis, she manages to enrol Julie into a progressive school in Hampstead, right by the heath, where she will follow an individualised curriculum that includes lots of outdoor exercise. It seems the perfect place for her daughter to absorb English. What's more, the school offers Stella a reduction in fees.

But the Depression makes sure her anxiety about money continues. That is, until Aylmer, now editor of the News Chronicle, hires her to write a weekly review of London's art exhibitions, called 'Round the Galleries'. Before she accepts the job, she warns Aylmer that she has little affinity with the contemporary British art scene. 'It's so different from my own style,' she says. 'I've always strived to create in my work an intense emotional response in the viewer.'

'And don't you think I'm aware of that? I know you're a traditionalist and considered unfashionable by some, but that's precisely why I think you're perfect for the position.'

That silences further doubts, but it gives Stella pause for thought. She decides to write under the pseudonym Palette, signalling yet again her place in the world. Not as an art critic, but as an artist. In galleries she looks for what pleases her eye. In her column she explains why she prefers Cézanne over Renoir and why she admires Bonnard and likes the work of Vanessa Bell,[23] which is free, fluid and glowing. And with every review, Stella's voice grows in confidence.

To her surprise, she likes the job. It not only gives her time to paint, time she needs while working towards an exhibition in Birmingham, but the regular income also provides her with stability. It allows her to put food on her table, which, in a country plagued by widespread unemployment, is heaven-sent.

Nevertheless, she's becoming more and more fearful. A sense of impending doom is sweeping across Europe. A civil war is raging in Spain. Sir Oswald Mosley, the leader of the British Union of Fascists, is becoming increasingly popular throughout the country. And Nazi Germany looks set to expedite its expansionist agenda. Stella is not alone in thinking that another war is inevitable.

goodbyes

It's early summer and Stella is sitting in the window recess of their hotel room looking down over the sun-lit port of Honfleur. She's waiting for Julie to return from visiting her father. They've been in France for six days now, having crossed the Channel as soon as they could after receiving a cable from Janice that Ford was gravely ill, and that Julie should come quickly.

Neither of them had been surprised by the news. Both were aware he had heart problems. Eighteen months ago, Julie had spent Christmas with him in Paris, and she couldn't help but notice how he was struggling with his health, especially when there were days he couldn't even walk unaided. But things seemed to improve for a

---

23. **Vanessa Bell**, née Stephen: (1879 - 1961) English painter & interior decorator, member of the Bloomsbury set & the sister of Virginia Woolf.

while after Ford was awarded an Honorary Doctorate of Comparative Literature from Olivet College in Michigan, and he and Janice moved to the States.

Then two weeks ago, he had written to tell Julie that he was about to return; that he missed France terribly. But he became so sick on the voyage back, that when their ship docked in Le Havre, Janice thought it best they stay put. Thankfully, she'd been able to find a small apartment across the Seine estuary in Honfleur, where she could get some medical assistance.

Stella checks the time on her watch: 4 o'clock. It's getting late. She wonders what's keeping her daughter. She should have been back by now. Not that she's worried about her safety per se. Julie's perfectly capable of looking after herself. She's blossomed since leaving school, thanks to the two years she's spent studying stage and costume design. And now, instead of enjoying the last few weeks of her final term at Michel St Denis' London Theatre Studio, she's here spending all day at her father's bedside, while at night she cries herself to sleep beside her mother in their hotel room's huge, mahogany sleigh bed. It's distressing to say the least.

The first day in Honfleur had been different. That morning Stella had gone with her daughter to Ford's apartment. A misty rain was drifting down between the buildings that lined the cobbled street. When Janice had answered their knock, she embraced them warmly. But it was clear to the two older women that Julie was intent on seeing her father immediately. They watched as she hurried towards the adjoining room, the air heavy with sickness. Stella had remained behind and after quickly exchanging pleasantries, came right to the point. 'Do you think he'd like to see me?'

'I don't know,' said Janice, without hesitation. 'But I'll ask him.'

'Thank you. Just send word back with Julie. I'll make myself scarce today. But tell me – how is he?'

'He's a terrible patient, as you probably know. But even so, he's very weak and in a lot of pain. I really do believe he's dying, Stella.' There were tears in her eyes.

'I'm sure you're doing everything that's humanly possible.' Stella squeezed Janice's hand. And as she moved to go, added: 'If there's anything I can do to assist you, in any way, you'll let me know, won't you?'

'Of course.'

Later that day, when Julie returned to the hotel, she had been all smiles and optimism. 'Oh, I think he's going to get better,' she said in a rush of joy. 'He was so happy to see me. He sat up in bed and held my hand, and we chatted away for ages. Of course, he had lots of little naps, but he took some soup and ate a small omelette for lunch. Which made Janice awfully pleased. And yes, I almost forgot. He told me he's been writing. So I think if he can still do that, he's going to be fine.'

'That's wonderful news, my darling.'

'He's really pleased to be back in France too. Said it was the only place he wanted to live because, against all odds, it was still the most civilised country in the world. I thought he sounded a bit like you then.'

Stella had laughed. 'Well, I think we should take full advantage of your father's recommendation, don't you? And see if we can find a little bistro near the water and have ourselves a feast of *moules à la crème* for dinner this evening. How does that sound to you?'

And that was precisely what they had done.

Back at the hotel much later that night, as they were preparing for bed, Julie had removed a note from her pocket. 'Oh goodness me,' she said, handing a small, neatly folded piece of paper to her mother, 'I almost forgot to give you this. It's from Janice.'

Stella read the message twice then refolded it and put it in her handbag. Its meaning couldn't have been plainer. Janice had asked Ford if he wanted to see Stella, and he'd answered by saying he was too sick to care about such matters, and his answer was no. Stella had accepted his response. For almost five years now they'd not been on speaking terms. For Julie's sake, she'd wanted at least to maintain the veneer of friendship between them, but that had been impossible. There'd been too many arguments and an awful lot of spite. When arrangements needed to be made about Julie, it was Janice she wrote to, and it was Janice who replied.

When Stella turned off the bedside lamp, their room snapped into darkness. 'I think, while you're visiting your father tomorrow,' she'd said, lying on her back beside her daughter, 'I'll do some sketching around the harbour.'

'That's a good idea,' said Julie, the bedsprings creaking as she kissed her mother's cheek goodnight.

But since then, their evenings together had not been so cheery. While Julie spent each day watching over a frequently delirious Ford, Stella sketched the tall, slender houses along the Quai Sainte-Catherine with their timber frames and slate roofs. She loved the way the light walked with her down the narrow streets and laneways, heralded by the cries from seagulls sweeping overhead. But she'd hated returning to the hotel, knowing her daughter may return to her even more upset than the day before.

Stella glances at her watch again. An hour has gone by. She scans the scene from the window, searching for any sign of her daughter. And then she sees her - hurrying along the quai.

As soon as Julie enters the room, she apologises for being late and after removing her jacket, pulls over a small armchair near the bay window where her mother is sitting. 'He'd been delirious most of the day, and I just couldn't leave him. But then when I decided that there was no point in staying any longer and I may as well come back here, he seemed to come to.'

'So how are you, darling?'

'I'm fine. But I don't think he's ever going to get better. Well, not in that apartment he won't.'

'Why? What's wrong with it? It looked fine to me.'

'But you barely got past the entrance. It's a bit like the Villa Paul – externally very beautiful with a great view, but with no conveniences whatsoever. It makes the simplest thing, like fetching water, an ordeal. And Papa, poor darling, is in so much pain, what good is a view to him now?'

'So you think he'd be better off in a hospital?'

Julie shakes her head. 'I really don't know. You see this morning when I first got there, he was sitting up in bed and he seemed so much better than he had been these last few days. He was really pleased to see me and he held my hand and kissed my fingers one by one and told me he loved me over and over again. That's when I realised that he knows he's dying. And then he told me he didn't care that I'd turned my back on the Catholic Church, that all he wanted was for me to be happy.' She pauses, takes a deep breath, exhales slowly then continues. 'He was exhausted after saying all this and went to sleep for a while, but then the pain came back, and he was crying out, and it was unbearable to hear and see. That's when Janice called for the local doctor again. And I can't tell you what a useless, horrible, little man he is. He took one look at Papa and told Janice that it was obvious Monsieur had done whatever he wanted all his life and there was nothing he could do for him now.'

'Oh dear. That's really quite shocking.'

'Yes, Janice was very upset about it. But she sponged Papa down, which seemed to calm him a little. I decided to go then and when I bent down to kiss him goodbye, he gripped my hand and said he hoped my mother had a good hidey-hole in some lonely place in England's countryside because he didn't want me living in London when the Hun started bombing the city.'

As Julie's voice starts to break, Stella puts her arms around her daughter's shoulders and holds her while she weeps.

Stella wakes early next morning. For some time, she lies in the semi-darkness listening to the persistent, lonely cawing of a seagull. The air is cold on her face, but she can feel the bed-warmth of her sleeping daughter beside her. She's glad she'd asked her if she wanted to stay longer because she doesn't want her to have any regrets later.

But Julie was adamant. 'Oh no,' she said. 'We've been here a full week, and Papa understands that I must get back to finish my course. In fact, he thinks it very important I do so. That's why we said our goodbyes yesterday.'

Stella feels an immediate sense of relief for her daughter. As for herself, that's another matter. If Ford had agreed to see her, she would've liked to have salvaged some of the wreckage of their failed relationship, to be at least on speaking terms at the end. But that would never happen now.

A week after their return from France, Julie receives a letter from Janice telling her that after she'd left, Ford had rapidly deteriorated, often thinking in his delirium, he was back in the trenches. And so she'd decided to place him in a pleasant, little hospital in Deauville to be cared for by Franciscan nuns. She promised she'd write again soon, which she did four days later, after Ford had died in her arms.

author! author!

Stella starts getting fan mail not long after her book hit the shops in June of 1941. Some are from writers like Rebecca West and her old friend, Edith Sitwell. But the ones she loves the most are the ones from strangers. Like the man who wrote to say that he'd gone on a pilgrimage to visit – of all places – Coopers Cottage in Bedham. And the elderly lady, who'd sent her a stamped self-addressed envelope hoping Stella would respond to let her know what she and Julie had been doing since they'd moved out into the sticks.

The fact that so many people had taken the time to write to say they enjoyed the book proves to Stella that it had resonated on some elemental level with ordinary people. Which is precisely what she'd hoped for. She considers it a vindication of sorts, that she'd been right to craft her life story without deliberate untruths or distortions of facts. Yes, there were a few evasions, but she's happy enough with that. Weren't some truths better left unnarrated?

Still, it's funny how she'd never considered writing her memoirs until just after Ford died when she was offered a £100 advance to do just that. Desperate for money, she had no choice but to accept. The war had just started. No one was commissioning portraits. She couldn't even afford to pay rent anymore in London.

But not for one moment did she kid herself. If it hadn't been for Ford and the life they'd shared, such an offer would never have been made. It was clear what her publishers expected of her. They wanted the pleasure and play of Paris, the Latin Quarter and stories of *la vie de bohème*. She knew, as did they, that there'd never again be anything like Paris in the Twenties. And although she aimed to please, she wasn't about to serve up a tale of unscrupulous tittle-tattle. There was no way she was ever going to demean her relationship with Ford or sully his name. He had enriched her life. So while acknowledging his faults, she took responsibility for the choices she'd made. After all, she and Ford had once been very much in love. That fact needed to be made.

And she also had her daughter to consider and her own self-respect to uphold. And as for using her memoir to settle old scores with other people, that simply was not her style. She'd leave that sort of wilful spitefulness to others, for she'd long embraced Ford's maxim to do what you want in life but take what you get for doing it. There would be no place for bitterness or complaints about her life in her book.

After she and Julie moved near the little hamlet of Purleigh in Essex, Stella had begun to write. For a modest sum, they'd rented an apricot-washed brick cottage called Green End, with a garden of fruit trees, wild berries and masses of roses. It was at the end of a little lane and with its high mansard roof and charming dormer window, it looked out upon the surrounding open farmlands. Stella filled it with all the furniture she'd collected over the years in France.

And even though Purleigh lay beneath the Luftwaffe's nightly flight path to London, Green End felt oddly safe and permanent - a quiet place to paint, to garden, to recall her past and of course to write. Thankfully, time had softened the edges of the pain Ford had caused her. And in the recounting of her memories, she curated her life in the way she and he had wanted it to be seen.

Naturally Stella is thrilled to hear that the initial 2,000 print run for Drawn from Life had completely sold out. The reviews too are glowing. What has appealed to critics most is her strong, clear voice, drawing her readers into her life and her thoughts and ideas. Had it not been for the war, it may have become a runaway success and put an end to Stella's financial struggles. But sadly, that is not to be. A desperate paper shortage makes it impossible for the publishers to reprint.

Still, thanks to the book, a couple of commissions come Stella's way, which force her to venture back to the city and face her fears of the relentless air-raid attacks. Luckily, she finds a small mews house to rent in Chelsea and by sub-letting the lower half of the flat, she's also able to retain her rural place of refuge.

As months go by, she moves back and forth between Green End and London with relative ease. And although the destruction she sees all around the city upsets her a great deal, she paints it, and discovers once again that when she immerses herself in her art, she grows less fearful. Somehow, by giving a classical shape and artistic design to the physical damage of war, she becomes less distressed by it.

In one of those paintings, The House Opposite, she depicts the effects of war in a view from a window. At first glance it looks like a peaceful domestic scene of a healthy potted pink primrose sitting on a windowsill bordered by billowing white lace curtains. But beyond those curtains lies a glimpse of the neighbouring bombed-out house, which is clearly uninhabitable.

Of course, Stella is aware that there isn't much demand for works such as this and so is surprised when Flight from Reason, a scene of buildings, monuments and statues destroyed by the Blitz, is sold for £15.50 to a high-ranking military officer after he sees it in a special wartime exhibition at Charing Cross. Even so, her income is still paltry. She subsidises what she earns from the occasional sale by teaching art to people with little drive and even less talent. There is little satisfaction there, but life for Stella is about to change.

As for Julie, when her hopes of finding work in the theatre had disappeared along with world peace, she decides to join the Army at the end of 1941. Because of her fluent French, she's given a post in London liaising with the Free French Forces. And it is through this work that she meets and falls in love with an American journalist and documentary film scriptwriter, Roland Loewe, who works on propaganda films for the Allies. They're married in February 1943, and Stella is delighted. She likes Roland very much and thinks he's a good match for her daughter. The couple set up house in a nearby rented flat, which means she can still see Julie as often as she likes.

Although it's the first time Stella has ever lived alone, it doesn't take long for her to appreciate her new-found domestic independence. She now has room to create a little studio in her Chelsea flat. Then she receives word that Louis McCubbin,[24] director of the Art Gallery of South Australia, who's already purchased her painting Embankment Gardens for the gallery, has been instrumental in her being recommended to the Australian War Memorial as an Official War Artist in England. She is fifty years old and in accepting this role she must agree that all her paintings during the term of her appointment will become the property of the Australian government. For this, she will be given a uniform with the honorary rank of captain and receive fourteen guineas a week plus allowances. She couldn't be happier.

painting ghosts

Stella hurries along the Strand. She loves this part of London but there's no time to window shop today. She has an appointment with the Admiral at 10am sharp in his office at the Australian High

---

24. **Louis Frederick McCubbin**: (1890 - 1952) Eldest son of artist, Frederick McCubbin and a WWI artist himself. As director of the Art Gallery of South Australia 1936-1950, he revitalized it through his many innovations and significant acquisitions, particularly in relation to Australian art.

Commission. As she passes King's College, she can see that a part of the building is still cordoned off from the public – another casualty of the Blitz. But she has no intention to fixate on that. Today of all days, it's important to stay calm and positive.

At the entrance to Australia House, she's greeted by a uniformed security officer, who checks her papers. 'Everything's in order, Captain,' he says, 'and if you'd like to follow me, I'll show you upstairs to the Admiral's office. I know he's expecting you.'

'I can't tell you how lovely it is to hear another Australian accent,' she answers, smiling. 'I almost feel I'm back home.'

'Well, in a way you are, Ma'am. Everything you see around you – the marble, the timber, the stone – all of it comes from Australia. Just like me and you.' And his laughter echoes down the corridor.

As Stella sets up her sketch pad and pencils, Admiral Sir Ragnar Colvin sits back in his dark wooden chair, a huge map of Australia on the wall behind him and tells her a little about himself. He's been a long-serving British naval officer and in 1937 was made head of the Royal Australian Navy. Unfortunately, when he had a patch of bad health, he had to return to England and was appointed the Naval Advisor to the Australian High Commission. 'And so, Captain Bowen, I consider it a great honour that the government of Australia should want a portrait painted of me.'

Stella relaxes a little. He isn't as intimidating as she'd imagined. 'Well, let's hope I don't disappoint them or you.'

'I'm sure that won't happen,' he says, then falls silent as Stella takes up her pencil. She senses his sincerity. But he's also very tense. A difficult, complex subject to be sure. Even though he seems serious and world-weary with his right elbow resting on his chair's armrest so his large hand can cradle his head, his left hand is a fist, resting on his lap. This is a man who is strong and determined - a man who's not about to give up.

She decides she'll include the map in her portrait. Australia is where his heart and his concerns are. That's what she wants to capture.

Since the Japanese bombed Darwin and then the battle in the Coral Sea, Australia's fear of imminent invasion is very real. She knows from Tom's letters that the entire civilian population is conscious of the country's isolation. And she can tell Admiral Colvin is aware of that too.

'I don't want to rush you,' he says looking at his watch, 'but I do have another meeting shortly.'

'I think I've got what I want. Would you like to take a peek?' Stella stands up and places three sketches on the desk facing the admiral. She waits.

'I say, I'm extremely impressed. They actually look like me.' He's beaming.

'Thank you, sir. I'm always relieved to hear that. You see, I'm intrigued by the human face. Always have been and when I paint someone's portrait, I try to drag out the heart and soul of that person and reproduce what they stand for, what they're feeling and thinking at that given moment in time onto my canvas. For me, anything else would be utterly false and untrue.'

'Well, I'm looking forward to seeing the finished product.' He rises to his feet. 'So what happens now?'

'I'll take these back to my studio with the notes I've made and hopefully produce something everyone will be pleased with. If I need you to sit again for me, which I think is very unlikely, I'll let you know.' As Stella gathers up her sketches, the admiral asks if she has any questions. She raises her head. 'As a matter of fact Sir, I do.'

Colvin doesn't move. 'Well, go right ahead, Captain.'

'I know I've been attached to the RAAF but I'm wondering when I might be posted somewhere.'

'That all depends on when you finish the portraits of me and of Air Chief Marshal Burnett.'

'Oh, that's very good, Sir,' says Stella. 'That won't be long then.'

A few minutes later she's walking back along the Strand.

Throughout the night of 27 April 1944, one Lancaster bomber after another thunders down the runway of Binbrook Station, the home to Australia's 460 Squadron, and then disappears into the dark night. They're headed for Friedrichshafen, an important German industrial town on the northern shoreline of Lake Constance. Next morning, well before dawn, most of the old town centre has been destroyed.

Back in Lincolnshire, Stella is in the canteen of the interrogation hut with a couple of officers of the Women's Auxiliary Air Force, whom she's befriended. They are quietly waiting, like everyone else, for the crews to return. Tea, hot cocoa, rum, cigarettes and biscuits are at the ready for the men when they come in. All eyes though are on the clock, and everyone is counting the names as the pilot of each crew enters the hut and writes the name of each of his men on the blackboard.

But as the sun rises, Squadron Leader Jarman has not yet appeared. When Stella is told Jarman's plane has been reported missing, she's too numb for tears. She hadn't expected her initiation into military life to be so grim. For over a week now, she's been working on preliminary sketches of all seven members of Jarman's crew. None of them had shown the slightest bit of interest in her drawing them. But that's what she'd liked about them – their youth, their vitality, and their natural reticence to stand in the limelight. To them, sitting for a group portrait was downright foolishness. There was a war to be won, and they had work to do preparing for their next flight.

When all hope dies that their aircraft will be found, Stella sets to work. These missing men were her lads, and she's determined to honour their bravery if it's the last thing she'll do. Her thoughts race back to her trip to Italy with the Pounds. Back to Fra Angelico and especially Giotto, who knew a thing or two about group portraits. She had experimented with their techniques when she'd done the triptych of the Lavignes and their restaurant. But this painting will be more ambitious, even though she feels like she's painting ghosts.

So with the initial drawings she's done of each of them and some official photos as well, she goes back to London to finish what she's started. She had already formulated a conceptual framework for the group portrait and she huddles the men together in the centre of the canvas. With their uniforms, parachute vests, helmets, and oxygen masks, she will unify them into a single identity. But she also wants each airman's individual humanity to be obvious, and the only way she knows how this can be done is by highlighting their fresh and vulnerable faces. She's glad that when she'd sketched them back at the barracks, she'd observed each of their unique facial features closely, just as Giotto might have done. But unlike her beloved quattrocento artists, who used the wings of angels to hover symbolically above the heads of their subjects, Stella paints a Lancaster bomber as an ominous black metal bird of prey instead.

The irony isn't lost on Stella that having been a pacifist during the First World War, she is now an official recorder of Australia's participation in the Allied cause. Concerned that her intentions with this, her first painting in the field for the War Memorial, may be misinterpreted, she decides to show it to Julie and Roland as soon as it's finished to see what they think.

'I've called it Bomber Crew,' she says, pivoting the easel towards them. 'And I'd like you to give me your honest opinions. Please?'

Several minutes pass as the pair look closely at the picture. 'One thing's for sure,' says Roland, 'it's incredibly moving. Even if you don't know that this crew didn't return, you can tell they're all casualties. You can see it in their eyes.'

'I agree. I think it's quite extraordinary, Mum. They're together but alone. And even though they've witnessed the terrible reality of war, they must keep fighting. There's something noble about that. But what about you? Are you happy with it?'

Stella's mouth forms a gentle smile. 'Oh yes, very happy. But I must admit to wondering what your father would've thought.'

'I think he'd be proud of you.'

Over the next few months, Stella works tirelessly. She's stationed for a time at the Pembroke Dock base in Wales and paints airmen coming ashore after being on patrol in their Sunderland flying boats. And she has a brief stint as a radio broadcaster for the BBC Pacific Service, Calling Australia, giving informal reports about her war work and life in general in England. She later spends some bitterly cold winter months in icy Nissan huts at the Driffield station in Yorkshire. And although the conditions of the barracks aren't altogether comfortable, she enjoys the camaraderie of her fellow officers, who accept her for what she is – an artist.

When in May 1945 the war ends in Europe, the War Memorial, pleased with her work, extends her appointment to recreate scenes of the repatriation of prisoners of war in convalescent hospitals and at Gowrie House in Eastbourne in Sussex. Although she's happy, she has noticed she's often extremely tired. Even after a good night's sleep, she wakes in the morning feeling drained of all energy. Obviously, she needs a holiday. But there's no time for that just yet. There's still work to be done. Only the other day, she chose to paint a portrait of a young POW.

In his khaki slouch hat with its leather strap positioned perfectly on the jut of his cleft chin, he's unmistakably Australian. The Rising Sun badges on the collar of his uniform are an unnecessary confirmation of his war service. Stella positions him at an angle with a three-quarter view of his head. She paints the background bright red with a slap-dash brush. It's there as a contrast - it's not the main event. The mood, the action is in his handsome face. And the big, brown eyes with their sad, faraway stare tell his story.

This indigenous Australian soldier must have seen things he wished he hadn't. But Hitler had to be stopped. There was no doubt about that. But after seeing so many of his mates killed and having years stolen from his life in a stalag, he must have wondered if it had all been worthwhile.

Stella simply calls the painting Private, Gowrie House.

green end

So this is it. She has been given notice to quit. And there's nothing much she can do about it. Except perhaps dry her tears and enjoy the time she has left, hopefully avoiding the kind of cruel and painful death that Ford had to suffer. What she hopes for is a more courageous, gentle end, one faced with composure and dignity. But there are plenty of things she needs to do before that day arrives.

Obviously, visiting Australia is now out of the question. And she's sad about that. Ever since she'd written her book, she'd thought a great deal about the land she'd left behind over thirty years ago. And despite Ford always saying that his country was anywhere artists and writers lived, she'd never really embraced that idea. How could she sever ties with her homeland when quite a few artists and writers she'd met in Europe made her feel excluded because she was a woman and a colonial one at that?

On meeting so many young Australians as a War Artist, she'd listened to their recollections of an Australia, which were very different from her own. And she'd started wondering if she'd preserved Australia in her mind like some kind of egg in aspic, when in fact it had changed. Or was it a case of her never fully knowing it in the first place? Gowrie House, in particular Private David Harris, had sown that seed of doubt.

The former POW had only just arrived at the repatriation centre prior to his embarkation to Australia when she'd caught sight of him in the reception lounge. He looked a little lost, so she offered him a cup of tea and struck up a conversation.

He told her he'd been badly wounded back in May 1941 in Crete and had been in a Casualty Clearing House when the Germans took him prisoner. He'd ended up in some terrible stalag in Silesia, where he spent the rest of the war. He didn't say much else. And Stella hadn't wanted to draw him out. His eyes looked dead. That's why she was surprised when he agreed to sit for her.

And while he offered up his face, naked and unselfconscious, she painted. Yet while she painted him, he never uttered a word. Nor did she, which was unusual for her. But when she'd finished, he asked her not to put his name on the picture, saying there was nothing special about him and that's the way he liked it. 'I'm just one of the ones who made it back alive,' he said. 'All I want to do is get back to Perth, to go home. Don't you want to do that too?' Then he smiled and warmed the room.

'Yes, I would love to do that,' she said. And meant it.

She'd never met an Aboriginal Australian before but a thread of connection with her homeland began to take hold. A visit was long overdue. And yes, yes, she wanted to see Tom again. But she also wanted to reacquaint herself with her country in every way possible.

From that point on she started to make plans to return to Adelaide, and even her diagnosis of colon cancer the previous year with weeks of extreme pain and discomfort post-surgery, hadn't weakened her resolve. Once she knew Canberra had received her last commission of the Victory Day Parade, making a total of forty-six paintings and drawings for the War Memorial, Stella applied for repatriation. When that was knocked back on account of her being appointed in England, rather than in Australia, she investigated other ways of financing the trip.

After several articles in various Australian newspapers sparked public interest in her work, the idea of mounting a touring exhibition was suggested. But too many prohibitive customs duties and government sales taxes on works of art being brought into the country quashed that proposal.

Thankfully, it doesn't take long for Stella to realise there's no use mulling over what isn't meant to be. It's time to put her house in order, time to prepare for the inevitable. But first she will have to tell Julie.

Not for nothing is the winter of 1947 named the Big Freeze. And on the icy January night when Stella tells her daughter she has breast and liver cancer, Julie howls like the wild storm outside. Eventually, Stella's composure quietens her. 'Darling, you must be sensible about this. My cancer is incurable and no matter what I do, I'll be dead by the end of the year. So I either subject my renegade body to further medical interventions that may – and do take note of that word may – prolong my life by a few weeks, or I can simply choose to have pain relief and take advantage of every moment I have left.'

Julie moves closer to her mother. 'It's just that I love you so much, I can't imagine life without you.'

Stella wraps her daughter in her arms. 'I know it's hard. I never wanted this either. And because you mean the world to me, I'd imagined a much longer life for myself too – one that would always be close to you. But it's not to be. And crying isn't going to change a thing. The only thing we can control is the way we spend the remaining time I have left. So let's have no more tears, aye?'

Wiping away her tears with the back of her hands, Julie tries to sound cheerful. 'I'll do my best.'

'Good. And there's one more thing I'd like you to do. I want you to promise me that when I'm gone, there'll be no fuss, no funeral nonsense, thank you very much. Just go and have a drink somewhere and raise a glass to me.'

By April, winter has worn itself out. Wanting to watch the roses bloom, Stella decides not to renew her lease on her place in Chelsea, as she'd prefer to live out what remains of her life in the serenity of Green End. No matter how tired she feels, she loves sitting outside on the old stone bench, that stands between two of her cottage windows. There she can take in the joy of her garden, which is a blaze of colour and loud with the buzzing of bees. Its profusion of flowers – dahlias, peonies, hollyhocks, and jasmine – some scented, some not, enliven her. And she needs and wants that feeling to continue. For Julie is pregnant and with the baby due in October, Stella's one wish is for her not to die before her grandchild is born.

She also doesn't lack for company at Green End. There's always someone visiting - be it her doctor or a friend. And thanks to Phyllis and Julie, who'd volunteered to take turns to tend to all her needs, Stella is as content as she can be. She even starts work on a still life of summer flowers that she's promised to do for Keith and Theaden.[25]

It is Phyllis, who spends August with her in Green End. But within the first few days of her stay Stella appears to be floating away in a morphine haze. The doctor is called and adjusts her dose. Thankfully Stella's equilibrium is restored relatively quickly. Just in time for Mop to join them for a week.

'Welcome to my impermanent home,' cries Stella in a burst of joy as Mop steps through the door, carrying a rather large leather portmanteau.

'You haven't lost your sense of humour, I see.'

'No, thank God. But I have lost some weight.' Stella's brown eyes are laughing. 'I can't tell you how delighted I am to see you, dear friend.'

'Now don't get all sentimental on us please,' says Phyllis. 'Margaret's brought champagne.'

'Well, we should open it right away because I might fall asleep soon and I don't trust either of you to save some for me.'

'Bloody charming!' Phyllis says, laughing now. 'I'll get the glasses and some ice, if you two wouldn't mind sorting out some music so we can have ourselves a little party.'

Except for Stella taking a nap after lunch each day, their time together begins this way and changes very little over the ensuing week. Remarkably, the weather is mostly fine, and the cottage fills with the warmth of long-term friendship. The three women move about together with ease. They talk and laugh, eat and drink.

---

25. [William] **Keith Hancock:** (1898 - 1988) was a prominent Australian historian, who received two knighthoods for his contributions to history in both Australia & Britain. His first wife, Australian **Theaden Hancock** née Brocklebank (1897 - 1960) was a producer with the Pacific service of the BBC during WWII - a rare position for any woman at that time. It was she who arranged for Stella Bowen to record talks for Australian audiences.

One evening, they decide to sit in the parlour, listen to records and do some serious reminiscing. Mop puts 'Cheek to Cheek' on the gramophone, and as soon as the elegance of Fred Astaire's voice fills the air, Stella rises to her feet and grabs Phyllis by the hand. Together they dance gently around the room while Mop watches on, amused.

'Oh, that was wonderful. I haven't danced for such a long time,' says Stella, collapsing back onto the sofa. 'And whenever I dance, I can't help thinking of Ford.' She looks wistful and is a little out of breath. Her friends exchange furtive glances but before either of them says a word, Stella continues. 'You know, I'm still awfully proud of my connection with him.'

And so she tells them how grateful she is for the years she'd spent with him. She speaks of the heady glory of their beginning and having the company of such a man, such a mind. 'I can't put a price on that,' she says. 'I don't regret any of it. He enlarged my understanding of the world, which in turn led to my understanding of myself. And what's more, all my experiences with him steered me towards making art. I can think of no greater gift, can you?' She looks at her friends, who both seem teary.

'There were times,' says Mop, steadying her voice, 'when Ford irritated me immensely. I have to tell you, Stella, I sometimes worried about you because he was such an outrageous flirt and oh, when he put on those airs and started telling those whopping lies of his –'

'Yes, but they were harmless and meant to be entertaining. They were just part of his imaginative life,' Stella says and waits for a response.

Again, Mop breaks the silence. 'Of course. Did I ever tell you that I once heard someone say that Ford's conversation was like caviar?'

'Must've been a poet who said that,' says Phyllis. 'It always struck me that beneath Ford's exterior was a deeply empathetic man.'

'Please don't get me wrong, I'm not such a fool to think Ford had no faults. And I can't deny he hurt me deeply,' says Stella, her voice a little croaky. 'But I've had plenty of time to think about falling in and out of love and like I said in my book, it's completely unacceptable the way girls are raised to believe that the road to happiness is to follow the dictates of their hearts, when they should be taught to stand on their own two feet. Nothing is secure in this world. So yes, by all means, fall in love, but be sure you understand that nothing stays the same forever.'

There's a momentary pause. 'God, I'm going to miss you,' says Phyllis, blinking back tears.

'Me too,' says Mop.

'In case I forget,' Stella's voice is quiet now. 'Thank you for helping me arrange my cremation in Golders Green. It's one less thing Julie will have to do. And I also want you to know, in case you don't already, that I love you both very much.'

Later that night, Stella falls asleep thinking about all the writers, painters, poets, philosophers, and mad men and women she'd met in her life and marvels at the complexity and beauty of them all.

But come September, she rarely leaves her bed. And it is there in early October, that Julie places her new-born baby in her mother's arms. 'Here is your grandson,' she says. 'We're going to call him Julian.'

Stella studies his face. 'He's perfect.'

Phyllis, who's standing on the other side of the bed, suggests they all wet the baby's head. 'Shall I fetch the champagne?'

Stella smiles and nods, then turns to Julie. 'I'm sorry I'll never get to mind him but at least I've had the chance to hold him, which is a wonderful thing.'

Just as they'd planned, Phyllis pours a small glass of champagne and holds it out for Stella to take a sip. Instead, she dips her finger into the bubbly liquid, dabs it on the baby's lips and whispers: 'This is for luck, my darling boy.'

Three weeks after the birth of her grandson, Stella, surrounded by the gentle balm of loving voices, drifts off to sleep and never wakes again.

Part Nine

December 2019

Rigid with shock, I had no voice, no words. I wanted to run but doubted my feet were up to the task. When asked later, I wasn't able to say how long I'd been standing there, taking it all in, unconsciously committing to memory the hideous, heartbreaking truth of it: Antoine ridiculous with his chinos around his ankles and his mouth agape like one of those rotating clown heads waiting to be fed a ball in sideshow alley; and Ange, definitely nothing angelic there, with her cold, deadpan stare, no doubt enjoying my discomfort, while waiting for me to say something. Which wasn't going to happen. Not then. Not there.

It wasn't meant to be like that. When I'd rushed downstairs to the studio, all loved up with the positive pregnancy test in my pocket, I'd envisaged an encounter very different from the one I received. It should've been just the two of us: a sort of intimate communion of souls in a long, euphoric embrace. Instead, I'd been hit by treachery. And while I watched the man I loved and the woman I'd thought was a friend scrambling to get dressed, I realised that my peerless, perfect life was being shown for the fantasy it truly was.

I felt broken and started to cry. Something Ange, far too self-contained for tears, would never do. The only thing she'd ever done with her eyes was to bat them at unsuspecting men. Not that I intended to lay blame for Antoine's duplicity at Ange's feet. Oh no, he'd have been a willing participant. And it was this that caused my heart to crack wide open. Especially now when I heard him call my name – once, twice. Saying he could explain everything. That it was all a terrible mistake.

That's when I turned round and made for the stairs. Once in my study, I locked the door and threw myself onto the couch beside my desk. Alone, I let myself howl. What a fucking fool I'd been - not to have seen this coming. I must've had my head completely up my arse. But then, how could I have guessed when only that morning, Antoine had been telling me how much he adored me, how he couldn't live without me, how I was the love of his life. I'd never thought he'd cheat on me. And never considered him to be a liar either. But there you go! There was no doubting what I'd seen.

Once the room grew dark, I sat up and drying my tears, closed the blinds and switched on the desk lamp. I wondered how long the two of them had been having these little afternoon trysts and whether Sacha knew. One thing was certain: I had to work out what I was going to do. At least for the next few days. First though, I needed to disengage my heart from my head. I'd been handed the victim role, but there was no way I was going to play it.

At least I hadn't physically attacked Ange, so I was no Polyphemus. Nor was I a Jean Rhys or a Violet Hunt. And no matter how appealing it seemed, I had no intentions of publicly humiliating Antoine, either by writing a revenge memoir or denouncing him on Twitter. It was just not my style. But I didn't know what to do. I certainly couldn't stay in my study forever - that was for sure.

And then I heard Antoine tapping on my door. Please Neve, let me in. We need to talk. I love you, Neve. You must believe me.

I stood up. I'd have to face him sooner or later.

More knocking. *Tu peux m'entendre?*

Yes, I can hear you.

He looked dishevelled and almost surprised that I'd opened the door. An awkward silence followed while I waited for him to speak. Can we talk?

Yes.

He asked me if I wanted something to drink. He spoke softly, as if we were in hiding.

A cup of tea would be nice.

I followed him into the living room and sat down on the sofa while he rattled around in the kitchen. When he brought out the drinks: tea for me and a huge serving of Scotch for himself, I hoped it wasn't going to be a long night.

He pulled up a tub chair and sat opposite me, our knees almost touching. When he tried to put his free hand on my arm, I instinctively pulled away. Instead, he settled his eyes on mine. And so he began: I'm not going to lie to you. But please hear me out.

He waited a moment for my response. When none came, he continued: I'd gone to buy bread and just as I turned the corner near the little stationery shop, I bumped into Ange, so we went to the café for a drink and because it was lunchtime, we ordered some food.

Spare me the culinary details, I said.

Antoine put his head in his hands. I wondered if he was about to cry. Then thought perhaps it was all an act, hoping I'd fall for this display of repentance. He placed his hands back in his lap and then looked up at me, his eyes pleading for comfort. I opened my mouth to speak again but didn't make a sound. Seizing the moment, he continued: *Alors*, while we were eating, Ange told me she and Sacha were splitting up. She was very upset, and when we finished our wine, I invited her back to my studio for coffee. My first mistake.

I gave a little snort of disgust and folded my arms beneath my breasts. Undeterred, Antoine pushed on: While I made coffee, I told her she should go home and try to mend things with Sacha. I felt sorry for her. She was really distressed, so I hugged her and the next thing I knew…

I raised my right hand, prompting him to stop. I was tired. My breasts felt sore. And my heart was beginning to calcify. Please, I said. I don't need to hear the rest.

But will you forgive me? His voice was trembling.

You made a choice so now you must face the consequences.

Oh Neve, you make it sound like I did it on purpose. But it wasn't like that. I made no big decision. What happened, happened. If I could change that, I would. You know Ange means nothing to me. Nothing. And the feeling's mutual. She regrets this afternoon as much as I do.

And that makes it so much better?

He raised a hand to his forehead. Of course, it doesn't. You know what I mean.

I swallowed but said nothing.

Look, he said. Except for today, I've never been unfaithful to you. In fact, I've never even thought of being with another woman. And I promise you, it won't happen again. *Jamais. Jamais.* I love you, Neve. Only you. Just please give me another chance.

But I don't think I'll ever be able to trust you again.

You mean you're willing to throw away the last five and half years we've been together, just like that? He clicked his fingers.

I really don't know what I'm willing to do, I said, knowing how lame that sounded. I need time to think. It's been a long day, and I'm very tired.

Shall we have an early night then? He sounded eager, almost hopeful. Then quickly added: I'll heat up some soup if you like?

That'd be good, I said. Anything to stop him talking.

Later that evening, the opening news story covered the day's national strikes against President Macron's planned pension reforms with 350,000 people marching in Paris alone. It's likely, said the news reader, that these strikes will continue over Christmas. Sitting side by side on the sofa, Antoine and I ate our soup and watched TV in silence until the report from Australia stated that 17 December was the country's hottest day on record. A whacking 40.9°.

Oh god, I said, I should ring my mother. But I didn't move. I was mesmerised by the footage of what appeared to be the entire country in flames. There was mention of bushfires in the Blue Mountains and Sydney suffering from extremely hazardous levels of smoke. The report finished by stating that Australia was one of the most vulnerable major industrialised countries in the world to climate change.

That's when I rose to my feet and started tapping my phone. Antoine reached for the remote and shutting down the television, remained silent while I spoke to my mother. Although emotionally drained, I couldn't keep still. I walked around the room, talking, listening. Then finally I said: I'm coming. I'll get the first plane I can. Yes, we'll spend Christmas together.

Once the call was finished, I turned to Antoine, who now looked ashen and somewhat agitated. I told him I had to go home as if he'd heard nothing.

But this is your home, he said.

I didn't respond but noted his eyes of devotion.

He tried again: I'll come with you if you'd like me to.

No, that won't be necessary. I could see that my tone frightened him. But clinging to my self-respect by a very fine thread, I turned and started walking towards our bedroom.

You're not leaving me, are you? You will come back?

Can we have this conversation in the morning? I think we both need some sleep, don't you?

Next day, I felt and looked like shit. I hadn't slept much, having spent most of the night beside Antoine wrangling with the complexity of my emotions. Despite everything, I knew I still loved him. But deeply wounded by his betrayal, I felt vulnerable and a little afraid. I wished I could just forgive him and leave it at that and even wondered if I'd been at fault, that somehow I hadn't been enough for him. Or perhaps my mother had been right all along: that all talented, creative men were two-timing arseholes. I'd also wondered if by retelling Stella's story I'd re-wired my own emotional patterning. Stella had worshipped Ford and had indulged his pursuit of the label genius, so for quite a while, she'd put up with his infidelity, happy to live in the shadow of greatness, just as Hadley had done with Hemingway. Along with countless others like them.

But times had changed, and Antoine was nothing like these men. He was no narcissist. I'd never seen him flirt with other women, let alone emulate his father's attachment patterns. What's more, my life with Antoine looked nothing like Stella's had with Ford.

Just before dawn, I'd finally fell into a deep sleep. When I woke again, I'd forgotten the previous afternoon and almost hugged Antoine from behind, the way I often did upon waking. But thanks to a slender gap in the curtains, light from the morning outside entered the room and brought back the truth. At least he'd kept his promise not to touch me during the night. If he'd tried, I was pretty sure I wouldn't have been able to resist. But knowing that, didn't mean I'd have changed my mind about going to Australia. Of that I was certain. And so, with only the sound of his gentle snuffling snores beside me, I planned what I'd say to him over breakfast.

I wouldn't be mentioning my pregnancy. It was very early days and still quite possible I could miscarry. Besides, telling him could muddle things. What I'd say to him was that I was confused. No lie or cover up there. Yes, I did want to see my mother. It was the least I could do, especially now that Rachel, having downsized and moved to the Blue Mountains, seemed incredibly jittery on the phone about all the heat and smoke and bushfires. And most importantly, being away from Antoine for a few weeks would be an opportunity for me to figure things out. Surely, he would see the sense of that.

Rachel's newly renovated weatherboard cottage was an easy walk to the village of Springwood. Nevertheless, it took me a week before I braved the early morning menace of glowing orange smoke that was hanging over the Blue Mountains. I'd sleep-walked through my first few jet-lagged days back in Australia, but the allure of barista coffee from a local café was finally too strong to resist. And so each morning I walked to the village for my caffeine hit before the heat of the day made even that impossible.

But when cafés were firmly shut on Christmas day, I instead sat at the desk beneath the windowsill in my mother's front room and made do with Earl Grey tea. For a while I stared out at the light filled garden with its profusion of lemon-scented tea trees and its narrow, gravelled path that led to a white picket fence. Beyond that was the busy sweep of Hawkesbury Road which, according to Rachel, was once a trade-route of the Darug people, pre-dating European settlement by over 40,000 years. On the other side of the bitumen was the parched fairway of the local golf course.

My brain soon switched off this scene and instead ran through the events of the last two weeks. I'd hoped to have reduced my mother's fears of the fires by now. But that had proved impossible. When the huge Gospers Mountain fire crossed containment lines at Mount Wilson, and the Grose Valley had become a mega-blaze, Springwood and all the other Blue Mountains townships were placed on high alert. But what worried me most was seeing Rachel's vitality being leached away by time and osteoarthritis. My mother had always looked more youthful than her actual age. But not anymore. It was only when I told her that an ultrasound had confirmed I was eight weeks pregnant did she visibly brighten. Oh, how wonderful, she'd said. I'm going to be a grandma!

It all made for a reasonably pleasant Christmas Eve dinner. Until after dessert, when my mother, fuelled by a second bottle of wine, suddenly turned on me and demanded to know what was going on.

I don't know what you mean.

Rubbish! Please don't lie to me. Something's going on… I can feel it. I've waited all week for you to tell me what's wrong…but you've said nothing. You're not yourself. Sure, you're pregnant, but that should've made you deliriously happy. And where the hell is Antoine? Why didn't he come with you? Too busy tickling the ivories, is he?

That's unfair, I said, feeling the heat of her vitriol sprayed in my face.

Is that so? Then explain why that is.

And so it all came tumbling out – the pregnancy test, the betrayal and my own torment, trying to decide whether to forgive him and simply calling it quits.

Does Antoine know you're going to have a baby?

No, not yet.

Why not?

I couldn't think straight. I was hurt, angry, confused. I needed time to process everything because I knew that whatever I chose to do would define me and my future.

So with your headstrong dignity intact, you took flight, leaving behind all the dreams you'd shared together.

If you put it like that… I reached for her glass of mineral water and gulped down a mouthful. Then continued: Look, I wasn't being impulsive. If that's what you mean. Far from it. I figured if I put some distance between us, I might see more clearly. And I didn't want to be influenced by Paris…you know, everything looks so much better in France than anywhere else. And I knew we couldn't continue the way we were. It was all too raw.

What did Antoine think about you coming here?

He accepted it. He understood why I needed to get away and, of course, to see you. He wants me to forgive him and promises it will never happen again. (I was about to say he probably hopes you'll be a sobering influence but thought better of it.)

Do you still love him?

Without pausing, I told her I did. Because, I said, I know if we do split up for good, there'll always be a special place for him in my heart.

Rachel smiled. Oh, I'm so pleased to hear this because if what you say is true, it's going to be very easy for you to forgive him.

Really? What makes you say that?

Because if you love him, you'll be able to put aside your ego. You don't have to forget what happened, but you can forgive it. Sure, you're wounded by Antoine's infidelity, but if he's begging for forgiveness, he's wounded too. Both of you have been damaged by this but that doesn't mean you allow it to devour you. Life's too short for such foolishness.

I didn't respond straight away. I was letting my mother's words sink in. Several seconds passed, then: You know, I'm a bit dumbfounded by what you just said. It's such a turn-around. I mean, five years ago you were warning me about pinning all my hopes on one bloke. Remember?

Well, I was trying to be a good mother. Like I am now.

You've always been a good mother, I said, smiling.

Rachel stood up and walked around the table and placing an arm around my shoulders said: Then you won't mind me saying that no matter what you decide, I think you should tell Antoine as soon as you can that you're expecting his child. He has a right to know.

I squeezed her hand, recalling the time in my early teens when a teary Rachel had told me that only one of two men could've been my father. But she hadn't been able to contact either one of them. They'd both been one-night stands, and she only knew them by their first names – Keith and Larry. Not a lot to go on.

I'll call Antoine now, I said and picked up my phone.

I'll leave you to it, said Rachel, as she stacked some plates and moved towards the kitchen.

Fifteen minutes later, I was beside my mother at the sink, tea towel in hand.

Well, that was quick. Was he pleased with the news?

I didn't tell him.

What?

It was weird. He barely let me speak. I just said hello, and then he launched into this monologue about how much he missed me; that he couldn't bear it any longer; that he needed to see me, to convince me to take him back; that he was going to buy a ticket and be in Australia as soon as possible. He asked me if that was okay, and I said yes. He sounded happy then and told me he'd ring back as soon as he had details of the flight.

Did he say how long he intended to stay?

No. But I doubt he'll stay any longer than a week.

February 2020

Antoine arrived in Sydney, two days before the New Year. After an awkward embrace in the airport's Arrivals Hall, I hurried him into the passenger's seat of my mother's car. With the windows shut and the air-conditioner blasting, I headed west back along the motorway. The closer we came to the Blue Mountains, toxic fumes of ash and cremated eucalyptus leaves rose to greet us. Smells like the perfume of the apocalypse, Antoine said, then a moment later he asked if we'd have an opportunity to talk privately once we were at Rachel's place.

What's wrong with now?

I'd prefer your complete attention, he said.

Well, you'll get it, if you can wait till this afternoon. My mother's going to the movies with a friend.

Antoine smiled. That's great, he said.

And I was pleased. I'd planned this well. But still I was wary and hoped my expression looked suitably impassive. It felt strange having him sitting there beside me, each of us on the brink of change. My mind was racing ahead, thinking of future possibilities, and then bizarrely wondering if he'd noticed my breasts had grown larger.

There's something I need to tell you, I said, as soon as Rachel had left after lunch.

Oh no Neve, please don't, he said. Not yet. I really need to speak first. If you wouldn't mind, that is.

I said okay and suggested we move into the living room because it was so much more comfortable there. It was also very large and being at the rear of the house, its back wall was made of glass sliding doors that opened out onto a patio that extended to a camellia sasanqua hedge.

Très agréable, said Antoine, who settled himself on one of two long couches. I sat in the one facing his. Taking a deep breath, a surge of apologies and declarations of love began. I'd expected such statements but not the distraught delivery.

I've done a lot of thinking, he said, and I don't want to live a life without you in it. Every part of my being aches for you. What happened, happened. It's in the past. Which is now just a memory. It's not real. And as for the future, it's only as good as our imaginations will allow. Like your Stella Bowen said, the only reality is what's happening now. He paused briefly, then asked: Do you love me?

Of course, I bloody well do, I said, placing my right hand on my belly.

Good. Because I've got this idea. I've imagined a future where you've forgiven me and might even trust me again.

Well…

No, no, no, let me finish. For the past five years we've lived in France. How about the next five years we try living here in Australia?

Are you serious? I'd not expected this. What about your apartment? Your work? Your studio?

I can work anywhere. We'll visit Paris occasionally, but our life will mainly be here. What do you say?

As he moved to sit beside me, I was about to say that I'd be taking a big risk to stay with him, but he was leaning towards me, and I thought better of it. After all, life was full of risks. I felt his breath on my cheek and then his mouth reached mine. It was a long kiss. When his hand moved between my legs, I said his name softly, and we both knew then what my answer was.

The sex was quick. But I knew there'd be more to come, which there was, after I told him I was pregnant.

Mid-January the NSW Rural Fire Service announced that the Gospers Mountain megafire was at last contained. A communal sigh of relief was heard across the Blue Mountains. Antoine spent the month not only fine-tuning arrangements with Finn for his Liberté tour of Australia in April, but also purchasing a piano for my house in Newtown. When the current tenants moved out early February, Antoine and I moved in amid torrential rain up and down the coast.

As most fires were now extinguished, it seemed to us both that the gods had decided to smile upon us. Even news that a novel coronavirus had been discovered in Wuhan, China and was now appearing in the north of Italy didn't overly concern us. We both knew Antoine needed to return to Paris to wind things up back there and to organise shipment of his equipment and other belongings to Australia.

Don't worry, he told me the night before he was to fly out. I'll be back by the end of March at the very latest. I promise.

I'm not worried about you, silly. But what if this virus is as bad as some people think. I heard someone on the radio this morning saying that this might be the pandemic scientists have been predicting for a while now. And that it may well be worse than the Spanish Flu and if it is, then borders will shut. I mean, what will we do if you're stuck over there, and I'm left here?

Oh, *ma chèrie,* whatever you do, you are not to panic. It's not good for the baby. If borders are closed, they won't be closed forever. He held me close to him then. I want to see my baby growing inside you. So, I'm telling you, whatever happens, I'll find a way to get back here. No matter what. And I knew this to be true.

Acknowledgments

While the amazing life of Stella Bowen, her art, her spirit and her heart, inspired me to write this novel, many people assisted me along the way. I am grateful to you all.

However, special thanks must go to my first readers – Wendy DePaoli for her superb attention to detail, and Kerry Herger for her insights. Their good opinion of my work meant a great deal to me.

Thanks also: to Sarah Sproule for sharing her professional knowledge of galleries, museums and libraries; to David May for his patience and willingness to assist me in all things digital; to Drs. Rhonda Barringham and Michael Fairley for advice on medical matters; to Deb Summerhayes, who provided me with a copy of Hemingway's story 'Up in Michigan' long before either of us knew I might one day use it in a novel; to David Williamson for his permission to use his words in the epigraph; to Mike Herger for some historical detail of both World Wars; to Cyril Chérencé and Rita Orsini for being helpful with all things French – merci beaucoup; to all my friends for their unflagging encouragement and support, in particular Jo Gardiner, Janet Harding, Annette Hollis, Anne Nicholson, Diane Taylor and Ann Woodward.

A big shout-out must also go to TROVE and Internet Archive. I couldn't have done the amount of research I did do during the pandemic without these two internet repositories of treasures.

And lastly, to my son, Angus, who is a continuous source of joy to me, and to Peter, my partner in love and in life – thank you both for everything.

References

The following texts were sources of information and inspiration for *The Only Reality*, which is a work of imagination. Scenes, thoughts and conversations in this novel were fabricated by me, though occasionally, I used the odd word or phrase that Ford, Bowen and others used to enhance the historical credibility of the narrative.

Angier, Carole *Jean Rhys: life and work* Penguin Books, London 1992

Belford, Barbara *Violet,* Simon & Schuster 1990

Bowen, Stella *Drawn from Life: A Memoir* Picador Australia Sydney 1999

Cochran, Karen & Stang, Sondra J ed *The Correspondence of Ford Madox Ford and Stella Bowen* Bloomington Indiana UP 1993

Delany, Paul 'Jean Rhys and Ford Madox Ford: What Really Happened?' *Mosaic: A Journal for the Interdisciplinary Study of Literature*, vol. 16, no. 4, 1983, pp. 15–24. JSTOR

Fitzgerald, F. Scott, 'Show Mr & Mrs F to Number –' *The Jazz Age* New Directions Books 1996

Goldring, Douglas *The Last Pre-Raphaelite. A Record of the Life and Writings of Ford Madox Ford London:* Macdonald & Co., 1948

Hardwick, Joan *An Immodest Violet – the Life of Violet Hunt* Andre Deutsch Great Britain, 1990

Hemingway, Ernest *A Moveable Feast* Arrow Books, London 2004

Hemingway, Ernest *Fiesta* Pan Books 1972

Hemingway, Ernest *The Short Stories* Scribner, New York 2003

McDowell, Lesley *Between the Sheets: The Literary Liaisons of Nine 20th Century Women Writers* Overlook Press, New York 2010

Mellow, James, R *Charmed Circle – Gertrude Stein & Company* Praeger, New York 1974

Mizener, Arthur *The Saddest Story: a Biography of Ford Madox* Ford Carroll & Graf, New York 1985

Modjeska, Drusilla *Stravinsky's Lunch* Picador Pan Macmillan Australia Sydney 2000

Modjeska, Drusilla *The Orchard* Picador Pan Macmillan Australia Sydney 1994

Nicholson, Virginia *Among the Bohemians: Experiments in Living 1900 - 1939* Penguin Books, 2003

Pesman, Ros Autobiography, Biography and Ford Madox Ford's Women' *Women's History Review* History Review, Vol 8, No 4, 1999

Pesman, Ros 'The Letters of Stella Bowen and Ford Madox Ford' *Overland* 139 -1995

Pizzichini, Lilian *The Blue Hour: A Portrait of Jean Rhys* Bloomsbury Publishing, London 2010

Rhys, Jean *Quartet* Penguin Books 1982

Saunders, Max Ford *Madox Ford: A Dual Life* 2 Vols. Oxford UP 1996

Stein, Gertrude *The Autobiography of Alice B. Toklas* Vintage Books, New York 1960

Thomas, Sue 'Adulterous liasons: Jean Rhys, Stella Bowen and feminist reading' *Australian Humanities Review* Issue 22, June 2001

Wiesenfarth, Joseph *Ford Madox Ford and the regiment of women* University of Wisconsin Press, Madison 2005

About the Author

Foreign Attachments is Roslyn McFarland's second novel. She lives in the Blue Mountains and has an MA in Creative Writing from UTS. With an abiding interest in the arts and having also spent a great deal of time in France, she was naturally drawn to the story of the Australian artist, Stella Bowen.

Her first novel All the Lives We've Lived was also published by Ginninderra Press in 2019. An earlier novella, The Privacy of Art, was published as an e-book. Several of her poems and short stories have appeared in various print and online platforms.

Milton Keynes UK
Ingram Content Group UK Ltd.
UKHW040638131024
449481UK00001B/45